1859

My thanks to Gerald Garland for his
encouragement and editorial suggestions.

CAPITOL CRIMES
A Novel of Suspense

K. L. Spangler

authorHOUSE®

AuthorHouse™
1663 Liberty Drive
Bloomington, IN 47403
www.authorhouse.com
Phone: 1-800-839-8640

First published by AuthorHouse 11/10/2009

ISBN: 978-1-4389-5845-3 (sc)

I am a longtime resident of Salem, Oregon. For my fellow residents,
please be advised that I have taken some literary license of
geography, places, and themes for the purposes of storytelling.

This is a work of fiction. Names, characters, places, and incidents either are the
product of the author's imagination or are used fictitiously. Any resemblance
to actual persons, living or dead, events, or locales is entirely coincidental.

Printed in the United States of America
Bloomington, Indiana

This book is printed on acid-free paper.

*For **A** and **Z**, my two most precious gifts.*

Contents

PROLOGUE

HER SCREAM ECHOED off the rotunda walls of the nearly empty Oregon State Capitol Building. This was not the conclusion to her life that she had expected or deserved. She had worked so hard to graduate from law school, to pass the Bar exam, and to land a prestigious job with a powerful state senator. Her dream was to live a fulfilling life that included a career, marriage, and children.

An early death was not something that 25-year-old Melissa Walker had ever contemplated—until now. As she continued her sickening 100 foot free fall through the air, she felt as though she had been catapulted into a state of near timelessness. Her entire life flashed before her eyes.

She remembered the little black lamb that her daddy had brought home one Saturday afternoon when she was barely two years old. Her daddy, Albert Walker, was the Sunday school superintendant at her church. He had borrowed the lamb from the local zoo. He wanted to create a memorable Sunday school lesson for the church children. The lesson was about Jesus being a good shepherd.

Her mind then flashed to riding in the old Studebaker pickup truck that her daddy used to drive. She recalled looking through the holes in the floorboard near the gear shift lever and seeing the pavement fly by underneath her feet. Once in a while, her daddy would place her in his lap and let her steer. He took her to all kinds of places when

1

she was a kid—to the hardware store, to the plant nursery, to his office, and to the Dairy Queen for a soft ice cream cone.

She then flashed to her big brother. Sure, they fought like cats and dogs in their adolescence, but underneath their sibling rivalry there was loyalty. She loved her big brother. "How will he cope with my death?" she thought. She felt empathy for him.

Of course, her mamma flooded her thoughts too. She could remember her mamma holding her against her soft chest. Her mamma would often rescue her when she had trouble falling asleep at night. She'd carry her in her arms down the first flight of stairs and into the kitchen. She'd then hold her on her hip with one arm while standing in front of the Sears Kenmore stove to heat some milk for her.

The movie of her life neared conclusion as it displayed her high school and college years, her graduation from law school, and her recent passage of the Bar exam. She was glad that her family had celebrated those moments with her.

Just before impact, she found herself at peace. She had these thoughts: "I am ready. I accept my fate. I forgive my transgressor."

The Rotunda

"DAVIS," I ANSWERED, as I drove along South River Road with my cell phone now pressed against my left ear. My full name is Terrence Jack Davis. I'm a homicide detective for the Salem Police Department.

"Good morning, Jack," said my longtime assistant, Phyllis Wilson.

"Morning, Phyllis."

"Jack, we just picked up a 911 call from a janitor over at the Capitol. He apparently found a dead body in the main lobby this morning. It's a young female. Forensics has already been dispatched and the Chief would like you over there ASAP."

"Okay, I'm on it," I said. "Never a moment's rest for Salem's finest. Thanks, Phyllis."

It was a Monday morning, just past seven-thirty. I'd had too many late night gin and tonics. On this particular morning, my plan was to quickly check in at the Department and then head up the street to White's Restaurant for breakfast. I favored black coffee, eggs, bacon, and hash browns. But, all of that was now going

3

to have to wait for another day. It sounded like there had been another murder here in the capitol city. "Advantage scumbags," I thought.

Turning east onto State Street, I could see flashing "blue and white" lights on up ahead. I turned into the Capitol Building's underground parking garage. After taking the elevator up to the main lobby, I was instantly greeted by a beefy young State Police trooper who asked me for my identification. It seemed to me that rookie cops were getting younger every year. Or, maybe I was just looking older? My salt and pepper hair didn't exactly take any years off of my face.

I walked past the yellow crime scene tape and into the rotunda with its bronze replica of the state seal embedded in its floor. Unfortunately, at the moment, that wasn't the only thing embedded in its floor—directly in front of me was the crumpled mass of a young woman's blood-stained body.

The scene was crawling with State, County, and City cops. "Too many," I thought. Over the years, I'd seen more than one crime scene compromised by too much foot traffic. Before I had observed much, I heard an all-too-familiar voice. Not a welcome one either. It belonged to Bradley Gunthrie Lewis III—a smug State Police detective. Within local law enforcement circles, however, he was derisively referred to as, merely, Bradley G. At the moment, he was in full swing—maniacally waving his arms in dramatic gestures, while chewing out some low ranking State Police trooper.

Fortunately, however, one of the cops at the scene was fellow Salem PD Homicide Detective, Curt Deford. Several years ago, Deford had worked as my partner for a brief stint. He was a respected detective, just shy of his

40th birthday.

"Hi Jack," said Deford.

"Mornin'. Whadaya got, Curt?"

"Well, we have the body of a white female, age 25. Name's Melissa Walker. She's a recent graduate of Willamette's Law School. She was interning for Senator Allen Jacobsen. It looks like she fell or was pushed out of one of the windows up there in the dome."

I tilted my head back and looked straight up into the Capitol Dome, which rose 106 feet above the rotunda floor. A series of long vertical windows, each divided into equal one-third sections about the size of a narrow doorway, evenly lined the sides of the dome.

"Do we have some people up there dusting for prints and doing a forensic search?"

"Yep," said Deford. "I haven't heard anything yet, however."

Slipping on a pair of latex gloves and squatting down to inspect the victim's body, I asked, "What's the time of death?"

"Doc's preliminary assessment is that she died around two or three this morning," said Deford.

"Any evidence of a bullet or knife wound?"

"None," said Deford.

"Strangulation?"

"No," said Deford

"What time did the building close last night?"

"4 p.m. – closes early on Sundays," said Deford. "After four, the only ones allowed in are legislators, executive branch officials, and building employees."

"Has anyone talked to Senator Jacobsen yet?"

Deford shook his head and said, "No. He apparently has a speaking engagement in Astoria this morning. My

K. L. Spangler

understanding is that he's currently en route to Astoria, via private aircraft."

Standing back up, I peeled off my latex gloves and said "Okay. Let's get hold of him as soon as possible."

"I'll get on it," said Deford. "Oh, one of the night janitors is over there. Name's Joe Martin. He's been a janitor here for eight years. He worked the graveyard shift this morning. Claims he didn't see anything unusual until he discovered the victim's body right here around six-thirty. He's pretty shaken up, but he seems like a straight shooter."

"All right. I'll talk to him. Have you talked with security yet?"

"Yes. They're compiling a list of names of the people that were still in the building last night after it closed," said Deford.

"Okay. Nice work, Curt."

Deford then added, "Oh, hey, you might wanna know that Bradley G's already complained about our presence here. He seems to think that the situation is solely within the State Police's jurisdiction. Our forensic people are pissed. So is Doc—Bradley G's been henpecking him."

"Wonderful. All right, thanks for the heads up."

Shaking my head, I turned and stepped away from the crime scene. The Walker girl's murder, if that's what it turned out to be, might have happened in the State Capitol, but it also had happened in the middle of my city. Bradley G knew better than to try and pull some jurisdiction crap on Salem PD. But, then, maybe he didn't know better—as he all too often made a fool of himself.

I approached the janitor. He was Hispanic, dressed in blue denim coveralls, and looked like he was in his mid-forties.

"Mr. Martin – Joe Martin?" I asked.

"Yes."

Displaying my badge, I said, "Detective Davis, Salem Police Department. I understand that you're the night janitor."

"Yes, that's right," said Martin. Then, nodding his head in the direction of the Walker girl's body, he volunteered, "I discovered her body around six-thirty this morning and called 911."

"I see," I said, as I jotted down Martin's name in my notepad. "Where were you just before you discovered the body?"

"Well, I had just completed my break down in the basement cafeteria. That's my custom. Our lockers are down there and that's where I keep my lunchbox. I was returning to the 4th floor where I'd been cleaning and I came across her body—right where it is now."

"You didn't take the elevator?" I asked.

Looking kind of sheepish, Martin put his right hand on his belly and said, "Well, I've been trying to take off a few pounds, so I try to take the stairs several times a night."

"Gotcha there, Mr. Martin," I said with a chuckle. "Did you at any time see or hear anything unusual?"

"No."

"All right," I said. "When did your shift start?"

"Twelve midnight. The earlier crew leaves at twelve and then my partner and I take over for the next eight hours. It's a lot of building to clean."

"Yeah, I bet," I said. "So you work in teams of two?"

"Yes. Jose and I work together."

"Got it," I said. "And your partner, Jose, you said his name was?"

"Yes."

"Do you know if he saw or heard anything?" I asked.

"I don't think so. But, you'll have to talk to him."

"Yeah, I'll definitely do that," I said.

Martin seemed credible, but a little anxious. I'd learned a long time ago, however, that almost anyone who is questioned by a cop got a little nervous.

I pressed on, "Where were you between two and three this morning?"

"Uh ... not sure. Let's see, I guess I would have been in the East Wing of the 3rd floor about then. I was probably mopping the restrooms and emptying trash cans. But, I might have been vacuuming."

"And where was Jose at that time?" I asked.

"Well, he would have been cleaning the West Wing. We start on the 2nd floor. We enter there from the service elevator with all of our equipment. We then work our way outward, before proceeding on up to the 3rd and 4th floors."

"Sounds complicated," I said.

Shrugging, Martin said, "Not really."

"Did either of you see the victim, Melissa Walker, at any time during the night, Mr. Martin? Uh, before you discovered her body this morning?"

"No, sir."

"All right," I said. "Oh, I hate to have to ask you this, Mr. Martin. It's just standard procedure. But, I assume that you underwent a criminal background check before you were hired here, correct?"

"Uh, well, it's been eight years or so. But, I think I did. Why?"

Trying to sound reassuring, I said, "It's just a routine question that I have to ask."

"Am I a suspect?"

"No, No," I said. "I just have to investigate this from the ground up. Sort of like the way you clean this place. You know, you start on the ground floor and then work your way upwards – isn't that what you said?"

"Yes, that's right."

"Do you clean the stairwell that leads to the observation deck?" I asked.

"Usually," answered Martin.

"Well, did you last night?" I asked.

"Uh, yeah."

"Okay, when?" I asked.

"Well, uh, that was the first thing that I did after I came on last night."

Looking up from my notepad and directly at Martin, I paused for a few seconds and then asked, "I thought you just said that you always cleaned the top floor last?"

"That's right. But, the observation deck really isn't a floor and it's closed until the spring. Usually nothing has to be done in the stairwell other than some minor dusting. Occasionally there's a piece of trash on one of the steps— like a candy wrapper or something. So, I always head up there first and get it out of the way. By the end of my shift I'm pretty tired and I don't feel like trudging up 121 steps."

"I see. Okay, Mr. Martin. Thanks for your time."

With a slightly worried look on his face, Martin said, "Sure, no problem."

As I was turning away from Martin, I unfortunately caught the unwelcome sight of Bradley G energetically approaching. He was easy to spot—short, stocky, and dressed in a three piece suit that had gone out of style along with the Average White Band.

"Hi, Jack," he said. "What are you city boys doin' here?

I wasn't amused by Bradley's G's clumsy attempt to be folksy. We had history. He had entered law school with me nearly a quarter century ago. I had gotten there the hard way—by working my way through college at the University of Washington. No one in my family had ever graduated from college. Bradley G, on the other hand, was a transplant preppy from the East Coast. Everything had been handed to him on a silver platter. His father and grandfather had been "distinguished" trial lawyers.

After that first year of law school, I had the good fortune to land an internship with the Salem Police Department. After working in the Homicide Division that summer, I knew what I wanted to do—I wanted to be a homicide detective. So, I dropped out of Willamette University's College of Law and enrolled in the Criminology Program at Chemeketa Community College. Within a year I was hired as a police officer with Salem PD.

Meanwhile, Bradley G went on to obtain his law degree and was hired by the Department of Justice. He couldn't hack it as a trial lawyer, however, and ended up finding a job with the State Police as some sort of Human Resources Manager. For reasons that escape everyone in local law enforcement circles, he was later assigned to work in OSP's Homicide Division.

Not feeling it necessary to even greet Bradley G, I said, "I've already heard that you've been impeding the access of my forensic people and interfering with the ME's investigation. You know how it works, Bradley G. So, why don't you stay out of everyone's way and let them do what they do best—which is to gather evidence. The Journal just loves it when you give them an excuse to bash the

State Police for elevating politics above crime fighting."

A little red faced, Bradley G pushed his horn rimmed glasses back up his shiny nose, looked up at me, and managed to say, "You never get it—do you, Jack? Forget protocol, forget rules—just barge in here like John Wayne!"

"I appreciate the comparison Bradley G, but, back to the task. Whadaya got?"

Begrudgingly, Bradley G replied, "Only 25, fresh out of law school. She's been an intern for Senator Jacobsen for the last year. Looks like a probable suicide. She jumped through one of the glass doorways up there in the dome. She died from head trauma and internal injuries." Sighing, Bradley G then said, "These kinds of losses get harder and harder to bear."

A little startled by Bradley G's uncharacteristic display of compassion, I solemnly said, "Yeah, I know. But, why do you think that she jumped through one of the windows?"

Smugly, Bradley G answered, "Experience. Look, there's no evidence that her body was moved. So, how else did it get here? Even Spiderman would have difficulty jumping from the 2nd floor balcony all the way over here. Besides, I understand that the ME believes that the damage to the deceased's body is consistent with a fall from 100 feet."

"I understand all of that. But, what makes you think that it was a *suicide?*"

Squirming a bit, Bradley G answered, "Well, I may have over spoke, but, I don't think so. There's no suggestion of foul play. You get a feel for these things, Jack—you know that. She was probably a depressed law student."

If I'd never previously seen Bradley G in action, I would have found his speculation appalling. But, unfortunately,

I'd worked around him for several years now. He was a half-wit and a sycophant—a bad combination of traits.

"Is that right? Do you have any evidence that she was having psychological problems?"

"Not yet," said Bradley G. "But, I'm sure that we'll find some."

"No doubt," I shot back. "How 'bout the forensics?"

"My unit is doing a sweep for all of the usual stuff— prints, fibers, hair shafts, blood, and semen."

Cocking my head a bit, I asked, "Is there any evidence that the victim was sexually assaulted?"

"She has traces of semen around her vaginal area."

"Uh-huh," I said. "Any sign of a struggle?" Looking a bit peeved, Bradley G said, "Not that we've found. Of course, the ME will have the last word on that.

"How 'bout security cameras? Are there any up there in the stairwell?"

"One," confidently answered Bradley G. "Unfortunately, it's not aimed at the window that she jumped through. Also, at night the interior lighting up there is very poor. So I doubt that the video is going to be of much help. Nonetheless, I've got somebody on it and they're viewin' the tape as we speak."

In truth, I was amazed that Bradley G. hadn't managed to foul things up worse than he already had. I considered myself lucky. "All right, Bradley G. Thanks. I'm gonna take another look at the body."

Something was bothering me. After working in homicide for nearly 20 years, I knew that convenient scenarios often did not pan out. As I walked towards the victim's body, I thought: "A pretty young woman, who just graduated from law school, decides to launch herself through an open glass doorway for a 100 foot free fall onto the state seal? Doubtful."

The way I saw it, a whole lot more had to fall into place before anyone should even suggest that the Walker girl's death was a suicide. As I knelt down next to her body, it was apparent that we'd have to wait for the forensics analysis and the autopsy report. "What a tragedy," I thought. Regardless of how many years I'd been a cop, a loss of life always got to me—especially when the victim was young.

Leaving the Capitol Building, I suspected that things were going to get a lot more interesting in this case – and in a hurry.

2

The Jacobsen Family

SALEM IS A government town—the State Capital of Oregon. As such, it has more than its fair share of prisons, jails, and mental health facilities. Even so, there are not enough prison cells to incarcerate all of the convicted felons. The result is that for a town of 140,000, it has a relatively high crime rate. So, while legislators love to get elected by touting their "tough on crime" platforms, the good citizens of Salem are left with the fall out—a vicious cycle of more convictions, more prisoners, more early releases, and more crimes.

After leaving the Capitol, I headed back to the Department located in the City Hall building between Liberty and Commercial Streets. I prefer to work alone, but detectives almost always work in pairs. Over the years, I'd grown used to that. My partner of three years, Eva Tolento, is a smart and attractive 34-year-old. She's divorced and has an adopted six-year-old Chinese girl, named Jiao, who will wrap you around her finger in about five seconds.

It's not easy for a woman to succeed in male dominated

professions such as law enforcement. But, Eva had already overcome that obstacle. She graduated first in her class from a Midwestern police academy and, since working here, she had already earned the respect of the top brass—including several of the "good ol' boys." While I confess that I'm a bit of a dinosaur myself, I'm not as far gone as some of the other relics here in the Department. I grew up in a strict family with a mother who seemed to have eyes in the back of her head and an older sister who always seemed capable of outwitting me. So, I knew only too well that it was a big mistake to underestimate a woman—just because she was one.

Returning from the crime scene over at the Capitol, I entered the Department and took the elevator up to the 2nd floor Homicide Division. After pouring myself a cup of stale coffee, I spotted Eva walking towards me.

"Jack!" she said. "Listen up."

"I'm all ears."

"Senator Jacobsen's plane never arrived in Astoria. His son, Michael, was apparently piloting. He's a commercial pilot. The Senator's wife was also aboard. They were on a business jet—a Cessna Citation. I just got off the phone with a guy up at the McMinnville Airport. The Federal Aviation Administration gave me his number. He's apparently a weather briefer and works out of something called a . . . uh . . . Flight Service Station."

I knew what Eva was talking about. At one time I had entertained the idea of scrapping my career in law enforcement to become an airline pilot. Flying is one of those endeavors that can grab hold of you—and it had done so with me. The way I saw it, life didn't get much better than when lifting off of a runway on a clear morning, or when descending through a layer of clouds "on the gauges" to see a well-lit runway directly in front of you.

Back then, when I was flying a lot, I had come across young Michael Jacobsen down at the airport. He was still in high school and was just learning how to fly. I'd spot him hanging out in the lobby of the Fixed Base Operator, or out on the ramp at Salem's McNary Airfield.

Eva continued, "Let's see, uh, he said that Michael opened an IPR . . . or . . . IFR flight plan to Astoria. I have something here about 'shot the ILS on two six'—don't know what that means. Anyway, the airport was apparently socked in with fog and Michael couldn't land. So . . . uh . . . he flew something called the missed approach procedure and then circled the airport. The guy said that Michael was holding in VFR conditions and that he 'cancelled IFR and declined flight following.' I've also written down something about the radar tracking of the aircraft's Mode C. Look, you're the pilot, Jack—maybe you should work this airplane stuff?"

"Was a pilot, Eva—was a pilot," I said. "And, you're doing fine—better than most."

With a, "Yeah, right!" type of look on her face, Eva continued, "Anyway, the aircraft is not considered either overdue or missing. So no search and rescue efforts have been launched. Oh, one other thing. The aircraft is privately owned by the Jacobsen family."

"So, does anyone in the Senator's inner circle have a clue about where he is at the moment—his secretary, or some family member?"

"Not that I've been able to discover," said Eva. "I've tried telephoning his home, his cell phone, and his office. All of the telephone numbers lead to voicemail. Also, Curt went up to his office on the 3rd floor this morning, but no one was there."

"Okay, let's keep trying. Seems a little too coincidental, doesn't it? I mean the suspicious death of the Senator's young intern and then his disappearance by aircraft a few hours later."

Eva replied, "No kidding. The FAA assured me that they will immediately contact us if they learn anything about the aircraft's whereabouts."

"Okay—nice work. Did you happen to get the call sign for his aircraft?"

"What's that?" asked Eva.

"It's just the aircraft's number that's painted on its sides."

"Oh," said Eva, flipping through her pocket-sized notepad. "Not sure, uh, what kind of number am I looking for?"

"It would start with the letter N and would probably be a four or five digit number that might end with a letter."

"You mean like N1732T?" asked Eva.

"That'd be it."

I then pulled the local telephone book out of my desk drawer and looked up the number for Corsair Aviation in Albany, Oregon. After receiving the number, I punched it in on my desk phone. A young woman answered, "Corsair Aviation, how may I help you?"

"Hi, this is Jack Davis. I'm one of Don Macky's former students. He wouldn't happen to be around would he?"

The woman said, "Yeah, he just came in from a flight. He's right here—hang on."

After a brief pause, Macky said, "Hello."

"Hi, Don. It's Jack—Jack Davis."

"Whoa—a voice out of the past!" said Macky. "Hi, Jack. What can I do for ya?"

"Don, I'm unfortunately calling on official business

with the Salem Police Department. Do you know a local commercial pilot named Michael Jacobsen? He apparently operates his own charter business out of Salem, and flies a Cessna Citation."

Macky answered, "Yeah, I do. I mean, not very well. But, I've come across him—sure. He's an ex-Navy jock. Flies in here and fuels up once a month or so. I've spoken with him here in the lounge—you know the usual stuff about weather conditions, and IFR currency."

"Okay. He hasn't flown in there this morning has he?"

"Not that I'm aware of," said Macky.

"Were you flyin' this morning, uh, around eight or so?"

"Yeah," said Macky. "I was getting a student ready to solo—lot's of touch-and-goes."

"Albany's on the same frequency as Astoria isn't it?"

"Yep. One Two Two point Six," said Macky.

"Did you happen to hear any radio chatter from Astoria?"

"Um, you know, I did," said Macky. "How'd you know?"

"Lucky guess. What'd you hear?"

"Well, there was an IFR aircraft up there that was having trouble trying to land. The pilot announced that he was flying the missed approach procedure. He did so at least a couple of times."

"Did you hear him say anything else?"

"No, I don't think so," said Macky. "The only reason I even remember it is because my student asked me about the transmissions. I had to keep her from keying the microphone while the pilot up there at Astoria was announcing that he was departing and flying the missed."

"All right. Listen, if you see or hear anything about Michael's Citation—anything at all—I'd appreciate it if you'd call me immediately."

"You got it," said Macky. "Can I ask what this is all about? Did something go wrong with Michael's flight?"

"I'm not going to bull shit you, Don. I'm conducting an investigation on behalf of the Salem Police Department. There's not a whole lot that I can disclose. I'd just like to talk to Michael's father, Senator Jacobsen—that's all. He was apparently on a flight to Astoria this morning, which was piloted by Michael. I'm pretty certain that it was the same aircraft that you heard on the radio this morning. There's no indication that the aircraft crashed. I just want to locate the Senator."

"All right," said Macky. "Well, I'll certainly keep my eyes open for anything."

"Thanks, Don."

I then telephoned the Air Traffic Control Tower at Salem's airport. The controller verified that Michael had departed Runway 31 earlier this morning on an IFR flight to Astoria. That's all he knew, however.

I turned to Eva and asked, "Have you had a chance to talk to Doc about the condition of the victim's body?"

"No, I haven't. But, I understand that he's a bit pissed off because Bradley G limited his opportunity to examine things at the crime scene."

"I already heard," I said. "Let's pay Doc a visit."

Dr. Nicholas Emmons is the State Medical Examiner. Anytime there is a suspicious death in Oregon, his office performs an autopsy. He is very well-regarded and is now in his early 60's. He's published several journal articles on crime scene forensics and he's a sought-after guest lecturer at police academies across the nation.

"Hi, Doc," I said, as Eva and I walked into his office, which was located across town on D Street near the old Salem Mental Hospital—the same Hospital that was depicted in the 1975 movie, One Flew Over The Cuckoo's Nest.

Doc looked up, gave Eva and me a nod, and then said, "That imbecile, Bradley G! He did nothing but obstruct my opportunity to collect evidence this morning." Shaking his head and appearing to gather even more momentum, he continued, "Did you hear his dumb ass remarks on the television news? Hell, if outsiders only knew that he couldn't find his ass with a flashlight!"

Chuckling, I said, "Hey, you're preachin' to the choir, Doc."

"Yeah, I know, Jack. The bottom line is this. I've found skin and clothing fragments under the decedent's fingernails. She fought, Jack—she fought hard! She resisted an attacker."

Doc tended to talk very fast. So, as soon as he paused long enough to inhale, I interjected, "So, she was sexually assaulted prior to her death?"

A bit irritated by my unsolicited intrusion into his higher thought process, Doc looked up for a moment, and then continued, "Perhaps. Oh, she resisted—that, I know. It's also obvious that the cause of the decedent's death was massive blunt force trauma to her head and internal organs."

"Why are you hedging your bets, Doc? It sounds like your autopsy findings point to aggravated murder."

"I don't think so," said Doc. "My findings show that the decedent had sexual intercourse shortly before her death. But, there isn't the usual evidence of bruising and irritation around her vaginal area that would suggest forced penetration, or some kind of an assault. However, her body was so damaged from the impact of her 100 foot fall that it compromises the physical findings."

"So, she was not sexually assaulted, but she fought off someone?"

"Looks that way," said Doc. "My guess is that she had consensual sex prior to her death, but that's a question of law—not forensic science."

"Will you be able to gather a DNA sample from the skin under her fingernails and compare it to a sample from the semen on her body?"

"I hope so," said Doc.

"Okay. Can you tell me with any precision when the decedent had sex, or how close in time it was to her death?"

"Yes," said Doc. "I need to study things further, but preliminarily I'd say that she had intercourse within four hours of her death"

"Are you still placing the time of death between 2:00 and 3:00 a.m.?"

"Yes," said Doc.

"Okay, thanks Doc."

"Uh, Jack, there's one more thing—a very significant thing," said Doc. "The victim was pregnant. I'd say that the embryo was close to a month old. The chromosome test shows that it was a male."

I felt as though I had just been kicked in the stomach. "Do you think that she would have known that she was pregnant?"

"Doubtful," said Doc. "The science is pretty sophisticated today in terms of being able to measure the size of an embryo and then deduce the date of conception. In this case, the embryo was not more than three weeks old."

"I assume that you will be able to do a paternity analysis, if it's needed?"

"Yes, of course," said Doc.

"Okay, thanks Doc."

After driving back to the Salem Police Department, I had barely sat down in my chair when I heard my name being paged over the office loudspeaker.

"Would Detective Terrence Davis please pick up Line 3? That's Detective Davis. You have a call on Line 3."

I punched the flashing light for Line 3, "Davis, Homicide," I answered.

"Hi, Jack, it's Officer Manion. Sounds like you've had a pretty busy morning?"

"You might say that. What can I do for ya, Keith?"

Officer Keith Manion was a good cop. He had been with Salem PD for only a couple of years, but he had already established himself as a young officer who was smart, competent, and resourceful.

"Well, Deford dispatched me over to the Walker girl's apartment. I'm there now. It's on State Street just past the Four Corners area. I think you'd better get forensics over here."

"Keith, Eva's standing next to me. Okay if I put you on the speaker phone?"

"Of course," said Manion.

"Tell us what you've got?"

"Well, the bedroom looks interesting. The bed is messed up and there's a video camera mounted on a tripod near the foot of the bed. There's a cassette inside it. I don't want to disturb anything, so I haven't viewed the tape. But, I think you get the picture?"

"Yeah, I do," I said.

Officer Manion continued, "Okay, well, as far as the standard stuff, there's no sign of forced entry into the apartment. My partner and I have canvassed most of the other tenants who are presently here. The woman right below the victim's apartment works for the State Motor Pool. She's in her 50's. Her name's Margaret Kautz. She heard a lot of activity around 10 p.m. last night. She's pretty certain that it was the victim's voice and that of a male. Not a fight, but just a lot of running around and laughing. Thereafter, she heard . . . well, she was a bit embarrassed to tell me this, but, she heard the unmistakable sound of a man and a woman getting it on. You know, the whole bit—creaking bed and moaning."

"Did Kautz say anything else?"

"Yeah, she did. She said that about an hour later, around 11:30 p.m., she heard the victim's apartment door slam shut followed by the sound of laughter and two people running down the stairwell. She remembers it well because it woke her up. She said that she was peeved and she remembers looking at her alarm clock."

"Did she see them—particularly the man?"

"No," said Manion.

"Okay, did you ask her if she had *ever* observed Walker with a man?"

"Yes, she recalls one guy in particular. She described him as Caucasian, average height, brown hair, and about 30 to 35."

"All right, nice police work, Keith. Secure the apartment. Eva and I will be over there shortly. Hey . . . How's Tonya?"

"Oh, thanks for asking. She's four days overdue, so anytime now I'll be takin' a few days off."

Tonya was Manion's wife. She was expecting their

second child. I turned to Eva and said, "We'll need to talk to the woman who lives below Walker. Maybe we can get enough of a description from her to get a sketch of the guy that Walker was hangin' with? It's a starting place anyway."

It was past the lunch hour. I turned to Eva, "You have lunch plans?"

"Nope," she said.

"How about headin' up to the Roadhouse—on me?"

"Sounds good," Eva replied. "Let's get outta here."

The two of us then headed down to the parking garage. I turned onto Commercial Street and drove the few blocks to The Best Little Roadhouse Bar & Grill. We were seated in a booth. I ordered a cup of coffee and a club house sandwich, while Eva selected soup and salad. While waiting for our food to arrive, Eva said, "So, how do we get this thing classified as a murder investigation, Jack?"

"By good ol' fashion detective work," I said. But, we're going to have to also dig into Walker's past to see if she was having some personal problems. While it doesn't look like a suicide to me, I don't want us to get blindsided by anything that Bradley G might uncover."

Back in my college days, I had worked on a suicide research team while completing my degree in Psychology at the University of Washington. We gathered all sorts of data from psychiatric patients who had been involuntarily hospitalized for attempted suicide. Nearly all of the patients were less than 30 years old, and many of them were teenagers. All of them had gotten to the point that they wished to stop their pain at *any* cost—including the taking of their own lives. As I wolfed down my sandwich, I found myself wondering if 25-year-old Melissa Walker had possibly reached a similar point.

"Well, I hate to say it, but the victim wouldn't be the first young lawyer to commit suicide—if that's what it was." said Eva. Then, shaking her head wistfully, she added, "You know, the twenties are just so hard. Everything seems so black-and-white at that stage of your life. But, you're too old to go cry on your mom or dad's shoulder."

"I know. We have to keep reminding ourselves of that. If she did commit suicide, our biggest hurdle in reaching that conclusion might be our own discomfort with the senselessness of it. We're going to need to interview the victim's parents."

Leaving the Roadhouse, Eva and I drove out to the Four Corners area to investigate the Walker girl's apartment. The Forensics Unit had already arrived. We headed directly into the bedroom. Everything had been dusted for prints. I inspected the camera and then hit the rewind button. After 20 seconds or so, I hit the "stop" button followed by the "play" button. Eva was standing next to me. The tape showed Melissa Walker and a Caucasian man laughing and having consensual sex. Unfortunately, however, the tape did not display the man's face. It showed only his backside from the neck down. The Walker girl was blindfolded. It was a little kinky, but there didn't appear to be any rough stuff. The scene was recorded with yesterday's date and the time of "10:37 p.m." I then rewound the tape to the beginning. There was a total of less than 10 minutes on it. It was more of the same—sex play with no view of the man's face.

Turning off the camera, I looked over at Eva and shrugged my shoulders.

"I'd say he's between 30 and 45, average height and weight," said Eva.

"Yep—that narrows it down to about half the male

population," I said.

I then turned to one of the forensic investigators and asked, "Are you comin' up with anything?"

"Sure," said the investigator. "We've got enough here from her sheets to get some DNA evidence."

"Good. Anything else?"

"Yeah, we've lifted several sets of prints too," said the investigator.

"Nice work. Thanks."

"You bet," said the investigator.

It was after four by now, and Eva and I were headed back down State Street towards the Department. When we arrived, Phyllis informed me that the head of security over at the Capitol had telephoned. His name was Tim Lawton.

I promptly returned Lawton's call. He informed me that yesterday evening 39 people had entered the Capitol Building after 4 p.m., which was when it had closed to the public. However, 61 people had exited the building after that time and before 7 a.m. the next morning, when police began to arrive. He explained that the differential in the numbers was due to numerous employees and public officials who were already in the building and who had not yet gone home when the doors closed at 4 p.m. He also said that after 4 p.m. only authorized persons could enter the building by the use of a key chip. He then informed me that the security camera over the main door facing Court Street showed a man and a woman entering the building just before midnight. He was presently compiling a list of the people that had entered or exited the building during non-business hours.

I asked, "Are the key chips individually coded?"

"You're gonna love this one. Yes, the key chips are

coded. But, the hardware system that we have here at the Capitol is obsolete and doesn't have the capability to read the codes. We've requested an upgrade to the system for years now, but the funds keep getting slashed. Maybe this'll cause that to change? Anyway, all we can do is identify *when* a key chip was used to enter the building, uh, you know, the time."

Shaking my head, I said, "You gotta just love bureaucracy—don't ya?"

"No kidding."

"Okay, thanks, sir," I said. "The information's helpful. I'd appreciate it if you'd fax over the list of names as soon as you compile it. I'll also have to view the tapes."

"Sure," said Lawton.

After hanging up the telephone receiver, I leaned back in my government issued chair. I'd taken some ribbing about it over the years—refusing management's several attempts to issue me a new chair. The chair squeaked every time I moved in it and was in severe need of new vinyl upholstery. But, none of that particularly mattered to me. I liked the way it felt. Propping my feet up on my desk, I looked up at the wall clock. I felt like having a drink. My mind began to drift towards the pleasant thought of driving home, loosening my tie, and relaxing.

However, I turned toward Eva and said, "I just got off the telephone with the head of security over at the Capitol. He said that a man and a woman entered the Capitol Building together around midnight. Thirty nine people entered the building after closing, but 63 exited."

Eva said, "We really need to ID the guy in the sex video. It's probably the same guy who walked into the Capitol with Walker?"

"Yep."

Before leaving work, Eva obtained the address and phone number of Melissa Walker's parents. While I had stepped away from my desk, she telephoned them. After a couple of unanswered calls, Mr. Albert Walker finally answered the phone. He had already been informed of his daughter's death. Given the rawness of it all, and especially given the emotional condition of his wife, Gloria, Mr. Walker refused to be interviewed until tomorrow.

Once back at my desk, I looked at Eva and said, "You need to go home. You've got a kid who needs you."

"Yeah, I know. Hey, I just got off the phone with the victim's father. His name is Albert Walker. He lives in Washington, near Bellevue. He and his wife are pretty messed up at the moment. He asked that we not talk to them until tomorrow."

"Okay," I said. "I'll have Phyllis reserve a flight for us up there tomorrow and to schedule a meeting with the Walkers. If she can get it, will a 9 a.m. flight work for you?"

Smiling, Eva said, "Whatever you say, boss."

Waving my hand at Eva with a mock frown on my face, I said, "Right. Get outta here, will ya Tolento?"

It was now past six and it had already been a long day. I buttoned up my P-coat and headed out of the office and into the cool evening air. The sun was a hazy orange ball sitting just above the Western horizon and was casting a sepia-like hue on the brightly colored fall foliage.

Instead of driving home I headed up Fairmont Hill to pay a visit to my former partner, Peter Gunnerson. "Gunny" was now retired, but he still put his detective skills to work by acting as a consultant for Salem PD's "cold cases" task force. By anyone's account, he was the best homicide detective to ever wear a Salem PD badge.

Although I'd learned my trade from him, I knew that I'd never fill his shoes. He was one of a kind. In his more than 30 years of service, he'd been honored with nearly every award available to a cop. He'd also solved every murder that he'd ever investigated—except for one.

Back in 1973, when Gunny had been a homicide detective for less than a year, a 12-year-old girl named Gabriel Henderson was murdered here in Salem. She was a 6th Grader at Bush Elementary School—now torn down as part of Salem Memorial Hospital's expansion. She lived just four blocks away from the school, over near 15th and Mission Streets. She was seen walking eastbound on the south shoulder of Mission Street, shortly after school had ended at two-thirty. But, she never made it home. About a week later, her naked body was discovered in a ditch in the Ankeny Hills Bird Refuge. She'd been sexually assaulted and strangled.

Gunny tracked down every lead in the case and obsessively kept the investigation alive for several years. But, no arrests were ever made. The unsolved murder tore him up inside. Long after I became his partner, he'd occasionally say something about the case—when everyone else had forgotten about it. He felt like he'd failed by not collaring the sadistic killer that had murdered little Gabriel. Over many lunches and coffee breaks, Gunny and I speculated that the murderer had probably been killed or incarcerated in another state.

That's probably why Gunny still works on the "cold cases" task force. He's still driven to solve that one case. To this day, he will regularly pull out the file on Gabriel Henderson—who would now be 45 years old.

I walked up the brick walkway to Gunny's stately home. The lawn was green and well-manicured. I rang the doorbell and Gunny's wife, June, opened the door.

"Well, hi there Jack," she said. "Come on in."

"Hi, June—nice to see you. I hope I'm not interrupting? I was headed home and I thought I'd stop in and talk to Gunny for a bit."

"You're always welcome, Jack," she said. Then, momentarily turning away from me, she hollered, "Peter! . . . Honey! Look what the cat dragged in."

Several seconds later, Gunny came around the corner wearing a cardigan sweater and holding a tobacco pipe in his hand. "Hey, Jack! Good to see you, son. Did you come over to watch the Monday night game?"

"Nah. I haven't watched a whole game in years. Who's playin'?"

"The Seahawks and Broncos," answered Gunny. "Seahawks are favored by a touchdown."

"Sounds like it'll be a good one. I'm actually pretty whipped. I was headed home, but thought I'd stop by and run a couple things by you—if that's all right?"

"Of course," said Gunny. "So, what kind of mess has Bradley G created for you this time?"

Chuckling, I answered, "Well, that's not too far from the truth, Gunny. A young woman, a legislative intern for Senator Jacobsen, was killed in the Capitol rotunda early this morning. She was probably pushed out one of the open windows up in the Capitol dome. I'm treating it as a murder investigation, but Eva and I haven't yet ruled out either a suicide or an accident. We also know that just hours before her death, the victim was intimate with a Caucasian male. But, here's the kicker—the Senator is currently missing."

Gunny's face uncharacteristically began to drop. I wasn't sure what to make of it. I'd worked side-by-side

Gunny for years, while rarely seeing him display anything other than a poker face. While trying to not look surprised, I continued, "He was on a flight to Astoria this morning, but the aircraft never landed. His son was piloting the plane and his wife was aboard. He ended up flying the missed approach procedure a couple of times and then cancelled his IFR flight plan and declined flight following. That's all we know. We've been unable to locate the aircraft or anyone on board."

Gunny listened and shook his head in silence. I then said, "Anyway, the real reason I'm here Gunny, is that I'm concerned about a possible backlash. I'll have to interview Senator Jacobsen—assuming he's still alive. I know that most longtime politicians have some skeletons in their closet. He may already be trying to avoid prosecution."

Going with a hunch that was largely based on Gunny's present demeanor, I finally quit beating around the bush and said, "Uh, you know him don't you, Gunny?"

Gunny took a few deliberate puffs on his pipe before responding. His pipe smoking had never bothered me. In fact, I kind of liked the aroma. It even reminded me of my paternal grandfather, Joseph Davis, who'd once in awhile smoke a pipe while tinkering in his woodshop.

"Yes, I do. Fairly well, in fact," Gunny finally answered. "He lives up here on the hill, just a block from here. You're gonna have your hands full on this one, Jack. The Jacobsen family has deep roots here in Salem."

As usual, Gunny sliced through everything and had gotten to the heart of the matter. The Jacobsen family was an institution in Salem. Back in the late 1800's, Elmer Jacobsen—the Senator's grandfather—had helped build the town from the ground up. Likewise, the current generation of Jacobsens served on all kinds of commissions and helped finance several high profile philanthropic endeavors. Moreover, Senator Allen Jacobsen's two brothers, Alex and Arnie, were both licensed lobbyists who wielded considerable influence. Back in 1982, Senator Jacobsen was a Republican contender for Governor, but he stepped out of the race when his young son, Michael, became seriously ill. Michael had contracted something akin to meningitis with a persistent fever of over 104 degrees. As a result, he slipped into an unconscious state for nearly a month. Miraculously, he pulled through it without any permanent damage.

Michael was one of those kids who grew up building model airplanes and dreaming of the day that he could learn to fly. He was also very intelligent and always did well in school. He obtained a college degree at Oregon State University and then entered the Navy. He was immediately routed to Officer's School. He wanted to learn how to fly jets off of aircraft carriers—and that's exactly what he did.

After serving in the Navy for six years or so, he left the service and began flying for Alaska Airlines. Although he was an excellent pilot, he didn't care for the long hours and the low beginning pay for First Officers. So, his father, Allen Jacobsen, used the Jacobsen family money to go into business with Michael. He purchased a Cessna Citation jet—the very same one that was now missing—to allow Michael to start a charter flight service at Salem's McNary Field Airport. Surprisingly, the entrepreneurial enterprise succeeded. Salem is a town of considerable size that is sandwiched between Portland and Eugene. So, with no air carrier service in-and-out of the City, Michael's charter jet business succeeded.

"This might get ugly, Gunny," I said.

"Yep. Listen Jack, tread slowly. You're dealing with a minefield. The nuts and bolts of a murder investigation are one thing. Power, wealth, and politics are another. The Jacobsen family is highly regarded. I don't think that there's any doubt that Allen and his family would call in all of its chips, if it felt that he was in harm's way. So watch your backside, play it squeaky clean, and keep that idiot Bradley G as far out of the loop as possible."

"Okay, Gunny. Thanks. I should really get goin'. I probably ruined June's dinner plans. Sorry for the intrusion."

"Nonsense," said Gunny. You're welcome any time, Jack."

3

Victoria

As I DROVE home, I turned over every detail of the Walker murder investigation. What stood out was that it appeared that the victim's death was not a typical case of sexual assault followed by murder.

Turning off of River Springs Road my headlights panned across the trees and overgrowth that lined my nearly quarter mile long driveway. I was home. My three bedroom house is tucked away in the middle of a narrow five acre tract of heavily wooded land. The prize is the backyard, which slopes steeply downward to the Southwest and opens up to a panoramic view of the Willamette Valley and the Coastal mountain range.

I walked into the kitchen and grabbed a bottle of beer out of my stainless steel refrigerator. After a couple of long swallows I headed up the circular stairway to the loft. I then yanked off my cowboy boots and stretched out on the futon. The local news was reporting the Walker girl's death. It was the lead story on every station. While I didn't think much of reporters, it wasn't every day that a dead body showed up on top of the state seal in the center of the Capitol Building's rotunda.

At the moment, Bradley G was being interviewed and was stating rather matter-of-factly that the girl's death was an "apparent suicide." I shook my head. I wasn't buyin' it. "Oh well," I thought, "maybe that'll dampen the press coverage." The overly enthusiastic television reporter then mentioned that Melissa Walker had been a legislative intern for Senator Jacobsen. Surprisingly, however, nothing was reported about the unknown whereabouts of the Senator, or that his aircraft had not landed in Astoria.

After mixing a gin and tonic, I tried to finish a book that I was reading about the Lakota Indians. But, within minutes I'd fallen asleep. As I did so, my mind began to inevitably drift towards Victoria Severson—as it almost always did in my quieter moments. "Vicki," as I came to call her, had been my longtime love of 15 years. She had now been gone for two years, one month, and 14 days. She had fought a valiant five year battle with the big C—cancer. She was only 41 years old when she died.

I woke up around 6 a.m. After showering and drinking a cup of coffee, I hurriedly packed a small overnight bag. It was wet and windy outside—an all too common occurrence here in the Northwest. Bright yellow maples leaves covered my driveway. After arriving at the Department, I was promptly greeted by Phyllis.

"Don't get settled in," she cheerily volunteered. "I have two airline tickets here for you and Eva to fly up to Seattle at 10:30 this morning."

Still feeling like I needed to sleep another hour or two, I tried to sound appreciative, "Oh, nice work. Thanks. Have you told Eva?"

"Yes, she was just here a moment ago."

Right then Eva walked briskly around the corner. She

had been on the telephone with the FAA again. They had just confirmed that Senator Jacobsen's aircraft had arrived late the previous night in Bogotá, Columbia.

"Bogota?" I repeated. "Shit, he didn't exactly stay in the area did he? Let's try to reach the good Senator. We need to find out if he's trying to avoid prosecution. Every hour that passes without him contacting us suggests that he's doing just that."

With a mischievous look on her face, Eva asked, "You think there might be an expense paid trip down to Bogotá in this for us? I hear that there are some great casinos down there."

"Dream on, Tolento," I jokingly said. "If that's what you're after, I think you're in the wrong branch of law enforcement. Try the CIA." Pausing a bit, I then added, "But, I have been to Tokyo on business—so you never know."

"I didn't know that! Are you pullin' my leg, Tokyo?"

"No—spring of '94," I said. "It was an international seminar on police methods. Gunny was invited as a guest speaker. He somehow convinced the organizers that the two of us could put on a better workshop than just him alone. So, they paid my way too. Hey, we gotta go. Grab your suitcase."

We then drove up the Interstate towards Portland International Airport. About half way there, just shy of turning off to the Northeast on I-205, my cell phone rang.

"Davis," I answered.

It was Phyllis. "Hi Jack. You're not going to like this."

Letting out a deep sigh, I said, "Okay, let me have it."

"Senator Jacobsen telephoned Bradley G late last night. It was reported on the local television news this morning."

"What?" I said. "He called Bradley G? All right, could you give me the number for Bradley G's direct line?"

"Got it right here," said Phyllis, and she then read the number aloud.

"Okay, thanks."

"Good luck, boss," said Phyllis.

While relaying the information to Eva, I punched in Bradley G's number on my cell phone and hit the speaker button. Even if he was a dolt, Bradley G knew how the game was to be played. Back in the early 1980's an inter-agency agreement had been hammered out between Salem PD and the State Police. Back then, I was entering law school. But, Gunny was already a veteran homicide detective. He'd seen the whole jurisdictional issue coming—before anyone else did. The out of touch bureaucrats over at the Department of Administrative Services (DAS) thought that it would be a good idea to exclude Salem PD from any involvement with crimes that that took place on State property. But, the legislature didn't see it that way. Consequently, DAS backed down in order to avoid adverse lawmaking.

Instead, DAS approached Salem PD with the idea of an inter-agency agreement. Fortunately, someone had the brains to put Gunny on the Joint Advisory Committee. Largely due to Gunny's efforts, the inter-agency agreement ensured that Salem PD would take on nothing less than an equal role when it came to a crime that was committed anywhere within the City limits.

That is, pursuant to <u>DAS/Salem PD Inter-Agency Agreement No. 83-011,</u> Salem PD had primary jurisdiction over crimes committed within the Salem City limits. In those cases, the State Police was to assume a subordinate role in the form of "assistance." The complicating fact in the Walker investigation, however, was that the victim's body had been found inside the Oregon State Capitol Building—a State owned building in the middle of Salem, whose security was the sole responsibility of the State Police. In those cases, the agreement specified that Salem PD and the State Police were to act "jointly and separately" in its investigation of any crime with "seamless" communication.

All too aware of the aforementioned policy, which apparently had satisfied the bureaucrats over at DAS, I found myself thinking about my old partner. Gunny always got a kick out of bureaucratic interference. While he was smart enough to play along, he usually did not alter his investigative approach. More than once it was his detective work that solved a murder, even if another agency had primary jurisdiction. In a way, that's what Bradley G was doing—just going about his business. I privately respected that. But, the difference was that Gunny was a top notch homicide detective, while Bradley G was not. Gunny helped solve crimes. Bradley G usually bungled them.

After two rings, Bradley G answered. "Senior Detective Bradley G. Lewis, may I help you?"

"It's Davis. The morning news stations are all a buzz about your fireside chat last night with Senator Jacobsen."

Sounding a bit rattled, Bradley G responded, "Okay, Jack, okay. I suppose that you have a right to be a little irked."

I shook my head, while Eva barely muffled her laughter. I then replied, "Just tell me what you've got, Bradley G."

"Look, Jack. He called me last night around 11 p.m. our time. He's in Bogotá, Columbia, with his wife and son. He had longstanding vacation plans to fly down there with his family. They own a condominium down there. When his aircraft couldn't land in Astoria, he just decided to depart early for Bogotá. They had originally planned to depart for Bogota after he finished his speaking engagement in Astoria. So, they just left a little early, that's all."

Never much of a diplomat, I shot back, "Gee, Bradley G, you sound like the Senator's defense lawyer."

"Give me a break, Jack. The Senator was shocked by the news of Melissa Walker's death. He denied any involvement in the matter and said that he'd be willing to take a polygraph. Although he was in his office at the Capitol that night, he said that he left the building just after 9 o'clock."

"All right, Bradley G, " I said. "If the Senator calls you again you might consider passing along to him that it would be in his interests to immediately return to Oregon."

"He knows that, of course."

"Look, Bradley G, the ME is of the opinion that the Walker girl resisted an attack," I said.

"Yes, I'm aware of that," said Bradley G.

"And you know about the video that we recovered from the victim's apartment?"

"Yes, I know about that too," stammered Bradley G. "I have a copy of the video right here on my desk. From what I understand, all it shows is that the Walker girl had consensual sex in her apartment the evening prior to her death. She's an adult, Jack. What's the relevance of that?"

This time, I had to do a full "10 count" before responding. Bradley G would have trouble managing a curbside lemonade stand. Yet, somehow, he had been steadily promoted within the ranks of the State Police.

It was obvious, however, that he had unwittingly helped Senator Jacobsen, who in my view had now become more than a mere "person of interest."

"Just look at the tape, Bradley G. The dude was in bed with her after 10:30 p.m. and he left with her around 11:30 p.m."

"Oh," said Bradley G. "Well, I still believe that the most likely scenario is a suicide or an accident."

"Why did she try to defend herself then, Bradley G?"

"Well . . . I'm not yet buying into the fact that she was attacked," said Bradley G. "I'll have to talk to the ME about that. Also, even if she did resist, maybe it happened while she was having fun with the guy in the video—whoever that turns out to be."

"Okay, Bradley G."

By the time that I got off the phone with Bradley G, I was pulling into PDX's long term parking area. I reached for my wallet. Something that Bradley G had said was tugging at me. If the good Senator and his family had innocently flown to Bogotá on a family vacation, then Michael would have filed an IFR flight plan. Fumbling through my wallet, I pulled out some remnants from my flying days. Buried underneath my pilot's license and my medical certificate, was an FAA card that listed the toll free telephone number of the McMinnville Flight Service Station.

Dialing the number, I identified myself and spoke to a congenial weather briefer. I queried the briefer and asked him to recheck the computer system for any and all IFR flight plans that were filed for Citation 1732T for flights on Monday, October 9th. The briefer reminded me that all flight plans were erased within one hour if they were not activated. He then informed me that only one flight plan had been activated for Cessna 1732T on the 9th—a morning flight from Salem to Astoria.

I turned to Eva and said, "It looks to me like the Senator attempted a stealth flight out of the Country. Jets fly along airways in what's called the IFR system—on instruments. The FAA doesn't have any record that Michael activated an IFR flight plan for his flight to Bogota."

Eva replied, "So, the longstanding vacation angle doesn't look legitimate?"

"Doesn't to me."

While walking into the main terminal, I telephoned Doc.

"Medical Examiner's Office, Emmons speaking."

"Hi Doc, it's Jack."

"Mornin', What can I do for ya?"

"Doc, I want you to be straight with me," I said. "How solid is the forensic evidence that shows that the Walker girl struggled prior to her death? I mean, would it be reasonable to take the position that the fragments under her fingernails were the result of rough sex that she engaged in around 10:30 p.m.?"

"What? Well, I suppose it's possible," said Doc. "But, there's blood, skin, and clothing fibers under her nails, Jack. I've been looking at this kind of stuff for over thirty years. Any credible forensic expert would tell you that to get that kind of material under your fingernails, you'd have to be seriously fighting, clawing, and grasping. So, excluding only the roughest stuff, the forensic evidence could not have resulted from consensual sex. Whoever the victim tried to fight off, you can rest assured that they have some serious scratches on their body. She drew blood Jack, and she clawed into what looks like a blue denim shirt."

"Okay, Doc. As usual, you do all the real crime

solving."

"C'mon, Jack. We both know that's a crock."

"Hey, I'll talk to you later Doc. Eva and I are boarding a flight right now. Take care."

"You too," said Doc.

Privately, I was worried. Events were moving too fast. I preferred a deliberate approach to homicide investigations. Sort of like a chess match, where you can study your next move. But, this investigation had already taken on a life of its own—just like Gunny had warned. I felt as though Eva and I were already playing "catch up." Presently, Senator Jacobsen was our only suspect in the probable murder of Melissa Walker—and he had fled to South America. Thus, time sensitive evidence, such as scratch wounds on the Senator, was forever escaping our detection. Moreover, it was always preferable to obtain statements from family members <u>before</u> they had an opportunity to "get their stories straight." Then, there was also the possibility that the Senator might go into hiding on foreign soil, thereby preventing his extradition back to Oregon.

As the Dash 8 lifted off Runway 27R at Portland International Airport and quickly climbed to a cruising altitude of 18,000 feet, the seat belt signs were turned off. I ordered coffee—black, no sugar. As I sipped the coffee out of a Styrofoam cup, I began to wonder what the Walker girl's parents would be like. I pulled out a folded piece of paper from my dress shirt pocket and examined their address. They lived on Hunt's Point, a very affluent and exclusive neighborhood just northwest of downtown Bellevue. I then began to think about my own parents—who also lived in Bellevue.

When I was only two years old my mother and father moved from Tulsa, Oklahoma to Bellevue, Washington.

That was back in 1960. My dad, Arthur Davis, is now a 77-year-old retired architect. As I sat there mesmerized by the hum of Dash 8's four turboprop engines, I recalled when my dad was starting his fledgling architectural business. Sometimes, he would have to work all night to meet a deadline. When he did, my mother, Alicia Davis, would make breakfast for him and would then drive the mile or so up to his office and deliver it to him. I remembered riding in the backseat of our family Volkswagen and seeing a tea towel draped across the hot biscuits, bacon, and eggs that my mom had prepared.

While I hazily reminisced about my childhood, one of the flight attendants came up to me and said, "Uh, excuse me, Detective Davis?"

"Yes."

"The Captain has received an emergency communication from our dispatch office." Looking down at a hand-written note, the pretty flight attendant continued, "Salem Chief of Police James Heathrow would like you to call him as soon as possible. It's urgent. You can just use the phone right there in the seat back."

The Chief and I go a long ways back. In fact, I privately call him, "Cap." When I began working for Salem PD nearly 20 years ago, he was a captain. So back then, it was common for all of us to refer to him as "Cap." The name stuck—even after Captain James Heathrow was promoted to the Chief of Police position. In public, however, I refer to him as Chief Heathrow, granting him the well-deserved recognition of his title.

"All right, thanks," I said. I then picked up the receiver and read the printed instructions. Next, I pulled out my City issued Diner's Club credit card and swiped it in the slot above the phone. I then punched in Cap's direct phone number.

"Chief of Police Heathrow," answered Cap.

"Hi Cap. It's Jack. I'm on a Horizon flight right now with Eva. You have an urgent message?"

"Yes, I do. You won't be interviewing the Walker girl's parents, Jack. They were both murdered last night right outside of their home."

"No!"

Cap continued, "I'm afraid so. From what the Bellevue Police Department is telling me, it was a very professional hit. Single gunshot wounds to the back of their heads. No prints, no witnesses, and no suspects. They probably never saw it coming."

"The timing sure as hell is suspicious."

"You're damn right. But, that's conjecture until we have some evidence," said Cap. "This latest job was done execution style. We also know that Senator Jacobsen has an alibi for this one—since he's in Bogota. But, I'd wager money that he's connected to all three of the murders. I'm using every official, political, and personal means that I have to exert pressure on him to voluntarily return to Oregon. At this point, we don't have enough to extradite him. So, I'd like you and Eva to focus on gathering evidence. It'll be a different ball game once we can interrogate him."

"Okay, Cap. Does the Bellevue Police Department know that Eva and I are on our way there to view the crime scene?"

"Yes, they do," said Cap. "The Police Chief there, Dan Cayce, is someone I've met in professional circles. He's top-notch and plays it by the book. When I spoke with him earlier this morning, he reassured me that you and Eva were welcome. He's smart enough to realize the benefit of having our two Departments work together. We need more people like him in law enforcement, and less people like Bradley G."

"No kidding. Did you know that Senator Jacobsen telephoned Bradley G last night from Bogotá? Of course, the prick neglected to tell us."

"Yeah, I heard," said Cap. "I've already made some phone calls. No one in the Executive Branch is going to admit that OSP has an imbecile in a supervisory position. If they could have easily gotten rid of him, they would have done so a long time ago. We all know there's something there—but that's another story. I'd bet good money that Bradley's G's balls are in a vise right now."

"We can only hope."

With some resignation in his voice, Cap replied, "Yeah."

Cap and I knew that the local press would soon pick up the increasingly sordid tale that was beginning to unfold—the murder of a state senator's young female intern, followed by his immediate flight out of the Country. However, as Gunny had warned, the Jacobsen family machinery had already gone into overdrive.

That is, the extended Jacobsen family was a major stockholder in the Sterrett Company—the parent company of the Statesman Journal. Thus, in the morning newspaper the Statesman had downplayed the news of Senator Jacobsen's dubious flight out of the Country. The Statesman was not as cautious, however, in its commentary about my investigation into the death of Melissa Walker. In essence, the editorial alleged that I was wasting the Taxpayers' money by treating the investigation as a murder. The editorial concluded by stating that I was "over the hill" and by calling for my resignation.

As if that wasn't irksome enough, the Statesman ran a

third article right below the powder puff piece about Senator Jacobsen. In doing so, the Statesman reported Melissa's Walker's death as "a tragic suicide of an emotionally depressed law student." Specifically, the reporter said that the Walker girl had been on anti-depressant medication and had regularly obtained counseling at Willamette University's Student Counseling Service. The reporter then went on to praise the State Police's handling of the investigation, as well as the outstanding leadership of its Senior Homicide Detective, Bradley G. Lewis III.

After arriving at Sea-Tac, Eva and I rented a car and headed along I-405 towards Bellevue. As we drove north past Renton, I couldn't help but marvel at the majesty of the area. Although every year seemed to bring more traffic and more development, the "Eastside" was still beautiful. Looking out my driver's side window, I could see Lake Washington's East Channel and the snow capped Olympic Mountains. "Not exactly the Kansas plains," I thought.

The Bellevue Police Department was located on Main Street near I-405. Chief Cayce was expecting us. As Cap had said, Cayce was professional and courteous. After introducing himself and a few of his homicide detectives, Cayce personally drove Eva and me out to the crime scene.

Hunt's point is a narrow stretch of land that juts out onto Lake Washington. Many of the homes have lakefront properties. As Cayce drove through downtown Bellevue, I was surprised by the amount of development.

When I was a kid, Bellevue Square had primarily consisted of only three stand alone department stores— JCPenney, Nordstrom, and Frederick & Nelson. Now, Bellevue Square was an immense indoor mall that was a magnet for shoppers throughout the Pacific Northwest.

It housed not only all major department stores, but also many other high end stores and restaurants. Moreover, the downtown core had steadily grown over the years to include several upscale office towers and hotel buildings, which appeared to almost rival Seattle's skyline.

Chief Cayce pulled his unmarked light blue sedan into the Walkers' driveway. It was a typical crime scene, with officers, detectives, and forensic experts milling about. After viewing the crime scene and discussing the preliminary findings with the forensic experts, Eva and I concurred with Cap—the Walkers had been murdered by a professional. After we examined their bodies, they were bagged and removed. We stood there looking at their chalk outlines with blood stains readily visible. The Walkers had arrived home late at night, while the killer laid in wait. They never made it inside their house, however. They were each shot once through the back of the head at close range. The killer obviously knew how to handle a gun and had killed the Walkers in a chillingly efficient manner. There were no footprints, no fingerprints, no tire marks, and no witnesses. As the ballistics report would later confirm, the killer had used a handgun with a silencer.

The only puzzling fact was that the killer had entered the Walkers' home—apparently retrieving the house key from the set of keys in Mr. Walker's right hand. Unfortunately, after carefully searching inside the Walkers' home, investigators could not identify anything that appeared out of place, stolen, or vandalized. For some reason, however, the killer had entered the Walkers' home. In short, after nearly a full day of painstaking forensic work, the group of investigators came up empty handed. Although they bagged and identified a few random items, none of the items looked like they were connected to the double homicide.

After having lunch with Chief Cayce and a couple of his lead detectives, Eva and I drove back to the Sea-Tac Airport. Fortunately, we were able to catch an immediate return flight back to Portland. Even so, it was past 9 p.m. by the time that we arrived back in Salem.

Before leaving the office, I asked Eva about Jiao. I was wondering who was taking care of her little six-year old daughter, while she was out of town. Eva replied, "Oh, I have a neighbor who picks her up when I'm running late. She has a little girl who's Jiao's age. So, it works out pretty well."

"That's nice. My sister is constantly juggling her schedule to make it all work with her two."

"Yeah, like a live wire act sometimes," said Eva. "It's probably a little easier for me, however, with only one kid."

I thought quietly to myself before saying anything further. I had always wondered why Eva had adopted, but I figured that it was merely the result of her divorce and her subsequent focus on her career. She was certainly attractive enough to garner her share of attention from other men.

"You ever think about another adoption?"

"Sure," said Eva. "I've looked into it. The problem is the nature of our work. You know . . . the threats, the irregular hours, the violence—not exactly conducive to a dependable home environment. It's tough enough for a single mom to raise just one. Add another . . . well, I don't know."

Noting that Eva's eyes were getting moist, I fumbled for a tissue and handed it to her. A few seconds of silence then passed between us. I could tell that there was something deeply personal that Eva was holding in. I knew better, however, than to ask another question.

Standing beside Eva, I said, "Hey, why don't you head home? Go give that kid of yours some attention. I'll shut things down here."

"All right. Night, Jack."

"Night," I said.

After Eva left, I sat back down in my chair. I was alone. The office was dark with just a few fluorescent ceiling lights still left on. You could barely see my silhouette. My feet were propped up on my desk. I reached into my lower left desk drawer and pulled out my flask of Jack Daniel's whiskey. After a couple of swallows, I unbuttoned my shirt collar, loosened my tie, and sat there for nearly an hour—slowly sipping whiskey.

Everyone has pain in their lives. It was clear that Eva had some pain, and I knew all too well about my own pain. Anyone who knew anything about me knew that my work was an escape. Perhaps it lessened my pain to help the families of murder victims obtain some closure and to get killers off the streets.

4

The Press Conference

I FINALLY STUCK the flask of whiskey back in my desk drawer and drove home. I wondered how it would look right now to get busted here in Salem for a DUI. Heck, I was already a poster boy "has been" for the Statesman Journal. I chuckled to myself and thought, "Might as well liven things up a bit."

When I got home, there was a message on my telephone answering machine. I hit the "new message" button. It was Cap. He had called to let me know that he was under mounting pressure to take me off of the Melissa Walker case. As I finished listening to the message, he called again.

"Hi, Cap," I said.

"Hi. Did you get my message?"

"Yes," I said. "I just listened to it."

"Look, Jack, I don't like interference with my Department. But, you and I both know that you hit bottom with Vicki's death. I'm getting a lot of heat, from the highest level, to reassign you and to classify Melissa Walker's death as a suicide."

Letting out a sigh, I said, "That's bull shit Cap—and you know it."

"Of course it is. I just want a little reassurance. I wanna know what direction the wind is blowin' before I enter a shit storm."

"All right," I said.

"Jack, the Governor has personally spoken to me. The Attorney General is reviewing whether the State Police has sole jurisdiction over the death of Melissa Walker. That prick Bradley G is apparently behind it all. He convinced OSP to request an opinion from the AG. Frankly, I'm mad as hell about it. Nonetheless, my neck's on the line."

"Okay," I said.

"The information that I've received is that Melissa Walker had a history of psychological problems. She apparently struggled in law school and became depressed. She sought counseling and was prescribed medication."

"Do you want me to close the case, Cap—is that what you're telling me?"

"No, I'm not," said Cap. "Don't kill the messenger here, Jack. There's more. I've got a copy of an affidavit in my hand. It's a statement from an individual named David Williams, who asserts that he was Walker's boyfriend in law school. He states that she enjoyed sadomasochistic sex. I've also got copies of four referrals for counseling, which were made out to Melissa Walker. They span the last couple of years."

"None of that smells right, Cap," I said.

"I know. Listen, I've scheduled a press conference for nine tomorrow morning. I want to get the AG off my back. However, I'm also plenty pissed off with the Statesman Journal for its hatchet job on you and my department. We're family here. So, look, tell me everything that you know."

"You already know it," I said. "Look, we've got an event that led to the death of a young woman who worked for Senator Jacobsen. The autopsy report shows that she resisted an attacker. We also have the Senator admitting that he was in the Capitol Building on the eve of the victim's death. Then we have the fact that the Senator fled the Country just a few hours later under suspicious circumstances. Let's not forget that the victim's parents were also murdered later the same day."

"All right, I agree that you've got enough to treat this as a murder investigation. The damn newspaper doesn't run Salem PD, and neither does the AG. I just want you to play it by the book, Jack—we've got a lynch mob on our hands."

"Okay," I said.

I had always despised both news reporters and politicians. Most reporters were like jackals—they could just as easily attack you as they could praise you. And it was all for the purpose of furthering their individual careers, although they routinely defended their sensational stories under the banner of "the public's right to know." Furthermore, I'd already been warned by Gunny about the political influence of the Jacobsen family. The local newspaper was obviously not outside its reach. What I hadn't counted on, however, was the involvement of the Executive Branch and the Attorney General.

The next morning arrived with a gray overcast layer of clouds. The press conference was being held at the downtown convention center. At 9 o'clock sharp, Cap and I walked up to the podium. There were two white linen cloth covered tables on each side. The podium had several microphones affixed to it. I sat down at the table to the right, while Cap stood and began the press conference. As I sat there, I found myself musing about how nice it would be to be fly fishing in Montana, rather than seated here in a stuffy conference room packed full of reporters.

"Good morning," said Cap. "I've arranged for this press conference in order to respond to the recent news stories that have criticized both my department and Senior Homicide Detective Terrence Davis, who is seated here to my right.

"First, I want to say that I have not asked for Detective Davis's resignation, nor will I be. Second, in my more than 30 years in law enforcement I have never had the misfortune of seeing the level of inaccurate reporting that was printed in yesterday's Statesman Journal."

The Chief paused for five or six seconds before continuing. "So, if you folks think that I'm a bit irritated over the unfair attack on my department and on Detective Davis, you are correct. At times, you folks, who call yourself news reporters, seem far more interested in sensational stories than you do in the truth. What the Statesman printed yesterday, and what the rest of you then carried, was not 'news' reporting. It had little resemblance to either the truth or the facts. Instead, it resembled a smear campaign. Both the editorial about Detective Davis and the article on Melissa Walker's death did a disservice to every fair-minded news reporter and citizen in this Country. Both of the stories were probably libelous. Detective Davis has served this city for nearly 20 years. He is the finest homicide detective that I have ever had the privilege of working with. The Statesman owes both him and my department an apology."

After a brief pause, Cap then said, "All right, questions? You ... over there ... with the purple necktie."

"Good morning, Chief. Steve Patterson, with the Columbia Gazette. Could you please explain how your department got so far off track in the Melissa Walker murder investigation? That is, why are you wasting the Taxpayers' money by assuming her death was the result of a murder, instead of a suicide? Also, why is your department harassing Senator Jacobsen, who by all accounts is merely on a family vacation?"

Cap shook his head and looked down for several seconds. With his arms outstretched on edges of the podium, he briefly looked over at me. I was sipping a cup of coffee from a Styrofoam cup. Cap could barely contain his anger. I just looked at him and shrugged my shoulders—it wasn't anything that I hadn't seen before.

Cap then responded, "Well, Mr. Patterson, was it? I guess you didn't hear anything that I just said. But, that hardly surprises me, since listening is apparently a lost art in the news industry. Let me address your questions one at a time.

"First, we are not off track in the investigation. We are totally on track."

"Second, Melissa Walker was very likely murdered. Although we have not ruled out either a suicide or an accident, we have solid evidence that she resisted an attacker."

"Last, we are not harassing the good Senator Jacobsen—far from it. In fact, we have probably treated him with more consideration than he deserves. No one is above the law simply because of their title. Melissa Walker was the Senator's legislative intern. We also know that a few hours after her death, the Senator's entire family fled the Country by jet aircraft. They are currently beyond our reach in Bogotá, Columbia."

"Now, does that shed any new light on this tragic event for you, Mr. Patterson? I think that the good Senator Jacobsen owes it to his Country, and to all Oregonians to immediately return home to cooperate with our investigation."

Silence pervaded the conference room—a very long silence. Not your standard fare for a press conference. Finally, a young woman dressed in a dark colored business suit and seated in the middle of the room, raised her hand. "Yes, you over there," said Cap.

"Chief, I understand that Melissa Walker's parents were murdered up in Bellevue, Washington, just a day ago. Could you comment on that?"

"Yes. But, I'm going to turn that over to Detective Davis." Turning towards me, Cap said, "Detective."

I stood up and awkwardly straightened my tie. "Thank you, Chief Heathrow. The investigation into the deaths of Melissa Walker's parents is ongoing and we are cooperating with the Bellevue Police Department. Since it's a current investigation, there's not a lot of detail that I can give you. What I can tell you is what Bellevue PD has already disclosed. That is, the Walkers were murdered right outside of the front door to their home. Their murder was not the result of some random act gone awry, such as a burglary. The killer carried out a deliberate act in a chillingly efficient manner."

"Do you believe that the two events are connected— the murder in Salem and the double homicide in Bellevue?" asked the woman.

"We don't know. But, it doesn't escape us that they were family members who were all killed on the same day."

Looking around the room, I then said, "Right there, in

the brown coat."

"Detective Davis, would you please comment on the editorial in yesterday's Statesman?"

"And your name is?"

"Oh I'm sorry. Tom Kitzel, with the Roseburg Herald."

"Okay. Well, Mr. Kitzel, I've been working in law enforcement for about 20 years now. I cut my teeth interning for the best homicide detective that Oregon has ever seen—the now retired Pete Gunnerson. I don't even pretend to be in Gunny's league. But, I did learn a thing or two from him. We have a top notch police department here in Salem, and I'm proud to be associated with it. If you bother to look at my career, you'll find that I've solved all but one of the murders that I've ever investigated. So, I believe that my track record and experience count for a lot. Yet, from what I've heard about yesterday's editorial, which I haven't bothered to read, I don't think that it reflected a whole lot of journalistic integrity. Now, it might have reflected a lot of journalistic weakness, or perhaps undue influence, but, it surely didn't reflect a lot of integrity."

Again, there was silence—several seconds of it. True to form, however, the pack of newspaper and television reporters quickly recovered and began frantically waving their arms and shouting out questions. But, Cap was done. He stood up, raised both of his arms, and announced, "That'll be all ladies and gentleman. The good detective and I have work to do. Jack?"

With that, Cap and I exited the Willamette Room on the main floor of the Convention Center. We strode shoulder-to-shoulder out of the room and through the lobby. As soon as we had turned the corner towards the stairwell to the parking garage, I said, "Thanks, Cap. I appreciate the vote of confidence. But, you didn't have to do that you know? It'll probably cost you."

"Bull shit," replied Cap. "The day I start kissin' ass is the day I turn in my badge. I did what was right. Anyone in law enforcement knows that you're a damn fine detective." Pausing a bit, Cap then added, "So did Vicki."

A little startled, I said, "What?"

"Jack, she was one helluva woman—brains, humor, and beauty. My wife and I thought the world of her. My Doris fought the good fight with breast cancer about 15 years ago. Remember? Thankfully, she was lucky enough to survive it."

A lump was beginning to well up in my throat. I nodded my head as Cap continued, "So, when I read the editorial garbage that the dimwits over there across the street wrote, I thought about Vicki. I asked myself what she would have done. I kept coming back to one thing— an image of her telling you that you needed to confront the newspaper because what it was doing was wrong."

"Yeah, you're right," I said.

Cap and I then exited the Convention Center's underground parking garage. Cap was driving his unmarked Ford sedan. Just as we turned north onto Liberty Street, his cell phone rang. It was Sophie Lawrence, the President and Publisher of the Statesman Journal. She had just watched our live press conference on the wall-mounted flat screen television set in her executive office.

Like most downtown business people, Lawrence was acquainted with the City's Chief of Police. She began the phone conversation by graciously apologizing for the editorial that had slammed both me and his department. She then explained that the editorial had not gone through the newspaper's normal approval process. To that end, she indicated that she would be investigating the matter and that the Statesman would be printing a retraction in tomorrow's edition—something that Cap knew was unlikely. She then asked Cap if she could speak to "Detective Davis." Cap obliged and handed me his phone. As he did so, he whispered, "It's the CEO of the Statesman."

I shook my head and rolled my eyes. While I knew that Cap would probably receive some criticism for being so outspoken, I didn't think that the crusade would start so soon. So, as I picked up the phone receiver, I let out an audible sigh.

"Davis," I answered.

'Hi Detective, My name's Sophie Lawrence—I'm the President and publisher of the Statesman Journal."

"Uh-huh."

"I wanted you to hear this from the top brass over here at the newspaper. I, and everyone on my staff, wish to apologize for the slanted editorial and the inaccurate reporting of your investigation. I just wanted you to know that I'm taking responsibility for it. I'm truly sorry. Without naming names, I can assure you that I'm already looking into the matter. The editorial in particular, but, also the news article, did not go through our normal screening process. I'm not sure why. This probably will sound very lame to you at the moment, but, as long as I'm here, the Statesman will remain committed to the ideals of accurate reporting and fair editorials. What was printed in yesterday's paper did not comport with those standards. I'm truly sorry."

I was a bit taken aback by Ms. Lawrence's apparent candor—not a very common characteristic in the news media. Hesitating a bit, I responded, "Thanks, Ms.

Lawrence. I accept your apology. We all make mistakes. I've tried in my 20 years here at Salem PD to be as straight with the Statesman as I can. That will continue."

Ms. Lawrence, replied, "All right, I appreciate that. Thanks for being so gracious, detective. Please don't hesitate to stop by here to talk with me—professionally or personally. My door's always open"

Cocking my head a bit and raising an eyebrow, I said, "Okay. I might take you up on that sometime. Thanks."

Handing the phone back to Cap, I asked, "What do you make of her?"

Cap replied, "She's actually okay. She's never burned me. She's also cooperated with me every time that I've needed the newspaper's help. I think she knows right from wrong."

I considered Cap's words without responding.

After returning to the Department, Eva and I met with Cap in his office. We discussed the problems associated with not being able to interrogate the Senator. Every hour that passed by while he was sequestered away in Bogota, meant that potential evidence was disappearing. For example, did he have any clothing that matched the forensic evidence found underneath the victim's fingernails? Did he have an alibi as to his whereabouts during the 2:00 to 3:00 a.m. time of the victim's death?

During the meeting, Cap informed us that he had been in contact with both the local Bogotá authorities and the American Consulate. He had also contacted the Oregon Attorney General about the possibility of beginning the extradition process. Needless to say, the AG wasn't being very cooperative. He'd already tried, but failed, to bully Cap into ordering me to drop my investigation into Melissa Walker's death. To that end, the AG informed

Cap that it would take weeks, if not months, to begin the extradition process.

In fact, however, new evidence was unfolding by the minute. I had assigned Officer Manion to return to Walker's apartment complex to canvass the tenants. After he did so, he obtained a similar description from three tenants of a Caucasian male who had been seen with Walker. So we were looking for a John Doe, in his middle years, with brown colored hair, and of average height and weight.

Also, Lawton had sent over the list of names of all the people who had entered and exited the Capitol Building near the time of Walker's death. In doing so, he had established that 27 individuals, mostly public officials, were already in the building when its doors closed at 4 p.m. Another 39 people then entered the building after it had closed to the public. Yet, only 61 individuals had exited the building after it had closed and before police arrived at approximately seven the next morning. Fortunately, however, Lawton and his staff had identified the five unaccounted for individuals.

They had done so by reviewing the surveillance tapes and by interviewing the four janitors who had worked a staggered shift that night. The five individuals included two janitors, two lawyers in the legislative counsel's office, and one state representative. According to Lawton, all five of the individuals had alibis and were not near the Capitol dome's stairwell at the approximate time of Melissa Walker's death.

Yet, in reviewing the surveillance tapes of people exiting the Capitol building between 4 p.m. and 7 a.m., Lawton determined that no one dressed like the man who had accompanied Walker into the building had exited the building. He had explained, however, that it would be possible for someone to exit the building without detection by using the stairwell down to the parking garage. That is, there is a blind spot in the security system that insiders know about and that has been on the list of items to fix for years. When I asked Lawton if Senator Jacobsen would have known about the blind spot, he said that he probably did. He then explained that the Senator had chaired the committee that approved the budget for the Capitol building's security system.

After the meeting with Cap, I headed back to my desk. Phyllis had already departed for lunch, but she had left a phone message for me to call an individual named Lynn Palmer, "regarding the Walker case." Without pause, I punched in the telephone number that Phyllis had written down.

"Sherwood, Baines, and Hollister, may I help you?" announced a polite sounding female receptionist.

"Uh, yes, could I speak to Lynn Palmer, please?"

"May I ask who's calling?" said the receptionist.

"Yes, this is Detective Davis with the Salem Police Department."

"Oh," said the receptionist. "I'll put you right through."

"Thank you."

After 30 seconds or so, Palmer answered, "Lynn Palmer, may I help you?"

"Hi Ms. Palmer, this is Detective Davis from the Salem Police Department—returning your call."

"Oh . . . yeah. Uh, I'm glad that you called. Uhm . . . I just learned about Melissa's death. God, what a shock! I'm going home early today, I'm just a mess. We were housemates in law school for the last two years. I mean,

God, we were really close. The newspaper is saying that her death was an apparent suicide, but that it's under investigation. Uh, I'm a little nervous about this. It's probably nothing. Oh, I shouldn't have bothered you."

I was tapping my fingers on my desk. These type of calls were typical. Sometimes they provided no relevant information at all, while other times they helped solve a murder. So, I was interested in whatever it was that this young woman had to say. But, she needed to relax. The poor kid was probably in her twenties—an age when you're not supposed to be experiencing the end of your best friend's life.

"Ms. Palmer, I've been a homicide cop for almost 20 years. Forgive me if I sound insensitive. I know that this is a difficult time for you. I can assure you, however, that I will leave no stone unturned in my investigation into Melissa's death. That's why I'm glad that you telephoned me. Many, many times a case will turn on a piece of information that an individual thinks is trivial. So, why don't you let me be the judge of whatever it is that you'd like to tell me—fair enough?"

"Well, okay," said Palmer, who I could hear sniffling. "Will you need to take my statement? And is there any chance that I would be called as a witness if there is a trial?"

"I won't mislead you. The answer could be yes on both counts. But, until I hear what you have to say, I won't really know. Obviously, you know something about the law. So, I'm sure that you're aware that the majority of criminal cases result in a plea bargain and don't go to trial."

"Okay. Well, here it is," said Palmer. "Melissa was very naïve. She was also extremely attractive, and men were constantly pursuing her. While she was very private about her personal life, I got the feeling that something was going on between her and the Senator. I never liked him—he was too slick. I'm not sure what was happening there, but I could see that Melissa was becoming uncomfortable. If I had to call it, I'd say that the Senator took advantage of her. Then, recently, there was some new guy that was pursuing her. She seemed interested and I could see that her mood was lighter. I think that she was falling for the guy. I know that it sounds pretty weird, but I think that the guy might have been the Senator's son, Michael Jacobsen. It's just a hunch. Melissa never talked about him. But, he called her once, and there was something about the way that Melissa acted when I handed her the telephone. She was sort of giddy—if you know what I mean? So, that's pretty much it detective. What do you think?"

I was thinking how lucky I was that this young woman had telephoned me. I was also now concerned about her safety. She knew some things—about a woman who, for some reason, had very likely been murdered along with her parents.

"I'm glad that you called, Ms. Palmer," I said. "I have one question for you. Was Melissa having any psychological problems?"

"Well, she was in some distress over her personal life. Like I said, she was very private. So, I don't know any details—she didn't share along those lines. But, generally, she was a very stable, even keeled, and upbeat woman."

"All right," I said. I didn't want to let on to Palmer that she might be in danger. But, she needed protection. "Ms. Palmer. I want you to listen very carefully. I appreciate the information that you've passed on. It's very helpful. Uh, you're in a law office right now, correct?"

With detectible concern in her voice, Palmer slowly

said, "Yes."

"In Portland?" I asked.

"Yes—downtown," she said.

"What's your address?"

Palmer recited her address and said that she was in an office building on the 26th floor. I jotted down the address in my pocket notepad.

"Are you near a window?"

Sounding a bit alarmed now, Palmer asked, "Yes, why?"

"Do exactly as I say, right now. Get outta there. Go to an interior room. Can you do that?"

"Uh, yes," she said. "There's a kitchenette about 20 feet from my office."

"Good. As soon I hang up, I want you to immediately go there and stay there. Understand?"

Now frightened, Palmer said "Oh my God! Am I in danger?"

"Not if you do exactly what I'm telling you. I'll be there in an hour. I'm five-ten, average weight, and I'm dressed in a dark sports coat and jeans. Go to the kitchen—now!"

Crying a bit, Palmer said, "Okay."

I then drove up the freeway to Portland in an unmarked police cruiser. After opening the law office's double doors, I flashed my badge at the startled receptionist. I asked where I could find Lynn Palmer. She nervously pointed behind her and said, "Third door on the left."

I walked briskly down the hallway, first passing Palmer's office, and then finding the kitchenette. There she was—seated at a small round table. She looked very pale. I showed her my badge. I then quickly escorted her out of the office, down the elevator, and into my car.

Now that Palmer was in my custody and we were

headed away from her office, I started asking some questions.

"Where do you live?"

"In a small apartment here in Portland, near Northwest 23rd and Burnside," said Palmer.

"You live with anyone?"

"My 4-year-old son," she said.

"You have a son?"

"Yes," Palmer said anxiously.

"Where is he?"

With her cheeks flushed, Palmer said, "In a daycare center about three miles from here up on Terwilliger."

Pointing off to the right, I asked, "That way?"

"Yes!" said Palmer.

With that, I slammed the gas pedal to the floor and turned sharply onto Salmon Street. With Palmer pointing the way I arrived at the daycare center within 10 minutes. It was now 1:40 p.m. I hurriedly escorted Palmer into the daycare center.

Fortunately, we located her son, Jarod, right away. The happy little towhead wasn't sure what to make of his mother, who was by now crying. While choking back her sobs, Palmer knelt down and hugged Jarod with all her might. I felt for her. While I wasn't a dad myself, I felt pretty protective about my two little nieces. As Palmer was signing out Jarod for the rest of the day, the weary daycare attendant said to her, "Hey, your work associate Stephan was just here and said that he was hoping to find you. Did you see him? He said that he had some urgent business to discuss with you."

"Palmer's face dropped. She then blurted out, "Oh my God!" as she raised her trembling right hand to her mouth.

Drawing my revolver, I stepped into the open doorway to shield Palmer and her son. I then asked, "You don't work with a Stephan, do you?"

"No," said Palmer.

I then grabbed Palmer and her son and escorted them into a storage closet and told them to stay put. Next, I turned to the now frightened daycare worker and displayed my badge. In a hushed tone and with our backs literally against the wall, I said, "Ma'am, I'm a police officer. When exactly did you have your conversation with the man who identified himself as Stephan?"

"Uh, he was just here," she said. "It was about 20 minutes ago, I guess—maybe less. Yeah, I'd say that it was real close to 1:30 p.m. Why, is something wrong?"

"Yes. Could you describe what the guy looked like?"

The wide eyed young woman said, "Uhm. He was Hispanic. Not quite as tall as you. He had a mustache and was nicely dressed. Let's see, I think he was wearing a black T-shirt with an olive colored blazer."

"Anything else that would help identify him— eyeglasses a scar, a tattoo?"

She said, "Uh, you know, I think that he did have a pair of sunglasses that were pushed up over his head."

"Did he say anything else or inquire about Jarod?

"No," she said.

"All right, ma'am."

I then told her that some uniformed police officers would be arriving shortly and that she should cancel daycare for the rest of the day. Next, I escorted Palmer and her son out of the daycare center and into my car. I drove towards Salem. While en route, I telephoned Cap and explained the situation. He immediately contacted Portland PD. Within 15 minutes four Portland police officers arrived at the daycare center. The center then began proceeding with its emergency closure plan, while the police officers searched the premises. They did not locate the man who had identified himself as Stephan. However, the officers bagged and sealed a few forensic items, such as a fresh cigarette butt found just outside the main entrance and a gum wrapper that was inside a hallway closet.

While driving back to Salem, I tried to calm Palmer's fears. I apologized for turning her day upside down. She hadn't yet heard that Melissa's parents had been murdered the previous day. She was beside herself with grief and worry.

After returning to Salem, I escorted Palmer and her son up to my office and introduced them to Eva. I figured that Eva's similar background as a single mother would be a good fit. Heck, all I'd seem to have done was to upset Palmer. After a brief discussion with Eva and Cap, it was agreed that Palmer and her kid would stay at Eva's house for a couple of days.

On a hunch, I left the Department on foot and walked along Pringle Creek towards Willamette University. I was headed for the Student Counseling Service office near the Mark O. Hatfield Library, in the eastern section of the campus. It was just before 5 p.m. and it was almost dark out. I walked through the doorway and into the waiting room of the small building. There was a young woman seated at the reception desk behind a sliding glass window. She was chewing gum and looked bored. She was college age, sported a crew cut with bleached blond hair, and had piercings in her lower lip and left nostril. Apparently for dramatic effect, she wore eyeliner that was caked on so heavy that she looked like a human version of a raccoon. Then, to top it off, she was wearing a black tank top that revealed a high-pro glow tan that could only be achieved by several hours spent in a tanning salon.

"Sorry, we're closing," she nonchalantly said, while blowing a bubble.

I held up my badge and said, "Hi, I'm Detective Davis with the Salem Police Department. I just have a few questions ma'am. I won't hold you up."

"Uh, I'm already late," she said.

"This'll just take a minute. How long have you worked here?"

"Since last year," she said. I went home for the summer and just started again."

"What'd you say your name was?

"I didn't," she said. "It's Samantha—Samantha Livingston."

"Okay, Samantha." Motioning with my hand to a clipboard on the chest-high countertop in front of me, I said, "Is this a sign in sheet for students who obtain services here?"

"Uh, yeah," she said.

"Okay. Can you tell me what kinds of services are offered here?"

With a shrug of her shoulders, she said, "Mostly student counseling. You know—academic or personal concerns. But, we also provide STD evaluations and birth control options."

"I see. So, is there a nurse or a physician on staff?"

"Yes, we have a nurse who screens for STDs, and two doctors," she explained. "One of the doctors is a psychiatrist."

"Okay, uh, Samantha, could you tell me if you ever saw a law school student in here named Melissa Walker?"

"Uh, I'm not sure that I can discuss that," she said.

"So you know Melissa Walker?"

"Uh, I didn't say that," she said.

"But, you read the newspaper, right?"

"Yeah, sure," she said.

"So, you know about the recent death of Melissa Walker over in the Capitol Building?"

"Are you kidding? Every student on campus knows about it," she said. "My girlfriends and I are all freaked. The rumor is that she didn't commit suicide and that she was the victim of a serial killer?"

"Samantha, I'm going to be straight with you. I'm investigating Melissa Walker's death. At this point, there's no suggestion that there's a serial killer on the loose. Okay? You can tell your friends that."

"Okay," she said.

Listen, I don't want you to reveal anything that would violate any confidentiality laws or that would get you in trouble, okay?"

"All right," she said.

"I could always get a search warrant and then come in here and seize the Clinic's files and records. But, I'd rather not do that. How about if I just ask you a few simple questions that would only require you to just give me a simple 'yes' or a 'no' answer, and that wouldn't require you to violate any laws?"

"Okay—you're the police," she said.

"Right. Okay, Samantha, did you ever see Melissa Walker come in here for services?"

"Yes," she said.

"Did she come in here for psychiatric counseling?"

"No," she said. "Look, if you promise to not rat me out, I can tell you what you probably want to know?"

"You got it."

"She came in here for the pill," she said. "You know—birth control. That's it. She met with our doctor once, obtained a prescription, and then came in every two months to get a refill."

"That's it—she was in here solely for birth control?"

"As far as I know, yes," she said.

Looking down at the tray of business cards on the countertop, I said, "All right, you've been very helpful, Samantha. I have just a couple more questions. It looks like the physician that you have on staff here is Dr. Kuenzi, is that right?"

"Yes," she said.

"All right, I know that what I'm about to ask you is going to require more than a 'yes' or 'no' answer. So, it's up to you, Samantha. You've already been very helpful. Can you make me a copy of Melissa Walker's prescription slip?"

Frowning a bit, Samantha said, "I need this job. I don't want to get fired."

"I can guarantee you that you won't get fired. In fact, I'll be sure to talk to your boss to let him know that you were very professional and helpful."

"It's a she—my boss is Lenora Parker," she said.

The spunky receptionist then walked back to a large file cabinet, pulled out a file, and opened it up. She then grabbed Melissa Walker's prescription for birth control, made a copy, and handed it to me.

I then handed her my business card and said, "Okay, Samantha. I appreciate your help. If you get into any trouble here at work for cooperating with me, I want you to call me. Okay?"

"Sure, thanks," she said.

5

Columbia

I woke up early the next morning and was at my desk by 6:30 a.m. It had now been four days since Melissa Walker's death. After making a pot of coffee, I checked my phone messages and began tackling the paperwork in my "in basket." Within 10 minutes I returned to the copy room and noticed that some faxes had been received. I nonchalantly picked up the three or four sheets of paper— not expecting to see anything important. To my surprise, the second piece of paper was a fax sent to me from the Central Intelligence Agency. The CIA had become interested in the apparent murders of Melissa Walker, and her parents Albert and Gloria, due to the possibility that they had all been assassinated by one or more foreign nationals.

To that end, both the Bellevue and the Salem Police Departments had requested the CIA's assistance. They were interested in whether any Columbians had entered the United States during the week of October 2nd.

The facsimile from the CIA read as follows:

CONFIDENTIAL MEMORANDUM
To: Chief Detective Terrence Davis, SPD
Fr: Agent Lee Coatsworth, CIA, Anti-
             Terrorist Task Force
Re: Walker Family Murder Investigation
Date: October 12th
Mr. Davis:

My task force has reviewed all of the passenger manifests on commercial airlines that flew into the Continental United States during the week of October 2nd. We found that 156 individuals entered our borders with originating flights from Columbia. 74 of those individuals landed in the Eastern United States. The 82 remaining individuals landed west of the Mississippi River. 33 of those 82 individuals landed on the West Coast and 8 of those 33 individuals landed at Portland International Airport, while 5 landed at Seattle-Tacoma Airport. We have contacted and interviewed all 13 of those individuals. None of them appear to be involved in the deaths of Albert and Gloria Walker, as they all have solid alibis. Upon your request, we would be glad to turn over the names of the 13 individuals.. But, candidly, I believe that any effort devoted to investigating those individuals would be a waste of your time.

However, with the cooperation of the Federal Aviation Administration, we have also investigated the entrance of any private aircraft that flew into the United States during the week of October 2nd, which originated from Columbia. There were nine such aircraft. Three landed east of the Mississippi and were connected with classified United States Army missions. Five others landed west of the Mississippi, *but appear as legitimate flights for either business or personal purposes.*

The one remaining flight landed at Seattle-Tacoma Airport. The flight originated in Bogotá at 9 a.m. on Monday, October 9th. It landed and refueled in Mexico City, and then arrived at Sea-Tac just after 5 p.m. It was apparently carrying one man and one woman. The male, Jorge Gonzalez, is 43 years of age. The female, Rosa Guerro, is age 31. We have done a background check on both of them. They each have ties to Columbian organized crime. The aircraft departed Sea-Tac on Tuesday, October 10th, at 3:30 a.m. and returned directly to Bogotá, with a brief fuel stop in Mexico, City.

If I can be of any further assistance, please do not hesitate to call me.

I sat back in my chair and sipped my cup of coffee. It now seemed very likely that there was some sort of a Columbian connection to the three murders. That is, the Jacobsens had fled to Columbia, and now the CIA had confirmed that there was suspicious air traffic from Columbia to Seattle on the eve of the murder of Albert and Gloria Walker.

The Bellevue Police Department had already pieced together the events surrounding the double homicide of Albert and Gloria Walker. On Monday, October 9th, Albert and Gloria Walker had been distraught over the recent news of their daughter's death. They had gone to an evening Catholic Mass service in Bellevue. They were seen departing St. Mark Church at 9:35 or 9:40 p.m. Their bodies were not discovered until early the next morning, when their newspaper delivery boy found them just after 5:00 a.m. Based on the degree of rigor mortis in their bodies, the Washington State Medical Examiner opined that the Walkers had died between 10:00 p.m. and midnight.

Next, I accessed our computer system to retrieve anything that I could find on one David Williams—as the AG had said an individual by that name had signed an affidavit about Melissa Walker's sexual propensities. Four matches surfaced. Two of them were single men under the age of 40, who lived here in town. One of them worked at the Starbuck's coffee shop on South Commercial, across from the Fred Meyer store. The other was listed as an employee of a law firm, Johnson & Flynn. I decided to "drop in" unannounced at both places.

I drove up Commercial Street to the Starbuck's shop. There was a young woman behind the till. I asked her if "David" was working. She looked at me with a puzzled look, and said, "Yeah, he's right here." She motioned towards a six foot tall dude with long hair, who was standing a few feet from her. The guy appeared to be in his mid-twenties. He was now looking straight at me.

"You're David Williams?" I asked.

"Do I know you?" he good naturedly asked.

Displaying my badge, I said, "I'm Detective Davis, with the Salem Police Department. I'm investigating a possible murder of a young woman named Melissa Walker."

"Whoa! You're the cop that I just watched on TV. You wanna talk with me?"

"Yes," I said. "I just need a few minutes of your time. Can you step over here for a few minutes?"

Looking at his apparent boss, the young man walked along the counter and joined me at a small table near the entrance door.

"Mr. Williams, do you know Melissa Walker?" I

asked.

"No. Or, yes. Well, I mean no, but I've read about her suicide in the newspaper. I know that she jumped out of one of the windows up in the Capitol dome."

"Okay, listen very carefully," I said. "Other than reading about Melissa Walker in the newspaper, are you telling me that you've never met her?"

"Absolutely—I've never met the chick."

"Did you attend Willamette's Law School?" I asked.

"What, are you kidding? I graduated from South Salem High School and then went down to OSU. I washed out before the end of my freshman year. I just enjoy livin' and I wouldn't know anybody over at Willamette—especially anybody over at the Law School."

So, you didn't sign an affidavit about Melissa Walker?" I asked.

"Huh? What's an affidavit? No, like I said, I don't know anything about her, other than what I've read in the newspaper or watched on television."

"Okay, Mr. Williams," I said. "Here's my card. I want you to keep it. If you are bothered at all, or questioned by anyone in connection with the death of Melissa Walker, I want you to call me. Okay?"

"Uh, yeah, sure. Am I in some sort of trouble?"

"No," I said. "But, someone with your same name has come up in our investigation."

"You know, I sometimes come across the name of another David Williams here in town. My bank gets us confused, and so does the Post Office, even Safeway for Christ's sake!"

"Do you know anything about this other individual?" I asked.

"No, other than that he has my same middle name of

'Steven.'"

"Okay," I said. "So, there's another 'David Steven Williams' here in town?"

"For sure!"

"All right, you've been very helpful, Mr. Williams," I said. "Would you like me to talk to your supervisor, to make sure that she doesn't make any wrong assumptions?"

"That might be nice."

I then took a few minutes to smooth things over with the guy's boss. After leaving Starbuck's, I headed back down Commercial Street for the law firm of Johnson & Flynn. The firm was located in a new building on Front Street, which housed condominiums on all but the 1st and 2nd floors. I walked into the posh law office with its marble wall fountain and identified myself to the twenty-something brunette receptionist.

"Hi, I'm Detective Davis, with the Salem Police Department. I'd like to speak to David Williams."

"Uh, sure—just a minute," said the slightly flustered receptionist.

After I had taken a seat and flipped through an issue of Sports Illustrated, a young man dressed in a nicely tailored suit stepped into the waiting room. He confidently asked, "Detective Davis?"

Standing up, I said, "Yes, if you're David Williams, I'd like to talk with you for a few minutes."

"Sure. I'm with a client right now, however. So, would you mind waiting about 20 minutes?"

Pretty suave, I thought. I had to hand it to the kid—he knew the art of psychological warfare and he wasn't about to give an inch.

"Yeah, I'm afraid that I would," I said. "But, just come over to the police department after five. It'll be easier to question you there anyway."

"Uh, that won't exactly work for me."

"Look Mr. Williams. I'm conducting a murder investigation. I'd like to ask you some questions. It's in your interest to cooperate. You can do this the easy way right now, or the hard way later on."

"All right, look. Give me a couple minutes here to talk to my client and move him out of my office."

Of course, the kid didn't really have a client in his office. He and I both knew that. He was merely trying to save face. While I waited, no one was ushered back out to the waiting room.

A couple minutes passed and then the kid reappeared in the waiting area and said, "All right detective, my office is now available."

Holding the door open for me, the kid seated himself comfortably in his high-back leather chair that was situated behind a traditional looking lawyer's desk.

"What can I do for you?" he asked.

"You're David Steven Williams, is that correct?"

"Yes," he said.

I asked, "You're a recent Willamette Law School Graduate?"

"Yes," he said. "Are you familiar with the Law School?"

I didn't feel like divulging anything about myself to the cocky brat. So, I ignored his question. "Tell me about your relationship with Melissa Walker?" I asked.

"What's there to tell?" he coolly shot back.

"Well, for starters, it looks as though she was murdered and I see that you have a history of beating her up. So, you can either start spilling your guts now asshole, or I can handcuff you here in your office and haul your ass over to the County Jail for processing—your choice."

"Are you serious?"

"Very," I said.

"Okay, look. I knew, Melissa. We were in the same class at Willamette. We dated for a year or so. What else do you want to know?"

"Your affidavit—who put you up to it?" I asked.

"Whadaya mean? No one put me up to it. The State Police talked to me and I cooperated."

"Anyone in particular?" I asked.

"Yeah, a senior detective with OSP. His name was Bradley Lewis."

"So, you have nothing to add or detract from your affidavit?" I asked.

"I don't understand."

"Are you standing by your affidavit, Mr. Williams?" I asked.

"Of course."

"So, if you were called to testify in a murder trial, you'd testify that Melissa Walker liked sadomasochistic sex and that the two of you engaged in that sort of thing for over a year?" I asked.

"That's not what I said. What I swore to was that Melissa enjoyed that type of thing and that there were times when she would become violent if I didn't agree to do certain things."

"Did she ever scratch you or assault you?" I asked.

"Yes, lots of times."

"Okay, I think I've heard enough, Mr. Williams," I said. "If I were you, I wouldn't try to leave town anytime soon. Here's my card, feel free to give me a call. You can count on me dropping in again in the very near future."

"My only aim is to help in the investigation."

"I'm sure it is," I mockingly said. "Oh, one more question. Where were you early last Monday morning, October 9th, between the hours of midnight and 5 a.m."

"I imagine in my apartment asleep."

"So you were alone then?"

"Yes."

After I returned to the Department, I informed Eva of my encounters with the two David Williams here in town. I wished that she'd been along. She can often rat out a liar better than I can. I had no doubt, however, that the Starbuck's dude was being truthful, while the lawyer chump was up to his eyeballs crapola.

Eva and I spent the rest of the day at our desks—painstakingly poring over the evidence that we had gathered. We ran different "who dun it" scenarios off of each other and looked for flaws in the direction of our investigation. As any detective knows, most crimes are solved by no frills police work and dogged perseverance. So, I began checking and rechecking witness statements, telephone bills, and forensic reports.

One of the things that stood out was Lynn Palmer's revelation that Melissa Walker had possibly been romantically involved with Michael Jacobsen—the Senator's son. Thus, Eva and I decided to go down to the Salem Airport where the Jacobsen family's Cessna Citation was hangared. We talked to local pilots, flight instructors, and fuel service attendants. In doing so, we learned that Michael had regularly departed Salem in his Citation and often returned several days later. Yet, everyone down at the airport thought nothing of it. They just considered it a normal part of Michael's air charter service. In truth, they were right—a charter pilot is often away from his home airport for days at a time.

Most of the individuals that Eva and I spoke to thought that Michael was flying down to Southern California. At least that's what he had told them, and the amount of fuel that he typically purchased was consistent with a flight of about three hours duration. The clincher, however, was when we retrieved the Flight Plans that Michael had filed and activated with the McMinnville Flight Service Station. For two years, Michael had made regular flights from Salem, Oregon, to Bogotá, Columbia, with fuel stops in either San Diego or Mexico City.

As Eva and I both knew, however, such evidence could be viewed as either supporting or detracting from what Senator Jacobsen had publicly claimed—that he and his family had flown to their private condominium in Bogotá, on a well-deserved and previously planned vacation.

By 4 p.m., my eyes were beginning to glaze over. I was staring at the autopsy report on Melissa Walker. Eva and I had already each gone over the report three or four times. At the moment, I was reading page three of the report. Doc had stated that he found traces of an "intranasal solution." His finding was annotated with a footnote. I let out a sigh. At 48 years of age, one of the concessions that I had recently made to Father Time was that my near vision was not what it used to be. For some reason, Doc always had his office staff print his footnotes in a ridiculously small font size. If I hadn't known better, I might have concluded that Doc was intentionally trying to make the damn things as hard as possible to read. To make matters worse, Doc also seemed to enjoy inserting footnotes. Thus, his autopsy reports always came with a lengthy footnote section attached to the back, which sometimes totaled three or four pages. My past experience was that the irksome footnotes were technical in nature and nearly always irrelevant—at least to a murder investigation.

Nonetheless, I slipped on my dime store reading glasses and turned to the back of the report to reread the associated footnotes. Trying to stay awake and to not daydream about leaving work early for a cold beer at the Roadhouse, I finally reached footnote 26, which stated:

> "*The subject has a documented history of cluster headaches. Standard initial treatment with oxygen therapy failed. Therefore, her attending physician, Dr. Simon, began administering a solution of intranasal cocaine. Exhibit 14-1. It is well-established that the prophylactic administration of a 10% solution usually decreases the frequency and severity of the clusters.*"

I shook my head and then muttered, "Wait a minute! What?" I had painstakingly reviewed Melissa Walker's medical history. Most of it was in the form of chart notes that were irrelevant, mundane, and personal. But, one of the seemingly mundane things that I had read was that Walker had gone to Dr. Simon just a few months after starting law school. Apparently the stress of being away from home and starting law school had caused her to experience severe migraine-like headaches. Eventually, Dr. Simon diagnosed her condition as cluster headaches. His diagnosis was based on the chronicity and severity of Walker's headaches. Fortunately, however, after almost two years of treatment, or by September of last year, Walker's cluster headaches had ceased. Thus, I recalled reading a chart note from Dr. Simon that had stated that Walker had not experienced any further problems with cluster headaches for *nearly a year*.

I hurriedly flipped through Dr. Simon's chart notes for the period from September of last year through the present. Just as I had thought, there was no indication that Dr. Simon had administered the intranasal cocaine solution during that period. In fact, as I had recalled, there was affirmative evidence that he had not done so. That is, in his recent July 21st chart note, Dr. Simon reported: "Melissa has not experienced any cluster headaches since last September, at which time I discontinued all further administration of intranasal cocaine."

"Eva!" I said. Catching her eyes, I motioned downward to the paperwork in front of me. She walked over to my desk and said, "Yeah? What is it, Jack?"

Still squinting through my reading glasses at the seemingly micro-sized footnote, I looked up and said, "You read the Walker girl's autopsy report a million times like I did, right?"

"Absolutely," said Eva.

"And you read her medical history too, right?"

"Of course," said Eva. "Did we miss something?"

"Looks like it. Recall that Doc noted that he'd found some traces of a nasal solution?"

"Sure," shrugged Eva. "Like I've got over there in my desk drawer."

"No. In the associated footnote buried at the end of Doc's report, uh . . . footnote 26, it says that it's a <u>cocaine</u> solution."

Eva began to furrow her eyebrows. I continued, "Eva, Melissa Walker suffered from cluster headaches. They're apparently painful enough to send somebody over a cliff— or, perhaps through a 100 foot high window opening in the Capitol dome? From what I gather, one of the standard treatments for the condition is an intranasal cocaine solution. So, although Doc found traces of cocaine on the Walker girl, he attributed that to her doctor's treatment of her cluster headache condition. But, here's the critical part: Melissa Walker stopped having cluster headaches back in September of last year—over a year ago—and at that time her doctor discontinued any further administration of intranasal cocaine.

"God!" said Eva, "I'll get Doctor Emmons on the phone."

"Yup."

It was already after 5 p.m., but Doc had not left his office yet. Eva and I went into Salem PD's conference room in order to talk privately with Doc, while he was on the speaker phone.

"Hi, Doc. It's Jack and Eva," I said. "We're calling about Melissa Walker's autopsy report."

"You two are mind readers. I was just going to call you. The DNA test results were just transmitted to me. You will recall that three samples were collected. There was semen on her body, skin underneath her fingernails, and semen on her bedroom sheets. They all match. Also, whoever the guy is, he's the father of the child that the victim was carrying."

"Great work, Doc," I said. "That's vital information. Listen, you're the expert here. So we may have merely stumbled onto something that we don't fully understand."

Sounding a bit impatient, Doc replied, "Go ahead."

"Do you recall that you found traces of some nasal spray or solution on the Walker girl?"

"That's correct," said Doc. "I found evidence of an intranasal cocaine solution. She had a history of cluster headaches. Her physician had treated her condition with the accepted frontline defenses. But, they didn't work. So he began regularly applying a 10 percent solution of intranasal cocaine. Cluster headaches are pretty rare, but we do occasionally see traces of intranasal cocaine on a murder victim."

"Sure. But, did you know that the Walker girl's headaches had ceased and that she had apparently not received any intranasal cocaine in over a year?"

"What! Are you pullin' my leg, Jack?"

"No, sir."

"Christ!" said Doc. "Maybe I'm startin' to slip a little bit. If that history is accurate, then I made an error—a rather embarrassing one. I'm going to stick around here and reexamine the sample that I collected from the victim's nostrils. Where'd you find the reference to the victim's cessation of intranasal cocaine treatment?"

"It's a July 21st chart note from Dr. Simon. Hey, Doc—just let me know what you discover, okay? You're the best in the business and everybody in law enforcement knows it. Lord knows I've made my share of mistakes, and I'll undoubtedly make plenty more before I turn in my badge."

"Well, thanks, Jack," said Doc. "But, it looks like I messed up. Let me review things, however, and then get back to you. It'll probably be tomorrow morning. It sounds like I'll be issuing a brief addendum to my report."

"Okay, Doc. Have a nice evening."

"You too," said Doc.

6

Life's Metamorphosis

IT HAD BEEN a long day, but a productive one. On my way home I stopped in at Thompson's Brew Pub to take the edge off. The pub is housed in a turn of the Century mansion with a virtual maze of different sized rooms that guarantees a certain amount of privacy. Just the way I like things.

I took a seat in a booth. There was a football game playing on the overhead television set. I glanced up only long enough to see that it was some professional game between the "Ravens" and the "Titans." When I was a kid, I had all of the old NFL team names memorized. It was a different world now, however. Los Angeles Rams' quarterback Roman Gabriel was no longer throwing touchdown passes to wide receiver Jack Snow.

After quietly sipping my beer and watching the game for several minutes, a perky female waitress interrupted my reverie and asked, "Another drink?"

I looked up, smiled, and said, "Yeah, how 'bout another one and then cash me out."

The waitress flicked me a smile and said, "You got it."

After finishing my beer, I crawled into my 1990 red Eagle Talon and headed south on Liberty Street. While driving, I pulled out my cell phone and punched in Eva's number. She answered after a couple of rings. I asked her how the Palmer woman and her young son were doing. She said that they were fine. We then discussed the advisability of letting Palmer and her son return to her residence in Portland. Portland PD officers had inspected her apartment and had kept it under surveillance for the last several days. Nothing had turned up.

On my way home I stopped at the Sunnyslope Shopping Center to pick up some take-out food from Love-Love's Thai restaurant. I then sat alone at my marble dining table and ate dinner, while looking at the twinkling lights of Independence and Monmouth.

The next morning it was raining. I put on my overcoat and climbed into the Talon. I had gotten up early so I'd have time to stop at White's Restaurant for breakfast. Once there, I read the morning edition of the Statesman Journal and came across the retraction that Lawrence had promised. In truth, I was genuinely surprised. Although Lawrence seemed sincere, I didn't think that she would actually follow through with a public apology and a retraction of the editorial that had bashed me.

After I finished my breakfast and arrived at the Department, I telephoned Lawrence. It was still early, 7:12 a.m.

"Sophie Lawrence, may I help you?"

"Hi, Ms. Lawrence. This is Detective Davis. I hope that I'm not interrupting your morning cup of coffee?"

"No, no. I'm glad you called," she said. "Did you see this morning's paper?

"Yes, I did. In fact, that's why I'm calling. I just read

your retraction. I, uh, appreciate what you've done. That sort of thing is rare. In fact, honestly, it's restored my faith in journalism a bit. Anyway, I just wanted to say 'thanks,' and to let you know that I respect what you're trying to do."

"Well," she said. "I think that we have a long ways to go here at the newspaper to even the ledger with you and the police department. The editorial never should have met with committee approval. But, I'll accept your compliment. Thanks, detective."

"You're welcome. You have a nice day."

"Detective . . . ," she said.

"My friends call me Jack."

"Oh, well, please do me the return favor of calling me Sophie."

"Deal."

"Uh," said Sophie. "You should know that the editorial was approved in my absence. I hadn't yet returned from a vacation in Cancun. But, my point in disclosing that is not to absolve myself of any blame—far from it. Rather, it's to let you know that my staff was pressured, intimidated, and lobbied by the Jacobsen family. Every one of the Jacobsen brothers, including the Senator, lobbied my staff and called in whatever chips they had with our parent corporation—the Sterrett Company."

"Sophie," I somewhat uncomfortably said. "Did the Senator telephone your staff there at the newspaper?"

"Yes, that's my understanding, as did his two brothers."

I then asked, "Do you have caller ID on your phones over there?"

"Of course," she said.

"Can you tell me the number that Senator Jacobsen

called from?"

"Sure," she said. "In fact, how about if I buy you dinner tonight so I can tell you even more?"

Caught off guard a bit, I managed to say, "Uh, yeah, sure—that'll work. You have a place in mind?"

"Bentley's at six-thirty, okay?" she asked.

"Yeah. Uh, I'll see you there at six-thirty."

"Great!" she said.

I hung up the phone and realized that I was feeling almost giddy about the thought of meeting Sophie for dinner. I thought to myself, "Okay, Jack. You're 48, and you're feeling like an 18-year-old high school kid who has a date on a Friday night. Relax, buddy."

In truth, I had been in such a state of malaise after Vicki's death, that I had lost all interest in dating other women. "Romance" just no longer mattered. Only by burying myself in my job and in my hobbies did I finally manage to get on top of the grieving process. In fact, I even became a bit reclusive. It was not unusual back then for me to spend entire weekends alone. Most of the time I'd busy myself in my small wood shop, which would become permeated with the smell of fresh cut wood. To me, it was comforting and peaceful as I toiled away in my shop and honed my skill. It allowed me to heal.

Shortly after 8 a.m., Eva and I discussed the course of our investigation into the three murders. As we were doing so, my desk phone rang—it was Phyllis.

"Good morning Jack," she said.

"Morning, Phyllis."

"I have Sophie Lawrence with the Statesman Journal on line 2. Shall I put her through?"

"Yes, please," I said, as I could feel my heart pounding in my chest and I nervously cleared my throat. I then heard Phyllis hit the transfer button.

"Hi, Sophie," I said.

"Hi Jack. I hope you don't think that I'm pestering you or anything, but we just picked up something over here on the wire service. Senator Jacobsen is going to give a prepared statement from Bogotá, at eight-thirty this morning our time. It's going to be televised on CNN. The national media is starting to pick up the story and it's being slanted as 'murder and politics.'"

"Really? Hey, thanks," I said. "I appreciate the call. Oh, and I wouldn't mind a little pestering."

"Hmmm," Sophie coyly replied. "Don't get your hopes up."

"Wouldn't dream of it. See you at six-thirty."

"Okay," said Sophie.

I then stood up, turned to Eva, and said, "Come on. Senator Jacobsen's holding a press conference in about 10 minutes and CNN is televising it."

The two of us then headed off towards the conference room where an overhead television set was mounted in the far corner. On my way there, I passed by Phyllis and asked her to tell Cap to join us.

At 8:30 a.m. Pacific Standard Time, CNN's coverage began. Senator Jacobsen was standing at a podium with several microphones attached. He was dressed in a suit. His wife, Susan, was standing just off of his right shoulder. She was dressed in a black dress with white trim. Michael was posted just off of the Senator's left shoulder. He was neatly dressed in a blue blazer, white dress shirt, and a red tie. Even I had to admit that the three looked like the All-American family. The Senator began by announcing that his purpose in airing a statement was to quiet any suspicion that he had any involvement in the apparent murders of Melissa Walker and her parents. He was playing it just right, I thought—not too confrontational, but not too weak either.

The Senator continued, "My family and I are greatly saddened and upset over the news of the tragic deaths of Melissa Walker and her parents. Melissa was my legislative intern and a promising young lawyer." Turning to his left, and looking at Michael, the Senator continued, "Just recently, while having dinner with all of us, Melissa announced that she wanted to follow in my footsteps and pursue a career in public service. My family and I have been deeply saddened by her death, and we extend our deepest sympathies to the relatives and loved ones of Melissa and her parents.

"While grieving, my family and I have also been deeply hurt by the vicious and unfounded rumors that I was involved in the murder of Melissa and her wonderful parents. The truth is, my family loved Melissa, as well as her parents. I had no involvement in their tragic deaths. To that end, I did not flee Oregon to escape prosecution. Rather, my family and I departed Oregon on the morning of October 9th, on a previously planned family vacation. We flew to Bogotá, the three of us, in our family owned business jet. My son, Michael, is a professional pilot—a former Navy pilot who flew combat missions in Desert Storm. He piloted our aircraft. The three of us have done this many, many times in the past. We are a close knit family, and we enjoy vacationing here in this beautiful part of the world.

"If I thought that immediately returning to Oregon would help the investigation into Melissa Walker's death, I would do so at once. But, that is not my understanding. After all, I am on a family vacation. But, I am fully cooperating with the Oregon State Police.

"While my family and I would do anything to help the Walkers, we will not be intimidated or made to feel ashamed for taking a long overdue family vacation in our privately owned condominium in Bogotá. My family and I cherish the South American culture, and Michael has been an exchange student here. We have also donated our time and resources to help the many beautiful and kindhearted people here in Bogotá. In fact, at this moment, we are standing not more than a quarter mile from an elementary school that my family and I have financed.

"My family and I plan to return to Oregon, within a week. In the meantime, we will continue to fully cooperate with the efforts of law enforcement officials. Thank you and good day."

I turned to Eva, and said, "Damn, what a spin-doctor! He's nearly a fugitive. Yet, he goes on national television and paints himself as a dedicated family man who's being unfairly pressured to cut short his well-deserved vacation. Oh, and let's not forget that his son is a war hero. Can you believe it?"

Nodding her head in agreement, Eva said, "Well, just remember—the mightier they are, the harder they fall."

Before either Eva or I had left the conference room, Phyllis hurriedly entered through the doorway.

"Jack," she said. "You have an urgent call on Line 1 from Senator Jacobsen."

I gave Phyllis one of those "Are you serious?" looks and then walked over to my desk and punched in Line 1 on my telephone.

"Good morning senator," I said. "Or, I guess it's probably the afternoon down there."

"Yes, yes," said the Senator. "This is Detective Davis,

correct?"

"The one and only," I said.

"Detective, I don't know how to say this any more directly. My family and I are in very real danger. In the event that we don't make it out of here alive, I just want you to know that my family and I would like nothing better right now than to be home in Oregon. Unfortunately, however, we are presently under house arrest by a Columbian Drug Cartel—right here in our own home. As you might have guessed, we can't exactly turn to the local police for assistance. Most of the police are subject to bribery and many of the officers are known Cartel sympathizers."

I was carefully considering everything that the Senator was saying. I wasn't a fool, however, and I felt like I was being played. I had just witnessed the Senator give a world class television performance wherein he had denied any involvement in Melissa Walker's murder and had also bashed Salem PD. Now, only a few minutes later, here he was telling me that he was in danger and that he needed Salem PD's assistance.

In truth, I was not particularly surprised to hear anything that the Senator had just revealed. It wasn't rocket science to see a possible Columbian drug connection to the three murders under investigation. After all, the Senator had fled to Columbia within hours of Melissa Walker's death. Also, the CIA had uncovered a flight from Columbia to Seattle, several hours before the double murder of Melissa Walker's parents in nearby Bellevue, Washington. The kicker, however, was the recent discovery that Melissa Walker had apparently snorted cocaine. I had worked in law enforcement long enough to observe the ravages of cocaine. It wrecked lives and compelled people to do things that they normally would not do.

Columbia is the world's largest producer of cocaine. It is a beautiful country set atop South America. It is surrounded by the Pacific Ocean, the Caribbean Sea, and the Atlantic Ocean. It has vast and magnificent mountain ranges, as well as seemingly endless plains and valleys. Bogotá, or Santa Fe de Bogotá, is the Capital City of Columbia. It is situated on a high plateau at 8,661 feet above sea level, in the Cordillera Oriental chain of the Andean mountains. Over seven million people live in Bogotá. Unfortunately, the Columbian Government has struggled with a long legacy of corruption. In 1948, the Mayor of Bogotá was assassinated, which resulted in rioting that partially destroyed the City. The uprising became known as El Bogotazo.

In the 1970's, Columbia gave rise to the drug cartels, including the Cali Cartel operated by the Orejuela brothers and the Medellin Cartel operated by the near legendary figure, Pablo Escobar. Although those cartels had long ago been destroyed and their leaders imprisoned or killed, newer versions of the cartels had taken hold. They were not the mammoth organizations of old. Instead they were smaller operations, each of which had control over one particular area of cocaine production and distribution.

For instance, one cartel might control the growth and harvesting of the Papa plant, another might control its production, and yet another might control its distribution. These smaller and highly efficient organizations were more difficult to infiltrate and to destroy.

In fact, many Columbians chew Papa leaves as a way of life. It is their livelihood and their custom—no different than a farmer in Oregon's Willamette Valley enjoying a fresh ear of corn at his family's evening dinner table.

Senator Jacobsen continued, "All I can say is that I'd

like you to give us 24 hours. If everything goes as planned, my family and I should be out of harm's way by then. I will contact you again as soon as I can. If you do not hear from me within 24 hours, please inform the necessary officials that you believe my family and I are either being held hostage or have been killed. We . . . ."

The phone line went dead. "Hello? Hello? Senator? Senator, are you still there?" I waited a bit and then the static emitted through the phone receiver fell silent and was replaced by a dial tone.

"Shit!" I said, as I grabbed Eva's hand and headed briskly into Cap's office. I then informed Cap about the substance of my telephone conversation with Senator Jacobsen. The three of us agreed that we could do nothing but wait—as we still didn't have enough evidence to extradite him.

Eva and I spent the rest of the day poring over every detail that we could find about Senator Jacobsen's life— his personal history, his political history, his employment history, and his financial history. We also looked into the life of one David Williams, who had recently become an Oregon Lawyer. Although it was late in the day, we decided to walk over to the Law School and pay a visit to the dean.

What we discovered was that Williams had been found guilty of cheating on a law school examination during his 2nd year at Willamette. While he narrowly escaped expulsion from the school, he was prevented from graduating with honors. Moreover, the individual who filed the complaint against him was none other than Melissa Walker.

Eva and I then telephoned the Oregon State Bar. We were ready to obtain a search warrant if necessary to examine Williams' application for membership to the Oregon State Bar. Fortunately, we didn't have to. Instead, we talked to the Bar's Chief Legal Counsel, who was glad to cooperate. When asked if Williams had reported any ethics violations that he had committed at Willamette's Law School, the Bar's lawyer answered, "No, there's nothing in his application that suggests that. He's checked the 'no' box for any such infractions."

Armed with new information, Eva and I decided to "drop in" on Williams. This time, the little prick was not as puffed up. We were immediately escorted into his office. Looking nervous, Williams weakly asked, "What can I do for you?"

Eva took the lead. "Look, Mr. Williams, we know about your cheating infraction in law school and that you failed to disclose the incident to the Bar."

The young man hung his head. For the first time, I felt an ounce of sympathy for the guy. But, my compassion didn't last long.

"Okay," he noncommittally said.

"Would you like to tell us the truth—the whole truth—about your affidavit that you signed at Detective Lewis' urging?" asked Eva.

"I guess the cat is out of the bag now? Look, I blew it in law school. I cheated on an exam. Melissa caught me. It was while we were still together. She felt conflicted, but she decided that she had to report my conduct. I plagiarized and she knew it. So did the school—once they took a careful look at my exam. The incident tore Melissa and me apart. I was afraid to report the incident to the Bar, because I thought that they might not let me sit for the Bar Exam."

"All right, tell me about Bradley . . . I mean Mr. Lewis'

involvement with you?" asked Eva.

He approached me a couple days ago. He said that he was with the Oregon State Police, and that they were investigating Melissa's death. He seemed to know a lot about me and everything. He knew that I'd dated Melissa, that she'd reported me for cheating, and that I'd failed to disclose the incident to the Bar. I can't say that he blackmailed me, but he certainly implied that things would go a lot better for me if I signed an affidavit saying that Melissa liked rough sex."

"All right, Mr. Williams. Is there any truth to that assertion—that Melissa Walker enjoyed rough sex and that she often clawed into you with her fingernails?" asked Eva.

"None. The truth is, Melissa is a great girl. Smart, funny, social, and very grounded. I blew it with her. I'm ashamed of what I did in law school—and what I did with the affidavit."

"You realize, Mr. Williams, that what you've done is a punishable offense and can be prosecuted?" asked Eva.

"Yes, I do," he said.

"Okay, well, Detective Davis and I are going to talk this over. Here's my card. If you'd like to talk to me or to Detective Davis anymore about this, you give either one of us a call, okay? We're going to leave now. Are you all right, Mr. Williams?"

"Yeah. I'll be fine," he said.

7

Desert Storm Revisited

It was now 6 p.m. in Bogotá. The sun was an orange ball sitting just above the western mountaintop horizon. The sky and clouds were painted with an incredibly rich violet hue. The low lying sun cast long shadows over the downtown streets of Bogotá. As the sun drifted further into oblivion, the halogen street lights in the downtown area began to flicker on.

The Jacobsens had helped build their 2-story condominium from the ground up. That was 11 years ago now. Their condominium was located about 15 miles southwest of downtown Bogotá, and was nestled against a mountain hillside. It was a virtual mansion—constructed out of adobe with a lot of glass windows to take advantage of the view.

At exactly 6:03 p.m., the Jacobsen family exited the condominium through a side garage door that was hidden from the main road. Earlier in the day, Michael had washed their two cars—a Jaguar and a Ford Expedition. After doing so, he had moved the Jaguar back into the garage. But, he had deliberately positioned the Expedition out of sight and near the side garage door.

Two linebacker sized Columbians stood watch next to their black Lexus sedan, which was parked just off the main road. They were armed with automatic weapons slung over their shoulders. A couple of hours earlier, Senator Jacobsen had invited the two men into the condominium. He did so under the guise of friendliness, offering each of them a Cuban cigar, a glass of brandy, and a couple rounds of pool. While he was entertaining the two thugs, Michael slipped outside and poured a small box of sugar into the Lexus' gas tank.

The Jacobsens walked single file through the unlit garage, and exited out the side door facing the west. They climbed into the Expedition. The Senator and his wife climbed into the back seat and hunched down. Michael got behind the wheel. He started the Expedition's V-8 engine, but did not turn on its headlights.

The entire Jacobsen family was very familiar with the surrounding terrain. They had regularly vacationed there for 10 years, sometimes three or four times a year. Moreover, Michael, in particular, knew just about every inch of the surrounding geography. As a kid, he had ridden his Honda 70 and Honda 175 dirt bikes down a nearby fire access road, hundreds and hundreds of times. The access road ran parallel to the main road, which led directly to the 3,900 foot asphalt runway where Michael's Cessna Citation was tied down. The north-south runway had been built by a Columbian Drug Cartel, called Los Hermanos ("The Brothers").

Over the years, the fire access road had become overgrown with deciduous trees, shrubs, and debris. But, earlier in the day, Michael had jogged along the access road to ensure that it was safe. Although it was overgrown, it was usable. There were no broken down cars, boulders, or other large objects to prevent passage. Although there were some old tires strewn over the access road, Michael just tossed them into the ditch. The access road was located about a quarter mile to the Northwest from the Jacobsen's condominium.

Michael slowly accelerated to 10 mph and headed the Expedition along the northwest edge of his family's property. Keeping the headlights off and straining to see, it took about two minutes for him to locate the entrance to the old access road. His mouth was dry and his palms were sweaty—just like he had felt when he had flown his first solo aircraft carrier landing during his Navy days.

Fear is a funny thing. You can detect it, even smell it in another. Michael was nervously glancing up at the rearview mirror, half expecting to see headlights and the bright light of machine gun fire. But, that didn't happen. He just hoped that the sugar that he had poured into the Lexus would derail the two Columbians long enough for him and his family to escape.

The Expedition bounced and lurched forward at 15 miles per hour. "There it is!" exclaimed Michael. He could now see the old fire access road. He swerved hard to his left and entered the old road. He let out a sigh, turned on the headlights, and immediately accelerated to 50 miles an hour. It was still difficult to see, however. The old road was thick with overgrowth and was in poor condition— with lots of ruts, potholes, and bare patches.

After proceeding along for about a minute, Michael hit the brake pedal and quickly stopped the Expedition. Earlier in the day when he had jogged along the old road, he had found a clearing where it would be easy to cross over to the main road. He had estimated that the clearing was about a mile's distance along the road. He had now traveled 0.9 miles according to the odometer. He set the gear shift lever in park, jumped out of the SUV, and began running along the edge of the road. Other than the light from the Expedition's headlights, it was pitch black. He tripped, landing hard on his left side. He got back up, however, and within a few seconds he found the clearing. It was about a 100 yards up the road. He ran back to the Expedition, drove on up the road, and turned left onto the crossing point. It was bouncy, but he made it safely across to the main road. Once there, he turned sharply to the right and accelerated to 90 miles an hour. His heart was pounding and he thought, "Okay, Lady Luck—stay with us!"

The Cessna Citation was tied down about 10 miles away. During the seven minutes that it took to travel to the airstrip, Michael mentally rehearsed the aircraft's startup and takeoff procedures that he would follow. He wouldn't have any time to read from the checklists. His only concern was to get his family airborne as quickly as possible.

"There it is!" he thought. The Expedition's headlights bounced off the white colored jet. Michael hastily parked the Expedition a few feet away. He threw open the car door and yelled, "Get in the plane, Mom and Dad!"

Holding his wife's hand, Senator Allen Jacobsen ran towards the Citation. Michael had already sprinted ahead to remove the wheel chocks. He then reached up and unlocked the entry door. The set of stairs unfolded in front of him and he screamed, "Get in!" The Senator and his wife hurriedly climbed into the cabin area and took a seat. Michael secured the door and turned for the cockpit. As he did so, he turned back and said, "Strap in for the ride of your life!"

Michael stuck the key into the ignition, hit the Master Switch, flipped "on" the Avionics and Fuel Flow toggle switches, and began spooling up the turbine engines. "Come on," he said under his breath. He was careful to keep all of the jet's exterior and interior lights off, except for the instrument panel lights. Looking into the cockpit from back in the cabin, all you could see was an eerie red glow.

As the number two engine began spooling up, Michael shoved the twin throttle pack forward. The Citation shuddered and then sprang to life. The tie down location was 500 feet from the end of Runway 31, which would mean a northwest departure. Unfortunately, before beginning their escape, Michael had observed that the evening wind was blowing out of the southeast. In pilot terms, that meant that if Michael took off on Runway 31 it would be with a tailwind—something even a 4 hour student pilot would know better than to try. However, Michael figured that he had little choice in the matter. If he took the extra time to "back taxi" down to Runway 13, he and his family would likely meet a fate worse than attempting a risky takeoff. Namely, a missile launched from an angry member of the Los Hermanos Cartel.

That's when Michael saw them—several sets of headlights rapidly approaching from the main road. He instinctively pushed the throttle quadrant full forward with his right hand and reluctantly hit the toggle switch to turn on the taxi lights. There was just no chance in hell that he could takeoff on the narrow runway without the use of the taxi lights—to say nothing of the landing lights.

As the Citation's tail-mounted jet engines roared to

life, Michael saw the flash of machine gun fire. He felt a sickening tightening of his stomach muscles. He wasn't a stranger to that feeling, however. He'd experienced it before while flying Navy combat missions. But, it was different when you were a civilian and you had your parents seated in your aircraft.

Michael stomped on the left rudder pedal and the Citation turned sharply onto Runway 31, about 200 feet shy of the threshold. In doing so, he knew that he might not be able to get the Citation airborne before running out of asphalt runway. But, he also knew that he was out of options. He thought to himself, "Well, if we make it out of this alive it'll sure make a great hangar story—3,700 feet of runway, Bogotá's density altitude, and a tailwind. Shit!"

The Citation rocketed down the narrow runway set atop a plateau in the southeastern hills of Bogotá. Michael was relieved that he didn't hear the clinking sound of machine gun fire connecting with Citation's airframe. The pursuing Los Hermanos Cartel henchmen were apparently not within machine gun range.

However, they were within missile range—and Michael knew it. He had flown several sorties over Baghdad in Desert Storm back in 1990. While the United States Air Force and Navy fighter jets had flown into Baghdad nearly at will, there were a few casualties. Before the Iraqi Air Defense System had been completely destroyed, one of their mobile missiles had "locked" onto Michael's F/A-18 Hornet. Although he had escaped that brush with death, he could remember the fear that he had felt.

"Come on baby, come on, come on!" said Michael. He could see the end of the runway approaching. The airspeed indicator read 78 knots. Rotation speed was 93 knots.

Michael knew that the Citation's performance envelope had some leeway built into it. But, this was pushing it. He needed to get the Citation off the ground before it ran off the end of the asphalt runway. If he didn't, it wouldn't be pretty. The landing gear would probably collapse and then it'd be all over for him and his mom and dad. They would likely all die in a horrific crash that would end in an explosive fireball.

"There it is!" thought Michael. He could now see the end of runway approaching. "Shit!" he thought. The airspeed indicator was displaying only 81 knots. He kept the throttles full forward. Finally, when it seemed that the end of the runway had already passed underneath him, Michael pulled back on the yoke. The airspeed indicator now read 87 knots. Michael had the flaps set at 10 degrees to add more lift. As he rotated, he felt a series of vigorous bumps as the Citation proceeded beyond the end of the runway and was still not airborne.

But, just as suddenly, the bumps stopped—and Michael knew that the Citation had lifted off into what is called "ground effect." Every 100 hour pilot knows that a premature rotation into "ground effect" can lead to disaster. That is, once the aircraft rises above that level it will inevitably lose some lift. So, if you rotate too soon and too slow—you risk an unceremonious stall back onto the runway. Worse, if that happens at 90 knots with the aircraft's wings loaded full of fuel, it's almost always fatal. But, Michael had no choice—in this moment, he had to try and coax the objecting Citation into the sky.

The Citation's twin turbine engines gulped in air, as the jet began to inch upwards at what seemed like glacial speed. Although the airspeed indicator was slowly climbing, it still read only 90 knots. Grimacing, Michael yelled out, "Too slow, too slow. Come on, damn it!"

The automatic stall horn then began to go off, intermittently at first, and then steadily. Michael knew all too well what was happening. He could feel his stomach muscles tightening.

Sometimes in aviation a chain of events unfold that make recovery impossible. In this case, the Citation had lifted out of "ground effect" and was now plummeting back towards the ground! The left wing was also starting to sickeningly dip down as the aircraft struggled to remain airborne.

"No!" yelled Michael. The Citation was just a 100 feet above the ground. But, Michael had no choice—he had to lower the nose of the aircraft to increase its airspeed. At such a low altitude, however, the smallest of mistakes would lead to an instant inferno. As he carefully flattened his angle of attack, the airspeed indicator stopped its decent. It hovered at 88 knots for several seconds. Then, ever so slowly, it started to inch back upwards. 91 knots, 93 knots . . . . .

As if Michael didn't have his hands full enough just flying the damn plane, the nearby terrain was beginning to rise in front of him. Nonetheless, he kept the wings level and slowly raised the nose again. He had now reached 95 knots and was 180 feet above ground. Finally, while feeling like the rising terrain was going to scratch the paint off the underside of the Citation, Michael made it over the first set of hills. As he did so, the Citation continued to accelerate beyond 100 knots. Michael then cautiously steepened his angle of attack and began a slight accelerating turn away from the rising terrain.

As the Citation reached 120 knots and 1,500 feet of altitude above ground, Michael yelled out, "Yes!" He then grabbed his kneeboard, fastened it to his right thigh, and began to quickly and methodically read over the pre-takeoff and takeoff checklists. At 5,000 feet above ground, he keyed his microphone and contacted the Bogotá Flight Service Station.

"Bogotá Radio," he said. "Citation one seven three two tango on 122.6."

"Go ahead Citation one seven three two tango," said the rapid speaking flight service briefer in English, with a heavy Spanish accent.

"Citation one seven three two tango is at one four thousand, one zero miles northwest of Bogotá, and would like to file and open an IFR flight plan direct Mexico City International."

"Roger, three two tango, standby," said the briefer. "Citation three two tango, go ahead with your flight plan."

"IFR, N one seven three two tango, Cessna Citation slash Gulf, 360 knots, Bogotá VOR, 2345 Zulu, two six zero, direct, Mexico City International, three hours thirty five minutes, Michael Jacobsen, kilo sierra lima echo, three, and white on white."

"Three two tango ready to copy?" asked the briefer.

"Affirmative, three two tango."

Five seconds later, the briefer read Michael's clearance. "Citation three two tango, you are cleared at 2345 Zulu to fly direct to Mexico City International airport, climb and maintain one eight thousand and expect flight level two six zero within 10 minutes, contact Panama Center on 113.70."

"Okay, 2345, direct Mexico City International, climb and maintain one eight thousand, expect two six zero within 10, Center on 113.70."

"Affirmative, three two tango. Good day," said the

briefer.

"So long, three two tango," said Michael.

8

Sophie

I LOOKED AT my watch—it was 6:12 p.m. I had almost forgotten about my "date" with Sophie Lawrence. Feeling a bit self conscious, I grabbed my electric razor that I kept in my office desk drawer and headed into the men's restroom. After shaving and putting on a fresh layer of stick deodorant, I left the office and drove downtown to Bentley's Bar and Grill. Bentley's is a higher end lounge and restaurant that is located in the Convention Center. Although I preferred the smaller neighborhood bars, I was trying to make a good impression on Sophie.

Entering Bentley's, I checked in with the hostess. She had a reservation for a party of two under the name of "Lawrence." She then looked at me knowingly, as if she was for some reason impressed, and said that "table fourteen" was waiting for me. I looked at her quizzically and deduced that it was not my looks that she was impressed with. Rather, she was apparently all giddy about the fact that I had been invited to "table fourteen." Always a bit of a nonconformist, I nonchalantly said, "Oh, well, I'll just take a seat at the bar. When Ms. Lawrence arrives, would you tell her that I'm here?"

"Yeah, sure" said the slightly dismayed waitress, who was smartly dressed in a tightly fitting black skirt.

"Thanks."

I then walked over to the bar and ordered a draft IPA. I'd drained about half of it, when I felt a light touch on my left shoulder.

"Hi Jack!" said Sophie.

A bit startled by the openness of this pretty woman, I said, "Hi, good to see you."

"C'mon," she said, as she turned and began walking through the lounge and up into the restaurant area. "I drop enough money in this place to expect them to treat me well. They always give me the same table over here."

"Really?"

I felt awkward—something that I wasn't used to feeling. Cops liked to be in control, and I had been a cop for nearly 20 years. I wasn't used to feeling less than "in charge."

As we were being seated, I pulled out Sophie's chair for her and she said, "Thank you." I then sat down and found myself a little tongue tied. For once, I wasn't the one asking all of the questions.

"So, detective," said Sophie. "Tell me about yourself."

Lifting my head and looking right at Sophie with a guarded smile, I said, "48, divorced, work as a homicide detective, and live in south Salem."

Playing along, Sophie shot back, "Wow that was efficient. Seriously, Jack. Uh, how long have you lived here?"

Pausing a bit, I said, "It's been 23 years now. What about you—how long have you lived here?"

"Well, I was born and raised in Sweden," answered

Sophie. "My father was a merchant marine and traveled a lot. I was a middle kid. I have a younger brother and an older sister. In high school I was a foreign exchange student and I traveled to the United States to stay with a family in Palo Alto. Basically, I've stayed in the United States ever since, although I regularly return to Sweden. Sometimes three or four times a year."

"Do your parents still live there?

"My Dad passed away three years ago," she said. "He had a stroke. However, my Mom still lives there. We stay in touch and we visit each other frequently. In fact, she was just here in July. She likes the Art Fair."

For reasons that escaped me, Sophie apparently found me interesting. The two of us talked for more than two hours, while polishing off a bottle of Willamette Valley Vineyard's 2001 Pinot Noir. When it came time to go, I knew how I was feeling about Sophie, but, I didn't know if she was feeling the same thing for me. "Probably not," I thought.

I walked Sophie to her gold colored SUV. As we reached her driver's side door, Sophie turned and faced me. She then said, "Well thanks for a great evening, Jack. I really enjoyed being with you." As she did so, she looked up at me with her gorgeous blue eyes and smiled. I felt a tingling sensation in my loins and I started to lean forward to kiss her. I then hesitated, however, reluctantly straightening my shoulders and said, "I enjoyed being with you too. Let's do it again."

Apparently sensing my hesitation and feeling similar adolescent sensations, Sophie softly kissed my right cheek. She then said, "I'd like that."

Afterwards, I drove home along River Road feeling like I was on Cloud Nine. I liked Sophie, and my pleasant thoughts of her lightened my otherwise jaded view of the world. After I arrived home, I made a pot of coffee and walked upstairs to my bedroom. I took off my shoulder holster that housed my Smith & Wesson Model 10 .38 caliber revolver, and slung it over the wall hook next to my bed. I always did that. I wanted my revolver close by while I was sleeping. In my line of work, I often created enemies—the dangerous kind.

Most of my fellow Salem PD officers carried the sleek Sig Sauer P229 pistol—standard issue in law enforcement these days. But, I preferred the older style Smith & Wesson revolver. It was heavier, solid, and seemed more reliable with its fixed sight. I had learned to use my Smith & Wesson Model 10, while training under Gunny. He always carried an original Model 22 that was introduced by Smith & Wesson back in 1951. Back then it was called the "1950 .45 Army." It wasn't until several years later that Smith & Wesson began assigning model numbers to its various revolvers. Gunny used to say that there was nothing wrong with technological advancements, but "if it's not broken, don't fix it." He also backed up his words by consistently outscoring every officer, young or old, at Salem PD's biennial shooting competition.

Although I certainly didn't make a habit of working late at night from home—tonight was different. There were three unsolved murders and one of them had happened in the middle my city. Consequently, with a pot of fresh coffee on the table and warm thoughts of Sophie still lingering in my head, I opened up the Salem PD "bucket" file on Senator Jacobsen.

I began with the Senator's phone records, credit reports, tax returns, campaign finances, and newspaper articles. I also had the CIA's background report. Back in

2004, President Bush had nominated the Senator to serve as the new Director of the Naturalization & Immigration Service. However, within a few days of his Senate Confirmation Hearing, the Senator surprisingly withdrew his candidacy. The public reason for his withdrawal was that he did not wish to vacate his Oregon State Senate Seat and that he wanted to spend more time with his family.

However, there had been longstanding rumors in the Capitol halls that Senator Jacobsen was a philanderer who had a penchant for younger women. While the background report dismissed such rumors as "not credible," the fact remained that the persistent rumors had forced an investigation. Moreover, Eva and I had been doing some digging of our own. What we found was that the good Senator had regularly engaged in 1-800 "phone sex" by use of his cell phone. We had also interviewed three former legislative interns, who each reluctantly admitted that the Senator had sexually harassed them on several occasions—including propositioning them for sex. One of the three former interns had also admitted to having an affair with the Senator, which had lasted a couple of years.

While reviewing the stack of paperwork on Senator Jacobsen, I became all too familiar with the Senator's political platform. Senator Jacobsen was a six-term Republican State Senator. He was also the senior partner in a successful law firm here in Salem. He specialized in immigration, personal injury, and workers' compensation. At the moment, illegal immigration was not only a hot topic nationally—it had also captured the attention of Oregonians.

Salem is located in the heart of Oregon's Willamette Valley—a rich agricultural setting. There are many farms, both large and small, in the Valley. The crops include grass seed, corn, beans, fruits, and nuts. Consequently, large numbers of foreign born Hispanics migrate northward to the Willamette Valley in search of a better living. Many of them remain here illegally.

Senator Jacobsen had capitalized on the fear of many Oregonians. That is, he passionately argued that illegal immigrants were draining limited government resources and depriving the State's natural citizens of their "fair share." While he touted his theme of Nationalism, his detractors accused him of racism.

Naturally, the issue was controversial and the local media devoured it. The newspapers, the television news shows, and the radio talk show hosts all seized on the issue—as it possessed elements of patriotism, race, and economics. Adding to the drama was the fact that Oregonians were fairly divided over the issue.

Always an astute politician, Senator Jacobsen had fine tuned his rhetoric. Thus, it was not unusual to see him on the local evening news trumpeting his call for "immigration reform." Although the Senator gave lip service to his love for the people south of the United State's border, he did little to ease the plight of Hispanic immigrants. In fact, his evolving harsh personal view of minorities had caused his father immeasurable pain and embarrassment in the latter years of his life.

9

Father and Son

MICHAEL HAD ALREADY entered the data for the Mexico City International Airport into the Citation's GPS unit and had punched the "direct" button. After receiving his IFR clearance, he pushed the throttles forward and eased the yoke back to establish a climb. He was flying at night, at 14,000 feet Mean Sea Level, and still not safely above the Andean Mountain Range. He didn't want to linger at that altitude any longer than necessary. Thus, he instituted a steep climb on a direct path northward towards Mexico City International Airport.

After leveling off at 18,000 feet Mean Sea Level, Michael keyed his microphone and said, "Panama Center, Citation one seven three two tango at one eight thousand."

"Good evening Citation one seven three two tango," said the controller. "Climb and maintain flight level two six zero direct Mexico City International."

"Climbing to two six zero, three two tango," said Michael.

With the Citation now configured for the 1,000 foot per minute climb, Michael began to breathe a little easier.

His mind flashed back to Dessert Storm. He recalled the many times that he had flown sorties into Iraq, and after dropping his bombs had then climbed out at max speed in his F/A-18 Hornet to return to the safety of the Saratoga. Although he had not taken on any enemy fire in those missions, he had experienced an adrenalin rush unlike any other. Until now, that is. Escaping from the Cartel henchmen and taking off on a short field had brought it all back. He had experienced that similar "juiced" feeling. After all, he was flying a sleek new jet that he had just configured for a steady climb away from some very bad hombres. But, more importantly, as the adrenaline rush was now starting to subside, he was beginning to realize that he and his parents had just narrowly escaped being killed by the Los Hermanos Cartel.

After Michael had leveled off at 26,000 feet above sea level, Senator Jacobsen walked up to the cockpit. He sat down in the right seat.

"Gotta strap in dad," said Michael.

"Oh, sure."

A period of awkward silence then followed between the two men—father and son. Neither spoke to one another for several minutes. They just sat there in the soft red glow of the cockpit with the background hum of the twin turbine engines. The two men understood the meaning of their silence. They were both feeling more than just relief over their narrow escape out of Bogotá. That is, one of them was feeling shame over his behavior and a lot of gloom about what was inescapably going to happen to him—public exposure, criminal conviction, and prison time.

Finally, the Senator broke the silence. "Mike, I'm sorry," he said. "I've really put you and Susan at risk. I've been down some pretty rough roads before, but this one surely takes the cake. I'm going to face the thing head on and cooperate with the police."

"Dad, there's something that I need to tell you. We'll need to talk when we get back to the U.S."

"All right, son," said the Senator.

Allen Jacobsen was a self-made man. He was the oldest son in a family of five children, three boys and two girls. He had grown up in Salem, Oregon, and had excelled in both academics and sports. His father, Thomas Jacobsen, had served four terms in the Oregon State Legislature and was well known as a conciliator and a diplomat. In fact, his father's political experience, skills, and popularity, had caught the attention of former President Gerald Ford, who in 1975, appointed him as the United States Ambassador to Mexico. Consequently, young Allen Jacobsen grew up enjoying the privileges of aristocracy. He attended private school and by age 12 was taking high school level math classes and was fluent in Spanish, Italian, and German.

While his father was still a vibrant force in American politics, 18 year-old Allen Jacobsen entered the University of Oregon. After obtaining his baccalaureate degree in Political Science, he entered law school at Stanford University. While there, he met and married his wife. He then returned to Salem, and began working as an associate lawyer for a mid-sized law firm. After only a brief stint as an associate attorney, he began practicing law as a sole practitioner. Although he could have just relied on the Jacobsen family's name and wealth for financial security, he wanted to practice law. So, he took just about any type of case that walked through his office door—domestic relations, personal injury, real estate, immigration, and probate.

The early years of his practice were difficult. He had high expectations for his career and his wife gave birth to a baby boy, Michael. Yet, he found it difficult to fill his father's shoes and privately felt as though he would never measure up. After his father died, he became restless. His fledgling law practice was not doing well and there were many months when he had little to show for his labor. Sure, he had a ton of money available by way of his inheritance, but he wanted to chart his own life course. Consequently, unbeknownst to nearly anybody else, 30-year-old Allen Jacobsen often contemplated suicide. He also began to act recklessly while self-medicating himself with alcohol. It was an isolated incident at first and then a pattern took hold. Soon, he was regularly engaging in adulterous affairs with college age women.

It was in the throes of one of those adulterous relationships that Allen Jacobsen took his first hit of cocaine. His accomplice was a beautiful olive skinned Latin American woman who occasionally snorted cocaine. He had met the young woman over at the Atkinson School of Business, where he served as a guest lecturer.

Inexplicably, however, just as Allen Jacobsen's personal life seemed to be falling apart, his law practice began to succeed. That is, he had the good fortune of securing a couple of sizable settlements from motor vehicle accident cases. More successes followed, and within six years he had built one of the leading personal injury law firms in Salem. With his fluency in Spanish, he also practiced immigration law, but he mostly did so to just round out his paycheck. He did not bring passion into that aspect of his job. Unlike his father, he didn't seem to really care about the plight of Hispanic immigrants.

Nonetheless, Allen Jacobsen gradually took on more

and more clients who had entered the Country illegally. He ran an advertisement in the Yellow Pages that included the phrase, "Hablo Espanol." Thus, he frequently received inquiries from Hispanic individuals who needed help on all sorts of issues—access to government assistance, unfair labor practices, obtaining citizenship, and avoiding deportation.

Eventually, as if influenced by his kindhearted father, Allen Jacobsen gravitated towards political office. With the advantage of the "Jacobsen" family name, he easily won a seat with the Oregon House of Representatives. He then lost a bitterly contested and expensive campaign to become Oregon's next Attorney General. Thereafter, he settled back into his law practice for a few years, while planning and successively staging a bid to become an Oregon State Senator.

During those years, the Senator and his family regularly vacationed in Bogotá. They enjoyed the beauty of Bogotá, as well as Cali. It was while on vacation in Bogotá that the newly elected Senator came into contact with some high ranking members of the Los Hermanos Drug Cartel. That is, on several occasions the Senator would venture into the poorer areas of Bogotá, looking for both drugs and sex with young females. Eventually, the risk of exposure from his addictive behaviors became too great. As he wrestled with his weakness, his intelligent mind began to see huge financial benefits from possibly assisting the Cartel. That is, he could see that he was in a position to help with the Cartel's distribution of cocaine into the United States.

Thus, by the time that his son, Michael, had grown up and entered the Navy, Senator Jacobsen had illegally secured millions of dollars by financing and overseeing a sophisticated network of cocaine distribution throughout the Western United States.

Michael, however, had no knowledge of his father's illegal activity until after he had returned home from his service in the Navy. Although he had once or twice come across some civilians who had snorted cocaine, Michael had never felt compelled to use the stuff. It was by accident one day long ago that Michael grew suspicious of his father's international dealings. That is, he innocently came across one of his father's bank transactions. The document was laying face up on his dad's desk. Out of curiosity, Michael looked at the document and saw that large sums of money—totaling 2.5 million dollars—had been deposited in an off-shore bank account in the Cayman Islands.

When confronted with the transaction, Senator Jacobsen tried to finesse the matter. But, Michael was too astute. He'd graduated with honors from Oregon State University and was the top student in his Naval Officer's Class. Thus, he'd sensed his father's uneasiness and his sincere questions played into Senator Jacobsen's psychological need for catharsis—and to finally confide in someone.

After Michael learned of his father's illegal activity, he knew that he had a choice to make. He could report his father to law enforcement authorities or he could remain silent. He chose the latter course, which he tried to rationalize as "family loyalty." But, greed had also played a role. So, it was that choice—made many years ago—that Michael was now reflecting upon as he flew his family towards Mexico City.

IO

Columbians

I HAD RETURNED home when my cell phone rang. It was just after 11:30 p.m. in Salem, or slightly after 2:30 a.m. the following day in Bogotá.

"Hello," I said.

"Detective Davis, is that you? It's Allen Jacobsen."

"Yes. Where are you?" I asked.

"Well, we've landed safely in Mexico City. We didn't have enough fuel to make it any further. I'm emotionally drained right now. It was harrowing flying out of Bogotá, to say the least. Thank God we have Michael as our pilot. We're all breathing a lot easier, but we're still on foreign soil and can't wait to get home."

"What are your plans?" I asked.

"We're going to refuel here and then I believe fly on up to Portland. We should be there in the morning, around six-thirty. Anyway, you have my assurances that we are trying to return to Oregon as soon as possible and that we will fully cooperate with your investigation."

"Good," I said. Pausing a bit, I then ventured, "Senator, I might as well ask this now. Tell me straight out—did you have anything to do with the death of Melissa Walker or her parents?"

"Absolutely not!"

"All right," I said. "I wanted to hear it from you personally. You should call me at this same number as soon as you arrive in Portland. Understood?"

"Yes, yes. I've got to go now."

After reviewing the Melissa Walker file, Case No. 06-32, and scratching out some notes, I turned to my bedside clock. It read 2:11 a.m. While not the least bit sleepy and with my mind racing, I forced myself to turn off the bedroom lights. I then flopped down on my bed fully clothed for a couple hours of sleep. Unfortunately, I was rudely awakened by the blare of my alarm clock at precisely 4:00 a.m. After groping for a cigarette and lighting it, I flipped open my cell phone and punched in Eva's phone number.

"Hi Eva, it's Jack. Sorry to bother you so early."

"What time is it?"

"Just after four," I said.

"You gotta be kidding me. This better be good, Davis."

"It is," I said. "Get dressed. We need to head up to PDX. Senator Jacobsen and his family should be arriving there around six-thirty this morning, and I don't wanna leave anything to chance."

"God, I just love this line of work. Yeah, I'll be there. You wanna just meet down at the station in about 45 minutes and ride up together?"

"Yeah, sounds good," I said. "I'll give Cap a call and get his blessing."

"Okay, bye."

I telephoned Cap. He agreed that the Jacobsens might

be in danger. He told me that he'd call the head of Portland International Airport's Security to let him know about the situation.

I pulled into the underground parking garage at Salem PD and caught sight of Eva waiting in her car. The two of us then departed together in my Talon. It was raining—not a particularly unusual event in the Pacific Northwest. On the way to the airport, I contacted the FAA. They informed me that the Jacobsen aircraft had departed Mexico City at 1:30 a.m. Pacific Standard Time and was scheduled to arrive at PDX at 6:45 a.m. In addition, they knew that Michael was currently cruising over Sacramento at 22,000 feet above sea level. So far, his flight had been uneventful.

Eva and I arrived at PDX just after 6 a.m. and headed straight to Flightcraft—the Fixed Base Operator for private aircraft. We entered the posh building and sat down in one of the oversized leather sofas. We could hear aircraft chatter in the background, as the building's public address system was tuned into the frequency for Portland Ground Control. About that time a gentleman dressed in street clothes approached us.

"Detective Davis?" he asked.

"Yes."

While displaying his badge the stranger said, "Hi, I'm Undercover Officer Monfield with Airport Security. My partner, Officer Cornwell is over there. There are also two uniformed officers on site, who are currently patrolling inside and outside the building."

"We appreciate the back up," I said. "Have you been briefed?"

"Somewhat," said Monfield. "All I know is that Senator Jacobsen and his family are expected to arrive here shortly and that there's some concern for their safety."

"That's correct. What you really need to know is that we have reason to believe that there may be a threat by two Columbians—possibly a man and a woman."

"Okay, Detective. Thanks for the heads up."

I then heard the following exchange on the overhead loudspeakers, "Ground, Citation one seven three two tango at Juliet, taxi to Flightcraft."

"Citation one seven three two tango proceed straight ahead to Flightcraft."

"Wilco, three two tango."

I looked at Eva and said, "That's it! Let's go."

The two of us then got up and walked through the double doors that led outside the building and to the tie down area. Here it came, a white colored Cessna Citation with the call sign N1732T. It was taxiing towards us. I scanned the area. Everything seemed okay. A Flightcraft employee in blue overalls and ear muffs was directing the Citation to a tie down space just off to our right. The two uniformed security officers were stationed about a 100 feet off to each side of us, while the two undercover officers were still inside.

The Citation uneventfully taxied into the tie down area. Nothing seemed out of the ordinary. You could hear the aircraft's turbine engines slowly winding down. The cabin door then opened and Eva and I hurriedly began walking towards the Citation. Mrs. Jacobsen exited first. She stepped down the plane's short set of stairs and then stood on the tarmac and waited for her husband. Eva and I were now just 20 or 25 yards from the Citation. Senator Jacobsen then appeared and began exiting the aircraft.

That's when it happened—the guy in blue overalls pulled out a pistol with a silencer and fired two shots at the Senator. One of the shots missed, but the other connected with the Senator's upper chest. He immediately crumpled downward—sickeningly falling head first down the stairwell.

I drew my Smith and Wesson revolver and fired three rounds at the guy in overalls. I dropped him instantly, placing two shots to his head. After I shot him, I yelled out to Mrs. Jacobsen, "Get down! Get down!" She immediately dropped hard on all fours and began screaming, "Allen, Allen!"

At the same moment, Michael stuck his head out of the aircraft—apparently startled and unaware of what had taken place. I then yelled out to him, "Get back inside! Close the door! Close the door!

Before he had to time react, however, additional sniper fire bounced off the side of the Citation—narrowly missing Michael. Consequently, he dove back inside the Citation with the cabin door still wide open.

I then turned towards the hangar where the sniper fire had seemed to come from. Eva had courageously reached Mrs. Jacobsen, and was pulling her behind the Citation's nose gear. The Senator, however, was lying motionless at the foot of the Citation's stairwell. Blood was oozing out of the right side of his chest.

I crouched down and ran towards the Senator to see if he was still alive. After I reached him, I began dragging him behind the Citation's stairwell. As I was doing so, I was fired upon twice from the direction of the hangar.

The additional gunfire had given me a good feel for the sniper's location. I hit the tarmac hard, rolled once, and with both of my hands aimed my Smith & Weston revolver. I fired off two shots at the sniper. I then motioned to the two security guards to close in on the hangar. As they did so, I turned back around and grabbed the Senator's limp body. He wasn't moving and I feared that he was already dead. Reaching under his armpits, I dragged him out of sight and behind the stairwell. I was relieved to find that the Senator's heart was still beating and that he was breathing. He appeared unconscious, however.

I turned my head upwards and yelled out, "Michael! It's Detective Davis. Can you hear me?"

"Yes!" he answered.

"Stay put! Don't move!"

While I was hunkered down behind the Citation's stairwell, the two PDX security officers were approaching the hangar. The time was right to close in on the remaining assassin. I sprinted towards the hangar. The two security guards had entered the hangar through the front opening. They each momentarily stood with their backs against the walls on opposite sides of the opening. With their pistols drawn, the two guards then began to move outwards.

A few seconds later, I reached the hangar and ran along its west side towards a small rear doorway. Before entering, I scanned the nearby parking lot. A woman was hurriedly opening the driver's side door of a gray sedan. I yelled, "Stop, police!" But, the woman gave no hint that she heard me and slammed her door closed. She then gunned the vehicle straight ahead, bouncing over a parking stop, and turned left towards the main road. I drew my revolver and was readying to fire, when another car entered the parking lot. My aim was obscured and I had no choice but to lower my weapon. As I did so, the woman in the gray sedan turned onto the main road and sped off to the east towards Interstate 205.

I shook my head in frustration and ran back to the hangar. One of the security guards hesitantly stepped out from behind an airplane with his pistol drawn. Once he saw that it was me, however, he lowered his weapon and hurried over to me.

Out of breath, I said, "Alert Portland PD that a gray sedan with Oregon plates and the first three letters QZK—that's Quebec, Zebra, Kilo—is fleeing a possible homicide at PDX and is headed east towards I-205."

"Got it," said the security guard.

"And get a couple of ambulances out here," I added. "We've got one or more seriously wounded or possibly dead."

"They're already en route."

With that, I ran towards the Citation. Eva was okay. Mrs. Jacobsen was sobbing, but otherwise appeared fine. The sirens from the emergency vehicles could now be heard. I headed towards the Senator.

I yelled out, "Michael—It's okay." But, I saw that he was already knelt over his dad vigorously administering CPR. I peeled off my sports coat and pressed it against the Senator's oozing chest wound.

The EMTs then arrived and began furiously working on the Senator. I was impressed by their efficiency. The Senator's heart had apparently stopped. One of the EMTs opened up a tool box like case, filled a syringe with norepinephrine, and injected it into the Senator. The other then set up a portable defibrilator. On the second attempt, the EMTs obtained a pulse. After working a few more minutes to further stabilize the Senator, they loaded him onto a gurney and quickly placed him in the back of their ambulance. The Senator's wife, Susan, then crawled aboard and the ambulance sped off.

I went over to the man in blue coveralls. He hadn't moved since I'd shot him. Two EMTs were vigorously working on him. As I approached, one of them solemnly looked up at me and shook his head. The assassin was dead—with two bullet wounds to his head.

On the ground a few feet away was a pistol with a silencer attached. I picked up the gun with my ballpoint pen and placed it in a plastic bag. Once the EMTs stopped working on the guy, I checked his pockets for identification. There was none. The only thing on his person was a car key hooked onto a Budget Rental Car keychain that displayed the license number QZK 519.

I headed straight for the Flightcraft building. I used the courtesy phone with all of the hotel and rental car information displayed to call the Budget Rental Car office. I identified myself as Detective Davis with Salem PD, but seemed to get the runaround.

Next, Eva and I questioned Flightcraft personnel about the identity of the man in blue overalls. Not surprisingly, no one had ever seen him before. We then did a routine search of the premises. I had a bad feeling in my gut about this one. Unfortunately, my instincts proved correct. The real fuel attendant, a 24-year-old kid who had worked at Flighcraft only a few months, was found dead—shot once in the head at close range. His body was found stuffed into a trash dumpster on the eastside of the hangar. The kid was in his underwear—absent his customary blue overalls. The body count in this investigation just seemed to keep piling up.

While securing the scene for the forensic investigators, I flipped open my cell phone to call Cap.

"Chief Heathrow, Salem PD," answered Cap.

"Hi Cap. It's Jack. We've had quite a melee up here at PDX. Have you heard?"

"I just got word," he said. "Some of it was picked up on

the scanner. I don't have any details."

"Assassins, probably two, were waiting in ambush here at PDX. Tolento and I had looked things over, along with the assistance of two security guards and a couple of plainclothes men from Airport Security. It seemed secure. But, one of them, an Hispanic male, apparently murdered one of the attendants here and then tried to kill Senator Jacobsen. I took him out, but the Senator is in critical condition and I don't know if he'll survive. What I believe was a second assassin, a female, escaped in a motor vehicle."

"Christ! Can it get any worse?" vented Cap. "This is Salem, Oregon, not Bogotá, Columbia!"

"Well, apparently some folks have forgotten that. Any chance you can dispatch a patrol car over to Lynn Palmer's apartment? It looks like it may have been premature to let her go back there. I'm not sure how contained this situation is right now. But with at least one probable assassin still unaccounted for, I think that we have to be concerned about Palmer. Whadaya think about puttin' her and her kid back into protective custody."

"Consider it done, Jack," said Cap. "To hell with today's Beaver game—I'm headin' into the office right now to work this thing. Keep me posted."

"All right, Cap."

"Oh, and Jack," said Cap. "We'll need to talk in the office first thing Monday morning. You know it would be standard procedure for me to place you on administrative leave. But, given the clear nature of what happened up there and my desire to keep you on this investigation, I'm not takin' you off. IA won't like it, but since when have we ever given a damn about those sanctimonious assholes?"

"Never, as I recall. Thanks, Cap."

"Hey, seriously, though. How are you doin' with it all, Jack?" asked Cap.

Shrugging my shoulders, I said, "You know how it is, Cap. Right now my adrenaline's still on overload. But, I feel like pukin' my guts out. I guess if you have to kill someone, you just hope that it's in a situation like this—where an assassin is trying to gun down an elected official and perhaps his entire family. Also, seeing the dead Flightcraft employee stuffed into a trash dumpster makes it a little easier too, if you know what I mean? Damn, he was just a kid."

"Okay, I got ya," said Cap. "When you talk to IA, however, don't suggest anything like that—they'd jump all over it. Listen, Jack, I want you to let me know if you need to take some time off. Deal?"

"Deal."

After buttoning things down at Flightcraft, Eva and I drove over to the airport Budget Rental Car office. We entered the office, displayed our badges, and asked to see the manager. A thin looking guy with slicked back hair stepped forward. He was the manager. We identified ourselves as homicide detectives and explained that we were investigating a recent murder. The manager quickly offered his assistance. In doing so, he promptly retrieved the information concerning the gray sedan. It was registered to a woman named Julie Parker. Her driver's license, address, and telephone number were all from Minnesota. I'd been doing this long enough to know that all of the information was probably bogus.

Sure enough, although I jotted it all down and later had Salem PD run it through every computer base available, nothing checked out. Oh, sure, all of the information pertained to one Julie Parker, who had truly resided in

Minnesota. The only problem, however, was that Ms. Parker had died eight years ago at the ripe old age of 92.

Nonetheless, Eva and I were not without some new information. That is, the dead man in the blue overalls was Hispanic, and the woman who had fled the scene had long dark hair. Eva and I theorized that the two were the same individuals that had flown to Sea-Tac Airport on the day that Melissa Walker's parents were murdered. Ballistics would be able to determine if the pistol that was used by the male assassin to gun down Senator Jacobsen, was the same weapon that had been used to kill the Walkers.

Furthermore, we now believed that we had enough evidence to detain the Senator for questioning. At the moment, however, we would just have to wait and see if he survived his gunshot wound. As to Michael, I had reluctantly read him his "Miranda rights" before leaving Flightcraft. It wasn't a very pleasant thing to do at the time, with his father's life hanging in the balance, but it had to be done. He fit the description of the John Doe identified by the tenants at Melissa Walker's apartment complex, and Palmer had provided credible information that he was romantically involved with Walker. I was just glad that there hadn't been any reporters on the scene when I read Michael his rights and placed him in handcuffs. They probably would have played it up as the big bad Detective Davis picking on the Senator's kid—a war hero, who was grief torn over the possible loss of his father. At the moment, however, Michael was presently being transported to the Marion County Courthouse Jail for processing.

Eva and I had worked the City long enough to know that a well-paid and experienced defense lawyer would promptly appear on Michael's behalf. To that end, we discussed whether to interrogate Michael right now, or wait until the morning. We opted for the latter tactic, on the assumption that he might be more eager to talk to us after spending a night in jail. We were also concerned about his safety, however. Whether he liked being jailed or not, we knew that an assassin's bullet couldn't reach him in the County Jail.

It had already been a long day anyway. It was now after 4 p.m. and it was a Saturday. Most of the good citizens of Salem had by now finished their weekend chores and were settling in for some evening leisure time.

"Hey, Jack," said Eva. "How 'bout callin' it a day and meetin' down at Da Vinci's?"

"You're a mind reader, Tolento. Four-thirty?"

"Yeah," said Eva. "See you there."

It was happy hour at Da Vinci's, a French-Italian restaurant situated near the downtown core about a block south of the Marion County Courthouse. I arrived there first and ordered a draft IPA for myself and a glass of chardonnay for Eva. It was "happy hour" and the place had just opened. It was quiet. I sat there by myself for a few minutes and sipped my beer. Eva arrived about five minutes later. After we shared some small talk, Eva asked, "Jack, is Heathrow going to place you on administrative leave?"

Pausing a bit, while staring into my now nearly empty glass of beer, I said, "Cap and I spoke briefly about it. Given the clear nature of what happened, he wanted me to stay on the case. If we didn't go so far back, he would have placed me on leave. You know—old school trust"

"Yeah, I guess," said Eva. "But, how are you doin' with it all, Jack—I mean, emotionally?"

"You know . . . we're cops. You compartmentalize, but

underneath it all you want to puke your guts out."

"Yeah, I hear ya," said Eva. It sounds a bit calloused, but no one survives in this business without being able to do that."

"This one's a little easier to swallow too. It's not as if I shot and killed some kid who flashed a squirt gun at me. The guy was a professional assassin. I mean, here's a family trying to exit their aircraft, but they start getting mowed down by a professional hit man. "

"Yeah, I know. Well, hey, partner, if you ever need to talk some more about it, I can be a pretty good listener."

I looked directly at Eva for a few seconds. But, said nothing—I didn't need to. She understood. I just nodded my head and smiled a bit.

The two of us talked a while longer with the pleasant buzz from our alcohol beginning to kick in. Our conversation had become lighter as we talked and laughed over the usual mix of routine topics. In a teasing manner, Eva then asked, "So, Jack, word has it that you're wining and dining Sophie Lawrence. Not bad. I guess you're actually not the reclusive burnt out cop that you hold yourself out to be."

With a feigned look of dismay on my face, I responded, "Funny, Tolento. No more alcohol for you."

Undaunted, Eva continued, "Ah, c'mon, Jack."

"Yeah, I had dinner with Lawrence. She genuinely felt bad about the Statesman's hatchet job on our Department. I had a nice time with her."

"Oh, don't get all serious on me now," teased Eva. "I'm just havin' some fun here. I'm truthfully glad for you—maybe even a bit envious. I mean, I sure haven't come across a prince charming in this town."

I looked at Eva and said, "Not that you couldn't. Really,

Eva . . . you know that, right? Don't forget to stop, breath some air once in a while, and have a life outside of work."

"I know," said Eva. "But, it's not exactly the easiest thing to do with a job like ours and a kid to take care of."

Shortly thereafter, Eva and I departed Da Vinci's. After stepping out the door and onto the cobblestone sidewalk, Eva turned to me and said, "Oh, I keep forgetting to tell you. I was looking over Senator Jacobsen's financial records and discovered that he regularly receives large sums of electronically transferred money, which he then wires to offshore accounts. We're talking <u>very</u> large sums of money, like $250,000 and more. It looks like the money is being concealed, Jack. At least, the wire transfers don't follow a route that's been easy to track."

"Undoubtedly dirty money. Nice work. Keep after it."

Eva replied, "Thanks, I will."

"All right, let's greet Michael Jacobsen at six sharp tomorrow morning."

Eva said, "I'll be there, tough guy."

"Go home," I said, while waving her off. "This your car?"

"Yeah," said Eva as she opened her car door and drove off.

Michael

It was Sunday morning. My custom was to sleep in until nine or so, and then make a pot of coffee and a Bloody Mary to go along with an easy glide through the Sunday newspaper. But, today was already stacking up to be anything but a typical Sunday. It was barely five and my answering machine was blinking with three new messages. I also had the interrogation of Michael Jacobsen scheduled for six.

The first message was from Cap, who reported that Senator Jacobsen was still in ICU at Portland's Good Samaritan Hospital. The bullet wound to his chest had narrowly missed his heart and he had lost a lot of blood. He had not yet regained consciousness.

The second message was from Bradley G. He had called about some concern that he had over one of the security video tapes that had been seized and stored by Salem PD. I promptly erased his message.

The last message was from Sophie, who said, "Hi Jack! I know it's late, but I was just thinking about you. Would you be interested in Sunday Brunch tomorrow morning at Eola Hills Winery? Let me know." It was too early for me to return anyone's call. I paused for a moment while I thought about Sophie's offer and how nice it would be to relax with her today. But, reality quickly set in and I headed back upstairs to get showered and dressed. I managed to depart my house just after five-thirty.

As I turned the Talon into the underground parking garage at Salem PD, I noticed that an unmarked federal government car was exiting—something was up. I took an extra long slurp from my 16 ounce coffee. As I walked out of the elevator and toward my desk, I was greeted by Cap and Eva.

"Mornin', Jack," said Cap. "You're not gonna like this. Hell, I sure don't, and I've been in this business longer than you."

I stood there surveying the look on Cap and Eva's faces. In police work, you learn very quickly to "expect the unexpected."

Cap continued, "I received a telephone call early this morning. It was from the Attorney General. It seems that the AG was contacted by the honchos at the Central Intelligence Agency. Your suspect, Michael Jacobsen, is apparently an agent with the CIA."

I took another swallow of my coffee. I wasn't really surprised by what Cap had said. The CIA often recruited agents from the military—especially the officers. Michael had a college degree, officer status, pilot training, and combat experience.

"The AG called me to let me know that one or more CIA agents would be descending on us this morning." Cap then nodded in the direction of the conference room. I turned my head and sure enough, there sat a smug looking federal agent with aviation sunglasses. Cap then continued,

"The goon handed me this—it's an Order signed by the President. It releases Michael into the custody of the CIA. The AG told me that the Governor expects my full cooperation. It seems that young Michael was recruited by the CIA to infiltrate the Los Hermanos Drug Cartel."

I could feel my blood pressure rising. Leave it to politics and "national interests" to protect a key murder suspect of a 25-year-old Willamette Law School graduate. While shaking my head with a growing look of frustration on my face, I asked, "So where does that leave us, Cap? Are you being ordered to halt Salem PD's investigation into the murder of Melissa Walker?"

Sidestepping my last question, Cap said, "You keep diggin', Jack—you keep diggin'. There are too many loose ends on this one. But, you need to understand that my hands are tied right now as far as the release of your suspect. If you determine that Michael Jacobsen was involved in the murder of Melissa Walker, we'll have to proceed very delicately. The Feds are already breathing down the Governor's neck."

I sighed with resignation and then locked my eyes onto Cap's. He frowned and shook his head, but didn't say anything—he didn't need to. He was as pissed off about the whole damn thing as I was.

As he turned to leave, Cap said, "Keep after it, detective. Just keep me in the loop."

I then looked at Eva. She was visibly upset. Like me, she was having trouble with the idea that politics and espionage could impede a murder investigation. I could tell that she didn't want to let the matter drop. But, the way I saw it, challenging Cap right now was not a very good idea. I didn't want Eva to say something rash—like I'd done once too often in my career. So, I nudged her towards the elevator and said, "C'mon, I'll buy ya breakfast."

We headed south on Commercial Street. I then turned right on Owens Street and began motoring along South River Road. The early morning darkness was beginning to give way to the first signs of light. Neither Eva nor I were talking.

After about 10 minutes, I drove under the second of two railroad trestles leading to Independence. The damn things were death traps—especially the northern one. Just about every year someone failed to negotiate the near 90 degree turn underneath the trestle and would collide head on into the wall of concrete.

Heading over the bridge to Independence, I parked outside of Andy's Café and opened the door for Eva. Andy's was my other favorite breakfast hangout. You couldn't find better hash browns mixed with onions.

While Eva and I were sipping our coffee and commiserating over the recent turn of events, my cell phone rang.

"Davis."

"Detective, this is Michael Jacobsen. Can we talk in person?"

"Name the place and time."

"Uh, how 'bout the Flight Deck Restaurant this afternoon at two?" said Michael.

"I'll be there with my partner."

"You mean the cute brunette?" retorted Michael.

I wasn't amused. "Yeah, and she hates smart ass rich kids."

"I've been warned," said Michael. "Yeah, that'll be fine."

"We'll see you at two."

After Eva and I finished breakfast, we headed back

to the Department. Once there, I dropped Eva off and simply said, "There's something that I need to do."

The two of us had worked together long enough to trust each other. Neither of us took offense when the other impliedly said, "get lost." We both realized that each of us held some things close to the vest in order to protect the other.

I shot through the underground garage and headed towards Fairmont Hill. I wanted to talk to Gunny. About halfway there, I recalled that Gunny and his wife regularly attended Church on Sunday mornings down at St. Luke's. "Shoot!" I said under my breath, as I immediately turned left onto Lincoln Street and then left again onto Liberty Street. I was now headed north and back towards downtown. I arrived at St. Luke's a few minutes later. Driving into the Church's parking lot, I got lucky and spotted Gunny's dark blue Toyota Camry over in one of the angled parking spaces on Winter Street. There was an open space beside it, so I pulled into it and waited.

It was nearly noon and I had sat through enough church services in my lifetime to know that the congregants would be exiting shortly. When I was a kid, I'd always miss the noon episode of the Lone Ranger that was broadcast on network television every Sunday. And it didn't get any better as a teenager, as I'd usually miss the broadcasts of basketball games, football games, and track meets. Now, as a grownup, I knew that even adults get a little restless when a church service continues much past noon. We feel our stomachs begin to growl, we become bored with the usual call from the pulpit for discipline and avoidance of fun, and we start to fret about the overdone pot roast that is cooking at home.

Sure enough at 12:18 p.m. the doors at St. Luke's

Church swung open and the congregants gleefully headed towards their cars—probably feeling all cleansed, I figured. After a few minutes, I spotted Gunny and June exiting the church. I stepped out of my car as they approached.

"Hi, Gunny."

"Well, Jack . . . afternoon! Must be somethin' good, huh?"

Chuckling, I said, "You could say that." Turning to June, I apologized and asked if it would be okay if I stole her husband for about half an hour.

Raising her eyebrows a bit and drawing upon all the courtesy that she could muster, she replied, "I've been livin' with this stuff for over 30 years. You two detectives go talk, but, Mr. Terrence Davis, I'm going to hold you to your half hour."

"You got it," I said—feeling like a kid who'd just been scolded by his Sunday school teacher.

"Oh, and you're welcome to join us for dinner," she said. "I have a ham in the oven."

"Hey, I'd love to, but I can't. Unfortunately, work is consuming my life these days."

"Man's gotta eat doesn't he?" replied June.

"I really appreciate the offer, June. Thanks, really—but I'll have to take a rain check."

With that, June Gunnerson drove herself home in the blue Camry to tend to her Sunday afternoon meal preparations. As she did so, Gunny stepped into my car and the two of us headed over to Magoo's Bar and Grill.

"What is it, Jack?" asked Gunny. "Sunday afternoon? Must be something' more than just routine bull shit from Bradley G?"

"It is," I said. "The Jacobsens returned yesterday. There was a shootout up at PDX when they arrived at Flightcraft.

There were two assassins of probable Columbian origin. I dropped one of them, but not before he put a slug in Allen Jacobsen. He's presently in critical condition. A probable accomplice, a female, fled the scene and is still unaccounted for. Eva and I were going to interrogate Michael this morning, but he was released by federal court order. He's apparently a CIA agent."

Shaking his head, Gunny said, "Shit!"

"Wait, it gets better," I said. "Michael telephoned me this morning and wants to talk. We're going to meet at 2 o'clock today. Any advice?"

"Jack, you're in the middle of a hornet's nest. Like I said, watch your backside. I presume that you're meeting him in a public place?"

"Of course," I said.

"Good. How do you plan on handling it?"

"Not sure—that's why I'm talkin' to you," I said.

"All right. If it was me, I'd take the direct approach. You don't have the usual tools in your arsenal. You know . . . the threat of arrest, interrogation, and jail time. However, you do have some leverage. The fact that he initiated contact with you tells you something. So use it."

"Yeah, that's the way I see it too," I said. "Hey, Gunny, can I ask you somethin'?"

"Of course."

"How the hell did you learn to let these type of things go? You know, seeing a murder suspect cut loose."

Deliberating for several seconds, Gunny finally answered, "You just have to, Jack. Don't waste your time worrying about things that you can't control. Focus on the things that you can. If you can no longer let this type of shit go, because that's exactly what it is, you should get out of police work. For diehards like us, homicide work is a damn good job. But, there's also a lot of politics—sort of a cesspool that you have to constantly wade around in."

"Thanks Gunny," I said. "Sorry to ambush you coming out of church."

"Are you kidding? After that service anything looked good—even you, Davis."

The two of us left Magoo's and I hurried Gunny home. As I stopped the Talon in front of his stately looking home, I said, "Hey, tell June thanks again for the dinner offer."

"I will."

Eva and I arrived at the Flight Deck just before 2 o'clock. As we entered the restaurant, we both spotted Michael sitting alone in the lounge.

"Hi, Michael," I said. "You know who I am and this is my partner, Detective Tolento. How are you?"

"I've had better times in my life," he said.

"I'm sure. Sounds like it was pretty hairy flyin' out of Bogotá?"

"Yeah," said Michael. "Worse than Desert Storm. At least I was in a fighter jet there. I was damn lucky to get my family out of Bogota."

"Well, I'd have no problem sitting here and talking aviation with you, Michael, but I know that's not why you're here. Why'd you want to talk to us?"

Michael looked up from his beer mug and said, "I want to explain."

"All right, shoot. Detective Tolento and I are here to listen and to be straight with you. Of course, you realize that you're a suspect in one, if not three, murders."

"Uh, not really," said Michael. "But, I guess I'm here voluntarily talkin' with the two of you."

"We're listenin.'"

Michael took his time before speaking again. Eva and

I were both beginning to think that we'd set the wrong tone and that Michael was developing cold feet. But, he finally began talking again.

"The CIA approached me a couple of years ago. I'd flown with Alaska Airlines for about three years by then. They apparently were looking for an ex-fighter pilot who could infiltrate the Los Hermanos Drug Cartel. As you know, our Country has spent obscene amounts of money to try and stop the distribution of illegal drugs. I guess they were looking for someone like me—who fit a specific profile. You know, a pilot, single, reasonably intelligent, and fluent in Spanish. I had all of that.

"Anyway, I turned them down. At that time, I had just quit my job with Alaska and was going into business with my father. We started a charter airplane business out of Salem. But, things changed for me about a year later. I came across some paperwork in my Dad's home office. It pertained to some electronic bank transactions. Very large sums of money were being deposited in various accounts, most of them foreign. The sums of money were large, like $200,000 to $500,000. Once I saw them, I began to mull it over. I then recalled seeing my dad act strangely when I was younger. You know … mood swings. He'd be euphoric one minute, then anxious and frantic the next.

"So, I confronted him. He hedged a bit and tried to stonewall. But, his answers didn't wash—and he knew it. Perhaps he needed to confide in someone? I don't know. But, he finally came clean and told me that he'd become addicted to cocaine during the early years of his marriage. He eventually went through rehab, however, and kicked the habit. He said that he hadn't used the stuff for 10 years or so. But, before he cleaned up his act, he'd gotten involved with the mob and in the illegal trafficking of cocaine. While vacationing in Bogotá and Cali, he made contact with the Los Hermanos Drug Cartel. One thing led to another and he soon became the point man in the distribution of cocaine throughout the Western United States. He used his influence, his familiarity with both the South American and North American cultures, and his knowledge of banking laws.

"Suffice to say that I was truly shocked by his revelation. I mean, Christ, he's my dad. So I was totally conflicted about what to do. I knew that if I reported his activity it would destroy both him and my mother.

"Then, while I was still trying to decide what to do, the CIA entered back into the picture. Somehow, the DEA had gotten wind of my dad's involvement in the distribution of cocaine into the United States. They apparently passed along the information to the CIA, who used the information to re-approach me with a new proposition. They offered to pay me a nice salary, $20,000 a month. But, more importantly, they said that they could guarantee my dad's immunity from prosecution for all of his drug related activities.

"Of course, that was huge to me. To be able to get my dad off the hook, to spare my mother the agony of watching her husband being dragged through the mud and then sent to prison. I know my mom, and it would have destroyed her.

"So, that's about it, detective. The CIA doesn't know that I'm having this conversation with you and your partner. And I'd prefer to keep it that way. I've always marched to the beat of my own drummer, and I don't particularly care for the CIA. But, they promised me something for the benefit of my family, which I could not refuse."

I said nothing. I'd been lied to before and I knew all

too well that killers usually tried to worm their way out of things. But, I had to hand it to Michael, because he came across as a person who had just spilled his guts with the truth.

While he was still cooperating, I decided to ask Michael about his frequent airplane trips down to Bogotá. He explained that he had been running cocaine into the United States on behalf of the Los Hermanos Drug Cartel. He added, however, that he sometimes informed the DEA in advance of his runs, so that the Agency could minimize the shipment's distribution. He said that he had to be careful, however, because he didn't want to compromise his status as a spy for the CIA. The DEA gave him its blessing, he said, because it was interested in the far bigger prize of taking down the Los Hermanos Drug Cartel. To do so, the DEA and the CIA were collaborating and they needed Michael to gather information.

I continued to press Michael for more details. He explained that the Los Hermanos Drug Cartel would load his aircraft with cocaine. They hid the stuff in the Citation's fuselage, which had been modified by an aviation mechanic who created hidden compartments in the aircraft's underbelly. Once the contraband was loaded, Michael would depart at night from the small airfield built by the Cartel. He would not file a flight plan and he departed only on days that had clear weather. He would then fly due west at altitudes that were extremely low, illegal, and risky for even the best of jet pilots. To avoid radar detection, he would turn off the Citation's transponder and would fly "in the blind." Once out over the Pacific Ocean, he would drop even lower—sometimes flying within 100 feet of the water's surface. He would fly approximately five miles westward off shore, before turning northward.

After crossing the border into the United States, Michael would turn back toward the shoreline. He would then continue flying at a very low altitude toward a remote airstrip northeast of San Diego. Once there, he'd land and a distribution network organized by his father would quickly unload the hidden cocaine. Michael would then contact the local Flight Service Station and file an IFR flight plan back to Salem. After becoming airborne he'd activate the flight plan and fly home on the gauges.

I couldn't keep from shaking my head as Michael revealed his "daredevil" nighttime flights. He was lucky to be alive. To be sure, I respected his pilot skills. I was skeptical, however, about his story.

Before leaving the restaurant, Eva asked Michael the million dollar question.

"Michael, did you murder Melissa Walker, or have anything to do with her death?"

"No," he said without any hesitation.

"Were you in the Capitol Building with her on the morning of her murder?" asked Eva.

"Yes," he said with the same credible demeanor.

"All right, tell us everything that happened that night?"

"Look," said Michael. "You can hook me up to a lie detector machine if you want. But, all of this has to be kept confidential—between the three of us. The CIA would shit a brick if they knew that I was talking to either of you. For all I know, the Agency may well be listening to our conversation right now. It would certainly be in character for it to be doing so."

Michael then continued, "Bottom line, I was in love with Melissa. I met her last summer. She was passionate, smart, and attractive. What was not to like about her? As far as last Sunday, well, we spent most of the day together. We made love in her apartment. Melissa's a bit wild—that's one of the things that I love . . . loved about her. But, she got the crazy idea to go up to the observation deck atop of the Capitol rotunda, get stoned, and make love. So, that's what we did.

"We went over there around midnight. We brought a blanket and headed up to the observation deck. We curled up together and we were talking and laughing. But, we were having trouble working up our nerve. So, sometime after midnight, we snorted some cocaine that we'd brought with us. We then got it on. It was all about the thrill factor. You know . . . the forbiddance of doing something so intimate up there on top of the State Capitol Building.

"Anyway, we fell asleep afterwards. I then woke up and needed to use the restroom. So, I left the observation deck around 2:15 or 2:30. Melissa was lying there, asleep. But, when I came back . . . she wasn't there. I became frantic. I ran down the stairwell and that's when I noticed that one of the rotunda glass windows was wide open. So I stuck my head through it and looked down and saw her body lying in the middle of lobby floor. I almost threw up, but I managed to run down the rest of the stairs to see if she was still alive. It was just more than I could take. I mean here she was, this beautiful woman that I was in love with all . . . all smashed up. I checked her pulse. She was dead. I then panicked and ran. I just didn't think that it would look very good if it was discovered that I had been with her right before her death snorting cocaine and having intercourse on top of the Capitol Building."

I then said, "Okay, Michael. We're almost done here. We appreciate your cooperation. Again, you realize that you don't have to talk to us, that whatever you say might be used against you, and that you may have a lawyer present, correct?"

"Yeah, I know. You read me my rights up there at Flightcraft. I got it. But, I have nothing to hide. Again, I'm just asking that you keep our conversation confidential."

"Okay, I respect that," I said. "If you're immune from prosecution and never end up charged, I can keep it quiet. But, I can't make any promises if things turn out otherwise."

"That's good enough for me."

"Michael, you've admitted that you were with Melissa on the morning that she died. We have forensic evidence that Melissa struggled. Can you explain that?"

"Yes, I can. Melissa and I had made love several times that day. Melissa can be a bit wild, like I said."

I interjected, "So that was you in the videotape?"

"I knew that you'd find that. Yeah, it's the two of us. It was my idea. It added some fun for us."

"Okay," I said. "You had just started to answer my question about the forensic evidence that shows that Melissa struggled."

"Well, we both ended up getting stoned and as I said we made love out on the observation deck. So, I'm not sure what forensic evidence that you are talking about? But, let's just say that it had been passionate between us all day long. Also, Melissa got really high and wanted to crawl up onto the ledge of the observation deck and walk around it. We sort of got into a brawl, if you know what I mean? I knew that she wasn't thinking clearly and that she could easily fall off the ledge, but she was damn determined to go up there. So, I had to restrain her."

"I see," I said. "Had she been depressed recently or on any sort of medication?"

Well, yes and no. She had talked about the stress of law school and the Bar Exam. I know that she had suffered from migraine headaches. But, I never saw her take any medication."

"All right," I said. "Michael, what do you know about your father's activities in terms of his affairs with other women?"

"You get right to the point, don't you, detective?"

"I try to," I said.

"Look, he's my dad. I'm not an idiot. I'm aware of the longstanding rumors about his indiscretions. But, I've never witnessed anything along those lines and he's never discussed the issue with me."

"Okay," I said. "Tell us what happened down in Bogotá? Why did you have to escape?"

"We got wind of the fact that the Cartel had probably discovered my involvement with the CIA. Our housekeeper told us that some Cartel henchmen had come in and searched our condominium. Then, two heavily armed goons showed up outside of our condominium. There were other more subtle signs too. Basically, we were told by the Cartel not to leave. I think that the Cartel was trying to figure out whether to kill all of us, or to kidnap us and ask for ransom money."

"Okay, Michael," I said. "Detective Tolento and I appreciate your cooperation. Keep your head down. We may run a black and white by your house every few hours just to make sure that you're okay."

"No problem."

I then added, "Oh, and, uh, it might be a good idea if you don't leave town."

"Taking a chapter out of the Cartel's book, huh? Have it your way."

12

Sunday Evening, October 15th

I LEFT THE Flight Deck restaurant feeling unsure of things. Michael's story seemed plausible, but a bit farfetched. But, if he hadn't killed Melissa Walker, then who had? We already knew that his father had exited the Capitol building by 9:30 on the evening that Walker was murdered. My fear was that Eva and I had focused too much of our attention on Michael and his father. It was a mistake that rookie detectives often made—becoming myopic and fixated on a certain suspect or two, while the trail leading to the real killer grows cold.

On my way home, I stopped at Thompson's brewery. I needed solitude. It was cold outside. This year's unusually warm fall was beginning to give way to Oregon's more customary weather—drizzle, gray overcast, and cool temperatures. I turned up the collar on my Navy P-coat and headed inside. It was a Sunday night, and there were several diehards seated at the bar. The bartender was discussing the latest new microbrew. At the moment, I didn't care about microbrews. I took a seat at the end of the small overcrowded bar and easily downed two "pounders" of some amber ale that I couldn't name.

As I stood up to leave and was placing a 10 dollar bill down on the bar, I heard a familiar voice, "Jack! Hi!"

I wheeled around—it was Sophie! She had just arrived with another woman. Although I was glad to see her, it was a surprise. I'd been mulling over the Melissa Walker murder case and was in a reflective space—might even say that I was in a bit of a funk. I wasn't expecting to come across anyone that I knew, let alone Sophie, here at one of my favorite "off the beaten path" pubs.

Trying to sound nonchalant, I said, "Hi, Sophie. I didn't expect to see you here."

"Well, you just never know, detective. I'd like you to meet Linda Samuelson. Linda and I are old college buddies—we attended Stanford together.

"Pleasure's mine, Linda," I said.

"Likewise."

Sophie then invited me to join Linda and her for a round of evening cocktails, which I honored. Thankfully, the conversation was light—for I knew that my mind was elsewhere. After a half hour or so, I politely excused myself.

"Pleasures been mine ladies," I said. "I'm afraid that I'm bone tired and should be getting home. It was nice to meet you, Linda."

I then looked at Sophie, bent over and kissed her on the left cheek, and said, "Good to see you, Sophie."

"Yeah, take care, Jack."

As soon as I got out the door, Linda turned to Sophie and with a mischievous grin said, "Okay girl, you've been holding out on me."

"No I haven't."

"Uh, I saw the chemistry between the two of you and

so would anyone else within a mile," said Linda.

"It's that obvious?"

"Yeah," said Linda. "So are the two of you serious?"

"Look, my newspaper roughed him up pretty bad. I didn't like it and it shouldn't have happened. So, I called him to apologize and to try and make things right."

"Did you?"

"Well, yes, but . . . Oh, Linda, knock it off! We've gone out once."

"Okay, my dear—whatever you say," said Linda in a teasing sort of way. Smiling, she then added, "You really did light up around him, you know?"

"Hmm. Well, I do like him."

As I drove home, I knew that something wasn't right with the murder investigation into Melissa Walker's death. While I couldn't put my finger on it, I'd been working in homicide too long to not recognize my uneasiness. It meant that I could expect to be surprised—and that was one thing that a cop doesn't like. After arriving home, I poured myself a gin and tonic and tried to ignore my sense of foreboding.

The next morning I got up early and headed into work. When I got there, the first thing that I did was to call the Good Samaritan Hospital to check on the status of Senator Jacobsen. Unsurprisingly, I ran into a roadblock with the nursing staff. After getting through to one of the administrators, however, I was finally able to get some information. The Senator was tenaciously clinging to life. He had suffered a serious bullet wound that had just missed his heart. In addition, the doctors feared that he might have brain damage and some paralysis from remaining unconscious for so long before he was resuscitated. He had undergone a brain CT scan, however, which was negative.

While talking on the phone, I noticed a facsimile on my desk from Portland PD. They had located the gray sedan with license plate number QZK 519. It had been abandoned at the Airport Days Inn Hotel parking lot. Portland PD's Forensics Unit had dusted the vehicle for prints, but found nothing.

It was now just before eight and I had already put in nearly two hours of work. I decided to head up to White's Restaurant for breakfast. Before doing so, however, I left a note on Eva's desk inviting her to join me.

Just after I had ordered bacon, eggs, hash browns, and sour dough toast—Eva walked through the door. She sat down in the booth seat across from me. Unexpectedly, she then pulled out a VHS video tape from her handbag. She dropped it on the table. It was labeled, "Senator Jacobsen's July 12, 2005 interview with KGW." She then said, "Jack, you need to look at this."

I picked up the videotape and read the title. Furrowing my brow a little and forming a quizzical look, I asked, "Whadaya got?"

Eva then explained that the videotape concerned an impromptu interview that Senator Jacobsen had given on the issue of immigration reform. The television station had covered parts of a speech that he had given to the Salem Rotary Club. Afterwards, the KGW reporter cornered the Senator and began peppering him with questions about immigration reform. None other than Melissa Walker was standing next to him. Moreover, the Senator's political stance seemed harsh—you might even say racist. He said that it was time for America to tighten its borders in order to avoid a further erosion of its government's resources, its land, and its low crime rate. In doing so, he introduced Melissa as his "Legislative Assistant." The reporter then asked her a question or two and she very articulately supported the Senator's position and even cited some statistics that ostensibly backed up his opinion.

I greatly respected Eva's instincts. But, I didn't think that the video tape was any sort of a "smoking gun." So, while taking a bite of my toast and washing it down with a slurp of my black coffee, I casually said, "And?"

Eva then handed me a photocopy of a newspaper story concerning Joe Martin, the night janitor at the Capitol Building. He was not who he claimed to be.

The news article explained that Martin was from El Salvador, and that he had illegally entered the United States in 1984. His real name was Hector Rodriguez. He had obtained a "green card" by way of a false social security number. With that in hand, he obtained steady employment here in Oregon. During his first few years, he worked as a tree planter and then in a cabinet shop. He then obtained work as a janitor for a temporary employment agency and applied for permanent residency as a United States citizen. Eventually, he became employed with Cascade Janitorial Service and was assigned to work exclusively in the State Capitol Building.

In 2004, Martin married Rosa Amana. Rosa was also from El Salvador, but she had entered the United States on a tourist visa. By that time, Martin owned a house and had a 20 year history of solid employment. Thinking that they could settle into a life here in Oregon, the newly married couple conceived a child, a girl that they named Gloria Martin.

The Martins were happy and hardworking Americans. They were just glad that they had found a better way of life, and that they had been fortunate enough to escape El Salvador's poverty and violence. Every Fourth of July, the Martin family proudly hung the American flag outside their front door. They also contributed to their community. That is, Joe helped referee youth soccer games for the Parks and Recreation Department. Likewise, Rosa taught Sunday school to 1st and 2nd Graders at St. Mary's Catholic Church.

Just into their second year of marriage, however, troubles began for the newly formed family. Somehow, a bureaucrat employed with the Immigration & Naturalization Service (INS) discovered that Joe Martin had gotten himself into a bit of trouble while he was adjusting to his first year of life in the United States. That is, shortly after Martin migrated to Oregon, he was charged with: (1) driving under the influence of alcohol (DUI); (2) driving without an Oregon driver's license; and (3) driving without automobile insurance. Unfortunately, Martin was nearly broke at that time and he was not able to hire a lawyer to fight the charges. Thus, he was convicted on all three charges.

Despite those mistakes, the INS never took any action against Martin. After 1984, he annually renewed his work visa without any problem. He also eventually obtained permanent residency. Thus, by 2005, Martin thought that the mistakes of his past were long forgotten and he believed in America. After all, he had been steadily employed, he had gotten married, and he had an excellent credit history. He felt grateful and patriotic. Unfortunately, however, the INS bureaucrats somehow discovered his illegal entry into the country and his long ago DUI related convictions.

Like most bureaucracies, the INS used the newly discovered information as an excuse to act stupidly and unjustly. So after determining that Martin had broken the law, the INS slated both him and his wife for deportation. Moreover, relying on some obscure and absurd provision of federal law, the INS took the position that neither Martin nor his wife had any right to appeal its deportation decision.

At that point, the news media picked up the story and Martin appealed for help from Senator Jacobsen, who was an able immigration lawyer. However, at that time, the Senator was regularly making headlines for his "get tough on immigration" stance. Thus, his politics were on the other side of the fence from the side that Martin was on. Further, his law practice was geared towards defending powerful interests, rather than representing migrant workers who usually had little money to pay for legal services.

Finally, out of desperation and fear for the welfare of his family, Martin personally approached the Senator one morning after he had finished his night janitorial shift. Melissa Walker happened to be in the Senator's office. As it turned out, on that particular morning the Senator was in a sour mood. As a result, he abruptly dismissed Martin and even threatened to contact his employer to complain about his behavior. The Senator then instructed Walker to escort Martin out of his office—which she did.

Over the next two years, Martin and his wife bitterly fought the INS. They did so by finally obtaining some help from another local attorney, who took them on as *pro bono* clients. In the end, the attorney succeeded in preventing the deportation of Martin. But, with all the absurdity and unjustness imaginable, he could not stop the INS from obtaining federal court approval for the deportation of Martin's wife, Rosa.

On top of all of that, immigration reform was currently a very hot topic in the Oregon Legislature and in the local news media. And as if to seal Joe Martin's anger about the mistreatment that was now being heaped on him and his family, he had to endure Senator Jacobsen's almost daily rhetoric about the need for immigration "reform." That is, the Senator was constantly asserting that the United States should tighten its borders and deport all illegal immigrants. So, it seemed to Martin that every time he turned on the local television news he would see the Senator, yet again, blasting immigrants for reducing the standard of living for all hardworking Oregonians. And more often than not, the Senator had the same pretty young woman alongside him. Joe Martin knew that young woman to be Melissa Walker.

Thus, despite seeking help on every front that he could access, and pouring what little money he had into the cause, Martin lost his bid to keep his wife from being deported. All along he knew that if Rosa was deported she could face torture, if not death, upon her return to El Salvador. The tiny third world country was in a constant state of unrest, and the El Salvadorian Government did not take kindly to people who migrated to the United States. Even worse, Martin knew that little Gloria would have to return to El Salvador with his wife. That is, while Joe worked, Rosa had stayed at home and had raised little Gloria. Also, Joe often worked overtime to bring home some extra money to pay the bills and to feed little Gloria. Since Joe was already considering filing for bankruptcy, the couple knew that Gloria would have to stay with Rosa—even if Rosa was deported. And that's exactly what happened. In the spring of 2006, Martin had to helplessly stand by and watch his wife and his two-year old daughter board an airplane bound for El Salvador.

After reading the news article, I felt like I had a large lump in my throat. Martin had clearly gotten the shaft from the INS, and I felt sympathetic towards him. But, my job was to solve the murder of Melissa Walker. And the information uncovered by Eva provided Martin with a motive for murder. Until now, I had pegged Martin as a hardworking night janitor who appeared a bit nervous, but whose story and identity were legitimate. I was now wondering, however, if my instincts had been wrong. Thus, I looked up from my plate and said, "I think that we need to pay Mr. Martin a visit."

"I think that you're right," said Eva.

After finishing our breakfast, Eva and I headed north on Liberty Street past the Downtown core. Once we reached Center Street, we turned right and headed east. Martin lived in northeast Salem, near Hawthorne and Center. It was about 9:30 a.m. and Eva and I hoped to surprise Martin at his home. We knocked on his door, which he answered. Displaying our badges, I said, "Hi Mr. Martin. We met over at the Capitol last week, remember? I'm Detective Davis and this is Detective Tolento. We'd like to ask you a few more questions. May we come in?"

"Uh, well, I just got off work and I was about to eat dinner. Could we do this later?"

"We didn't mean to interrupt your mealtime, Mr. Martin," I said. "However, we do have some things that we need to ask you. It should only take a few minutes."

"Well, all right. Come on in, I guess."

With that, Eva and I entered Martin's second story studio apartment. He seemed fairly relaxed, although he was definitely acting put out. Once we were seated in the small and sparsely decorated living space, I asked, "Mr.

Martin, may I call you Joe?"

"Yes, yes."

"When did you change your name from Hector Rodriguez?"

Looking a little startled, Martin said, "What? Oh, well I guess that's no secret. Uh, around 1990, I believe. I just started calling myself that. You know, filling out forms with that name. It just seemed to make things easier."

"So you never formally changed your name—you just began going by the name of Joe Martin?"

"Yes," said Martin. Looking tired, he continued, "It just made things easier. Creditors treated me differently if I told them that my last name was Martin, rather than Rodriguez."

"I see. Joe, are you acquainted with Senator Jacobsen?"

"Whadaya mean?" he asked. Then, shrugging his shoulders, he added, "He works in the Capitol. I know who he is."

"Is there anything more than that, Joe? Have you ever talked to him or socialized with him?"

"No, no," said Martin, who was by now becoming visibly irritated. "I mean, sure, we've said hello to one another over at the Capitol—all of the folks over there know me."

"You mean the Senators and the Representatives?"

"Yes, of course, and everyone else over there," said Martin. "Now and then, I'll work the day shift. You know, to get some overtime in. So, I've been there eight years or so now. New faces come and go, but, I'm one of the familiar ones there at the Capitol."

"Well, Joe, didn't you ask Senator Jacobsen to represent you on your immigration troubles—as your lawyer?

Martin continued to look anxious. However, without any hesitation he answered, "Uh, well, sort of, my wife telephoned his office. I think that she spoke to his assistant, who told us that he was not taking on any new clients."

"Okay, Joe. Let me see if I've got this straight. Other than some occasional 'hellos' in the Capitol, you had no other face-to-face contact with the Senator. Is that right?"

Martin answered, "Well, none that I recall."

"I see. So you never walked into the Senator's Capitol office and asked him to help you with your immigration troubles?"

"Oh! Yes, I forgot," said Martin. "It was just a spur of the moment type thing. I had just emptied the trash cans in his office and I saw him enter. I said, hello, and tried to talk with him. But, he said that he was too busy. So, I left."

"Did things get a little tense? I mean did he have someone escort you out of his office?"

"What?" asked Martin. "No, no. I do seem to recall, however, that he was a little angry that morning. But, there wasn't a scene or anything. I think that there was someone else in his office, however, who I briefly spoke to."

"Might that person have been Melissa Walker?"

Both Eva and I saw Martin's face drop and his cheeks flush. We'd both interviewed enough people to not jump to any conclusions. However, we both instantly knew that Martin's reaction meant one of two things: either he was guilty of something and feared getting caught, or he understandably feared how things might look. Either way, Joe Martin was no fool.

"What?" asked Martin. "Uh, I don't think so. But, I suppose it's possible."

"Why's that, Joe?"

Unconvincingly, Martin said, "Uh, because you are asking me about it and I've read in the newspaper that Melissa Walker was Senator Jacobsen's intern."

"I see. Joe, you have access to the stairwell behind the Capitol dome don't you?"

"Well, yes, of course," he said.

"And you've already admitted to me that on the day that Melissa Walker was killed, you had gone up to the observation deck at the start of your shift—sometime just after midnight."

"Yes, that's correct," he said.

"Okay, Joe. I'm going to have to read you your rights and bring you downtown for questioning."

After reading Martin his Miranda rights, I handcuffed him and placed him in the backseat of our patrol car. Eva and I then drove back to the Salem Police Department. We had Martin placed in a holding cell. We figured that we'd stall a little bit, to give him some time to ponder his fate.

After pouring myself a cup of coffee and returning to my desk, my telephone rang. It was Phyllis.

"Jack, the Chief is on line two."

"Thanks," I said, as I punched the button for line two. I then answered, "Hi Cap."

"Jack, I've got Johnson and Cutright with IA in the conference room. They'd like to talk to you. I've already met with them. We knew this was comin'. I don't care what they think—they're always full of shit. I know you. What I'm more concerned about is how you are doin'. Do you still wanna stay on the Walker investigation?"

Without any hesitation, I said, "Yes."

"Good. I'd like to keep you on it. The thing's a God

damn mess. But, your wellbeing comes first, Jack. So, I'm just sayin', now's the time to take some paid leave if you need to."

"Thanks, Cap," I said. "But, I'm really okay. It wasn't a situation with a whole lot of gray area. The guy I took out was a professional assassin."

"Yeah, I know. And IA knows it too, but they always have their heads stuck way too far up their bureaucratic assholes to let the truth stand in the way of their zeal to prosecute."

"I know, Cap," I said. "But, that's nothin' we haven't seen before. I'll be okay."

"All right then. Let's get it done. See you in the conference room."

"Okay," I said.

The 45 minute session with the IA zealots went about as expected. Johnson was a career bureaucrat who had barely made it through police academy training and who'd never worked the streets. He'd always accepted pencil pushing jobs that never required him to walk a beat, investigate a crime, or place him in harm's way. Cutright, on the other hand, had briefly worked as a real cop. But, he quickly developed a reputation for being nervous and unreliable—not exactly the kind of traits that a cop would look for in a partner. So it didn't take him long to transfer out of the ranks and into a low level entry job with IA. Over the years, he somehow managed to work himself into a lead investigator position, as did Johnson. The two were, of course, loathed by the rank and file officers and were jokingly referred to as the "Keystone Cops."

At the moment, the two IA flunkies were doing their best to threaten me with several "doom and gloom" scenarios. Although their ploy wasn't working, I figured that I'd play along for a bit in order to let the two numskulls save face. Once I'd done so, however, I walked out of the conference room. In truth, I was more concerned about my upcoming interrogation of Joe Martin.

After grabbing a stale sandwich out of the hallway vending machine, I headed downstairs to join Eva in the briefing room. We wanted to use the next 30 minutes for a chalkboard session. It always seemed helpful to write down the pieces of information and then look at it all. After doing so, it was apparent that there were a lot of loose ends. We mulled things over, such as whether the two murder scenes in different states were necessarily connected, and whether Michael Jacobsen's "tell all" revelation was credible.

While still discussing things, Cap entered the room. He informed us that Martin's lawyer had just arrived. His name was Daniel Griffin. He was a well-known local lawyer, who specialized in personal injury and immigration law. He had helped Martin avoid deportation. But, he was not an experienced criminal defense lawyer.

Eva and I proceeded back upstairs with Cap. We entered his office. Griffin was already seated and was looking entirely too comfortable—the way that only a lawyer can. I was acquainted with Griffin, but didn't really have an opinion about him.

After the obligatory round of polite introductions, Griffin asked Cap if Salem PD was going to charge Martin with anything. Cap told him that we needed to interrogate him. In doing so, he agreed that Salem PD would not hold Martin for more than 24 hours, unless we found cause to charge him.

What Griffin didn't know, was that Eva and I had recently spoken with the State Medical Examiner's office.

Doc was out-of-state at some convention, so we had no choice but to speak with one of his deputies. We went over the autopsy report, and then reviewed the evidence that Doc, as well as the Forensics Unit had gathered. That is, the fingerprints, the skin and hair samples, and the clothing fibers. We'd also managed to obtain a search warrant to gather evidence from both Martin's apartment and his locker down in the Capitol basement. We wanted to see if we could obtain a match between the forensic evidence collected from the Walker crime scene, and anything in Martin's apartment or locker. Moreover, we already knew that Martin was wearing blue coveralls on the morning of Walker's murder, which sounded like a match for the fibers that Doc had collected.

While gathering up my files to take into the interrogation room, my telephone rang. It was Phyllis. "Good morning, Jack. I have a call for you from Sophie Lawrence on line one."

Normally, I would have inquired no further and would have just thanked Phyllis and punched in line one. But, at the moment, I was up to my eyeballs in work and was about to head into the interrogation room to question a murder suspect. So I asked, "Did she say what it was about?"

"Well, sort of," said Phyllis. "She just said that 'you'd want to know.'"

"Okay, thanks Phyllis," I said. I then promptly punched line one and said, "Good morning, Sophie."

"Hi, Jack."

"My assistant said that you had something urgent?"

"You mean I can't call my handsome police detective to just say, 'Hi'?"

Surprised to find myself laughing, I said, "Uh, well, yes, you can. Is that why you called?"

I certainly didn't consider myself any prize to members of the opposite sex. Oh sure, I had a square jaw line and I could fumble my way through a reasonably engaging conversation with a woman. But, the way I saw it I drank too much and I didn't particularly like to get close to people.

Sophie answered, "Hmmm. Well, in part. But, I thought that you'd also like to know that the local media has discovered that you are detaining Joe Martin in connection with the Walker girl's murder. You can expect a pack of journalists and probably several television reporters to arrive there at any moment. Mr. Martin's immigration battle with the INS was extensively covered by the local news media, and his plight generated a lot of public sympathy. This isn't going to do your bruised public image any good sweet guy. I just thought that you'd appreciate a heads up."

"I do, Sophie. Thanks. I don't mean to sound distrustful here, but I assume that these kinds of conversations between us are "off the record.""

Caught off guard by my remark, and maybe even a little hurt, Sophie said, "I guess you don't know me very well, Jack Davis. Hey, how about dinner tonight at my place? I make a great dish of sun dried tomato pasta that goes great with a bottle of red wine."

"That sounds nice," I said. "Can I call you after we've completed our interrogation of Martin? It might be pretty late."

"Sure."

"Okay," I said. "Thanks again for the heads up."

"Anytime, detective."

As I concluded my phone call with Sophie, Eva began motioning for me to head into the interrogation room. On the way in, she said that Martin's blue coveralls had been retrieved from his Capitol locker and the Forensics Unit was currently performing a fiber analysis. They expected to have results within an hour or two.

The interrogation of Joe Martin, aka, Hector Rodriguez, began at 11:46 a.m., on Monday, October 16th. After asking some preliminary questions, I handed things over to Eva. While the "good cop, bad cop" routine occasionally worked, that was mostly a script furthered by Hollywood. However, over the years, Eva and I had worked out a routine.

Interrogations were often more art than science. Of course, there were required questions that needed to be asked. But, beyond that, it was usually three human beings in a room—and one of them, the suspect, always felt like a cornered rat. In this case, there was a fourth person present, Martin's attorney, Dan Griffin.

Eva quickly got to the heart of things. "Okay, look, Joe. You were pretty angry with Senator Jacobsen weren't you? I mean, shit, when a father like yourself sees his wife and kid being deported you'd have a right to be pretty pissed off about the situation, right?"

"I'm not denying that I was angry at Senator Jacobsen. That's not a crime, is it?"

Eva, couldn't resist, "No, but murdering his young assistant is!"

I saw it coming. Griffin couldn't help himself. He bolted upright out of his chair, all red faced, and almost stumbling. He recovered quickly, however, and sputtered, "Detective, unless you want to charge my client with murder, I'd suggest that you stick to the 'where, what, and when' format. Otherwise, if you resume trying to intimidate him with baseless allegations, this interrogation will end. My client is cooperating because I've told him to. But, that can change."

Cops try to solve crimes. Defense lawyers try to prevent crimes from harming their clients—whether their clients committed them or not. The lawyer's job isn't to worry about "guilt" or "innocence" and all that lofty stuff. That's better left to juries, or even the State Legislatures and the Federal Congress. The juries weigh the evidence in the courtroom and the politicians enact the laws, the penal codes, and the measure of punishment. The lawyer's job is to zealously represent his or her client. At the moment, that's exactly what Griffin was doing. Although I knew that, I still thought that he looked pretty lame standing up and waving his arms, while acting all indignant. He should have known better than to come uncorked like that. Cops don't like it. It's usually just all show and only serves to impede the investigation and to piss off the interrogators. Fair or not, cops know that they have the ability to make a suspect's life very unpleasant. It's a fine line—between intimidation and harassment. But, pressuring a suspect often results in the discovery of a key piece of evidence or even a confession.

Eva ignored Griffin's tantrum and methodically continued with her questioning, "Okay. Joe, you were also pretty mad at Melissa Walker weren't you? We already know that she escorted you out of Senator Jacobsen's office on the morning that you approached him. That must have been humiliating?"

"That's not the way it happened. Yes, I was disappointed and upset. But, I didn't threaten anyone. His assistant, the girl that was murdered, just walked me to the door, that's all."

Eva then asked, "So, your memory has now improved,

huh? You now admit that Melissa Walker escorted you out of Senator Jacobsen's office?"

"She walked me to the door, yes," said Martin. "And I voluntarily left. There was no scene."

"You were working in the Capitol building on the night that Melissa Walker was murdered, weren't you, Joe?"

"You know that I was," said Martin. "I discovered her body early in the morning and called 911."

Relentlessly, Eva continued, "And your story is that during your entire shift you never saw Melissa Walker, until you found her body around 6:30 a.m.?"

"Yes."

Pausing for a few seconds, and then lowering her head with her arms crossed and resting on the table in front of her, Eva looked right at Martin, and said, "Do you really expect us to believe that, Joe?"

"That's up to you. The Capitol is a huge building. It takes four people, working two back-to-back full-time shifts to clean the thing. We start downstairs and work our way up. Sure, a lot could happen there that we would never see or hear."

"Okay, Joe," said Eva. "Where were you between the hours of 2:00 and 3:00 a.m. on the morning of Melissa Walker's murder?

"Well, uh, I usually finish the east section of the 3rd floor by 2:15 or 2:30. So, I was probably vacuuming up there, or emptying trash."

Eva continued, "Did you clean the rotunda stairwell leading to the observation deck on the morning of October 9th—the morning that Melissa Walker was murdered?"

"Don't believe I did."

"Uh, you earlier told Detective Davis that you did," said Eva. Which is it, Joe?"

"Okay. There are two teams that clean the Capitol building. Jose and I are one team. We work the midnight to 8:00 a.m. shift. The other team, Rick and Jorge, work the earlier shift. They start at 4 p.m. We rotate our duties every month. The basement cafeteria takes a long time to clean. So, the teams split things up. One team cleans the basement, the cafeteria, the 1st floor, and as much of the 2nd floor as they can. Then, Jose and I clean the remainder of the 2nd floor, as well as the 3rd and 4th floors. This month, the other team cleans the basement and the cafeteria. The team that cleans the upper floors always cleans the rotunda stairwell. But, as I initially told Detective Davis, the outside observation deck is closed this time of year. So, we don't clean it. We only do that during the late spring, summer, and early fall when it's open to the public."

"I don't understand," said Eva. "I'm not talking about the outside observation deck. If you and Jose are cleaning the upper floors, then wouldn't one of you have cleaned the rotunda stairwell on the morning that Melissa Walker was found dead?"

"Oh, yes, I'm sorry. I got confused by your questioning. I'm pretty nervous—and tired. I'm usually asleep at this time of the day.

"So let me see if I've got this straight, Joe," said Eva. You admit that you cleaned the rotunda stairwell during your shift of October 9th?"

"Yes."

"And when exactly did you do so?" asked Eva.

"Well, like I said, when I first came on shift—so shortly after midnight."

"And what did you find?" asked Eva.

"Nothing."

K. L. Spangler

Eva and I weren't at all sure about Joe Martin. His credibility had seemingly been going downhill ever since we began questioning him at his apartment earlier in the day. On the one hand, we didn't have any hard evidence linking him to the crime. What we did have was motive and opportunity. Yet, after continuing to grill Martin for three additional hours, we still didn't have anything more. It was now closing in on 5 p.m. and Griffin had become increasingly put off with the interrogation. He was now demanding Martin's release.

I decided to throw the dice. "You murdered Melissa Walker didn't you, Joe?"

"No," he emphatically said.

"You were mad as hell about losing your family weren't you? You'd endured enough from the likes of Senator Jacobsen—so you just snapped and decided to murder his assistant who was rude to you in his office."

"No, no!" said Martin. "I mean, yes, I was mad. But, no, I didn't kill anyone."

"U-huh. And since you've cleaned the Capitol Building for eight years now, it's probably fair to say that you are quite familiar with dome's stairwell, correct?" I asked.

"Of course," said Martin.

"I'll bet you even have a wrench down in your basement locker that you use to open the rotunda windows, correct?"

"Well, yes," said Martin. "I'm supposed to open them at times for ventilation. But, I didn't . . . . ."

Griffin interjected and cut off, Martin. He stuck out his hand in front of Martin's face. He then said, "That's enough. My client will not utter another word. This interrogation is over. He's cooperated—more than he should. You've grilled him for nearly five hours. Either charge him or release him!"

Eva and I got up and left the room. We discussed the situation with Cap. The three of us all agreed that we had little choice but to release Martin. We simply needed more evidence and, right now, we didn't have it. Thus, Martin was released at 6:15 p.m. and was warned not to leave the State of Oregon.

As Martin and his attorney departed down the main steps from the Salem PD offices, they were flogged by newspaper and television reporters. Unfortunately, the local news stations were still on the air and they were covering the event "live."

Griffin seized the moment. Displaying surprisingly savvy public relations skills, he stepped in front of the sea of microphones and said, "My client, Joe Martin, has just been released from the Salem Police Department. He was questioned by homicide detectives about the recent death of Melissa Walker. My client has not been charged—as there is no credible evidence implicating him. Joe Martin is a hardworking American who has been mistreated by the Federal Government and who is now being mistreated by the local police. He is innocent of any wrongdoing and had no involvement in the tragic death of Melissa Walker. We ask the Salem Police Department to refrain from any further harassment."

13

Monday Evening, October 16ᵗʰ

I WAS ABOUT to reach into my desk drawer to pull out my flask of whiskey. It was nearly 7 p.m. and almost everyone at Salem PD had gone home. Before taking a drink, however, I remembered that I'd told Sophie that I would call her. A bit unsure about what to say, I picked up the telephone receiver and dialed her number.

"Hello," answered Sophie.

"Hi, Sophie, it's Jack. We just finished here. What a day. Are you still up for dinner?"

"Sure . . . if it still works for you?" said Sophie. "I guess you probably know that the local television stations interviewed Martin and his lawyer as they were leaving your building just a little while ago? God, Jack, you must have a dark cloud hanging over you or something. The press adores Martin for his fight against the INS and the right wing. His lawyer was trying to paint your department as an evil empire."

"Yeah, I heard," I wearily said. "I'll be over in 10 minutes."

"You want directions?"

"Nah, I got it right here—one of the perks of the job," I said.

"See you soon."

"Okay," I said.

Absent mindedly I drove out of the underground garage to the east and was forced to turn left onto the one-way Liberty Street. Back in the 1940's, the Salem City Planners had "vision" and decided to make the City's main arterials into one-way streets. Thus, I had to drive on down past the Convention Center before I could turn back around to the south and head up Commercial Street.

The fog was thick tonight. I couldn't see more than about 10 feet in front of me, so I switched on the Talon's fog lights as I drove through the Candalaria area. Sophie lived in the affluent Croissan Creek neighborhood. The homes there were built on a steep hillside, some with panoramic westerly views. The only problem, as I saw it, was that the houses were all packed in too tight. Although that was apparently the City's answer to urban sprawl, I knew that suburb living wouldn't work for me. I was just fine with my rustic house that was situated on a remote five acres.

Sophie's home was elegant on the outside and warm on the inside. Kind of like her. When I arrived, she had a Toni Child's CD playing softly in the background. She greeted me at the front door.

"Hi, Jack! Come in."

Fortunately, I had stopped at Roth's grocery store along the way to pick up a dozen red roses. While generally baffled by women, I had learned a few things over the years from the school of hard knocks. One of the "no brainers" was to regularly buy flowers for your sweetheart. As I walked through the doorway, I handed Sophie the long stemmed roses.

"Why thanks, Jack! How sweet. They're beautiful!" Sophie then leaned into me and softly kissed me on the cheek.

I managed to mumble, "Sure. Thanks for inviting me over."

Sophie then led me into the kitchen and began cutting the rose stems. Afterwards, she put the dozen roses in a vase and placed it in the center of the kitchen island. I hadn't smelled home cooked food in a long time. For the last couple of years my supper routine had revolved around fast food, TV dinners, and an occasional steak grilled on my outdoor barbecue. So I was relishing the heavenly smell emanating from Sophie's kitchen. She had some concoction of sun dried tomatoes, garlic, and seasonings simmering in a skillet. And the aroma made me painfully aware that I hadn't eaten all day. As I stood there feeling a bit awkward, Sophie poured me a glass of Merlot from Willamette Valley Vineyards. The two of us then talked and sipped wine together for nearly a half hour.

The whole atmosphere was intoxicating—a beautiful woman, good conversation, and plenty of gourmet food. It was long forgotten territory for me. But, Sophie and I seemed to work well together, easily moving back and forth in her kitchen in near proximity. Now and then we'd innocently brush against each other—wondering if the other was feeling similar sensations.

After dinner, we were still seated at the table and well into our second bottle of Merlot. I wanted nothing other than to make love to Sophie. It had been a long time, however, since I'd even tried to read the subtle cues that a woman gives off. I thought that Sophie liked me, but, for a detective, I felt pretty inept at the moment.

The two of us had been flirting all evening long. But, we were each not sure about the other. We'd share some of our past, some of our personal matters, and then safely retreat by laughing about something benign. It was like a tango between two nice human beings, who were in their middle years and who had experienced the highs and lows of life.

I then asked, "Tell me about your life in Sweden, Sophie."

"Well, I grew up in Stockholm. I learned English at an early age—we all do over there. The public school system requires it. I was fascinated by America and was an exchange student during my last year of high school. I stayed with an American family in Palo Alto. I fell in love with the area down there and the family that I was staying with helped me get into Stanford. I was lucky. Although my grades were very good, I'm not sure that I would have gotten into Stanford if the school hadn't been trying to round out its student body with a certain amount of overseas students. I just happened into it at the right time."

"What'd you major in?" I asked.

"Journalism. That's where I got my start in the newspaper industry."

Sipping my glass of wine, I asked, "How'd you end up here?"

"Two reasons—a job here at the Statesman as a fledgling reporter and the business school at Willamette."

Opening the door to intimacy a bit wider, I asked, "Ever marry, Sophie?"

With a hint of sadness in her voice, she answered, "No—not that there weren't some opportunities along the way. I was just very intent on completing my education and on starting my career in journalism. I had a few hard knocks along the way too, which caused me to rethink the whole 'happily ever after' idea."

"I understand," I said.

"How about you, Jack?"

I didn't answer for several seconds. I wasn't all together comfortable divulging very many details about my personal life. Not that I was still grieving or anything, but just because I was a skeptic at heart and I barely knew Sophie. I was more comfortable asking questions, than I was giving answers.

"I've been married once," I said. "It was a mistake. I married too young and too quickly."

"Well, you certainly have a lot of company on that one."

I wasn't ready to discuss Vicki. That was still too close to home. In fact, it was near midnight and I found myself trying to say goodnight to Sophie, while making my way to her front door. After Sophie handed me my overcoat, I placed my arms around her waist and kissed her—exploring her sensual lips and mouth with a long goodnight kiss. Everything inside of me was screaming to stay the night and spoon with this lovely woman, but I didn't. Instead, I politely told her "good night."

The next morning I headed into work early—lately, an all too common occurrence. Although I was a morning person, I'd found that with age I increasingly enjoyed the virtues of sleeping in a bit. But, I never really minded an early start. Everything seemed quieter and more vibrant in the mornings. So, it wasn't unusual to find me sipping coffee and eating breakfast at one of my hangouts as early as 6:00 a.m.

On this particular morning, however, I got up early

for one reason—to start working on the Melissa Walker murder investigation. There were several aspects of the investigation that were troubling me. As a result, I'd resorted to my old habit of keeping a notepad on my nightstand to write down my thoughts that came to me during the night. I always did that when I felt buried by the nuances of an investigation.

With the sun still hidden behind the eastern horizon, I motored along northward on Liberty Street passing Madrona Avenue. As I approached Roth's grocery store, I turned into the parking lot to get a triple shot cup of coffee at the drive up window. Although I'd kicked the coffee habit several times over the years, I'd never managed to find any suitable replacement—especially in the morning, when my brain needed a jump start.

As I took a large sip of my coffee and began to exit the parking lot, I recalled a quote from the late singer and actor, Dean Martin. Commenting about why he felt compelled to drink, he reportedly had stated, "Well, you wake up in the morning and you realize that this is as good as it gets." While it was rare that I took a shot of booze in the morning, I sure understood the nature of Martin's thinking—especially when it came to that first cup of coffee in the morning, or that evening cocktail to take the edge off.

Arriving at work, I turned on my desk lamp in the otherwise dimly lit office. After powering up my computer, I glanced at my phone messages. There were two of them. One was a message to call Good Samaritan Hospital regarding Senator Jacobsen. I telephoned the hospital. I was promptly transferred to a nurse who informed me that the Senator was out of ICU and appeared to be stable.

That was good news. I could almost feel myself relax

a bit. I knew that the Senator could provide a lot of useful information. Thus, I was relieved that I would probably be able to question him. There had been a security guard posted outside of the Senator's hospital room ever since he had arrived. The Senator had undergone two lengthy surgeries to remove the bullet from his chest and to stop the bleeding. The bullet had punctured his right lung and had narrowly missed both his heart and his spinal cord. Simply put, he was lucky to be alive and it remained to be seen whether he would ever fully recover. He had been unconscious for a long time out there on the tarmac at PDX.

I knew that it was critical to talk to the Senator as soon as he was lucid and able to communicate. So I asked the nurse if I could talk to the him this morning, and she gave me the green light to do so.

The other message was actually a manila envelope from the Joint Forensic Team. Salem PD, Marion County, and the Oregon State Police all had their own forensic experts. Sometimes turf battles took place. But, in complex investigations, all three units typically cooperated with one another—unless Bradley G got in the way. The OSP laboratory is second to none. So Salem PD and Marion County often ship their forensic evidence over there for analysis. In those situations, I often come across Bradley G. I always feel fortunate, however, when he's not around and I can speak to one of the hardworking OSP forensic experts. They're truly top notch.

I pulled out the contents from the envelope. It concerned the suspected Columbian male that I had shot at Flightcraft. There was an OSP cover letter attached to the front of the materials. The letter was signed by Bradley G. I could see that it was a boilerplate letter with a few pertinent details thrown in concerning the decedent. The materials consisted of an autopsy report, a ballistics analysis, and an identity search.

I skipped the autopsy report, knowing full well that the decedent had died from multiple bullet wounds fired from my revolver. It was the ballistics report that I was interested in. When I saw it, I immediately flipped to the Conclusions section. The OSP forensic expert had concluded that neither the pistol that the decedent had used to shoot the Senator nor the revolver that was found holstered to his ankle had been used to kill Melissa Walker's parents. That is, the impression left on the .32-caliber slugs that were removed from the bodies of Mr. and Mrs. Walker did not match the size and spacing of the lands inside the barrel of either weapon.

Turning to the identity report, I noticed that there was some information that had been obtained from Interpol. The suspect's fingerprints were used to identify him as one of Interpol's "most wanted" criminals. His name was Felipe Guerez. He was from Columbia, and he was a known assassin with ties to the Los Hermanos Drug Cartel.

As soon as Eva arrived, I stuffed the reports back into the manila envelope, grabbed my overcoat, and whisked her out of the office. A bit disgruntled with me, she said, "Hey, Jack, what's up?"

"A lot—we need to go over things."

We took the elevator down to the parking garage and got into the Talon. We headed south towards the Sunnyslope Beanery—a favorite coffee house of Salem PD officers. After grabbing a table against the wall, I plopped down the manila envelope.

"Okay, here's what we got," I said. "Senator Jacobsen is stable and out of ICU. We need to head up to Good Sam and interview him. Also, the assassin that I killed up at Flightcraft is a known mafia hit man from Columbia. But, the forensics analysis shows that neither of the weapons found on him match the slugs retrieved from Melissa Walker's parents."

"God!" said Eva. "When are we going to get a break in this investigation? An entire family was murdered . . . one of them in our State Capitol Building, and all we've done is piss off the news media and rule out every suspect."

"I hear ya. But, we haven't exactly 'ruled out' anyone. I doubt that we're going to find a 'smoking gun' in this investigation."

Eva sat back in her chair with her arms folded across her chest and shook her head back and forth several times.

"Maybe we're making this too difficult and overlooking the obvious. We both know that other than random acts, most victims are murdered by people that they know and usually for the most elemental of human emotions—rage, jealousy, or greed."

"I know, Jack, but all that leaves us with are suspicions and hunches."

Feeling glum and frustrated, Eva and I departed the Beanery and headed north on I-5 for Portland's Good Samaritan Hospital. We quickly found Senator Jacobsen's room on the 8th floor. Sitting right outside the doorway was a beefy "twenty-something" police officer who was sleepily looking at the latest copy of "Guns & Amo." Eva and I got a kick out of it. The kid, about six-two with arms like tree trunks, probably had visions of becoming the next Dirty Harry. It was a rite of passage that most young cops go through. There's nothing wrong with carrying some passion into your work. But, after dealing with the darker side of humanity day-after-day for a paltry government paycheck, many rookie cops don't make it past two years of service.

I took pity on the guy, however. Within three feet of him, I dryly said, "Good work, officer. Everything okay here?"

Startled, the young officer ditched the magazine, stood up, and officiously asked, "And who might you be?"

"Detectives Davis and Tolento, Salem PD."

The ruffled officer stammered, "Got some ID?" But, Eva and I were already displaying our badges in front of his nose and simply walked past him.

The Senator was eating lunch and watching Headline News on the overhead television. A nurse was just finishing up with her check of his vitals. As we walked into his room, the Senator gazed warily at us. He looked pale and wrung out—the way a person looks when they've been sick for an extended period. Eva and I tried to be respectful of the situation. Regardless of whether the Senator had engaged in any criminal wrongdoing, he had nearly lost his life.

I finally broke the ice and said, "Good morning, senator. I'm Detective Davis, and this is Detective Tolento, with Salem PD. How are you feeling?"

Senator Jacobsen looked at us without responding. It made us both feel a bit uneasy. Clearly, we were up against a worthy adversary—a powerful politician that we wouldn't be able to easily manipulate and who had developed a sense of purpose as a result of nearly dying.

Impatiently, I said, "We'd like to ask you a few questions, Senator Jacobsen. Are you up to that?"

"I guess so," said the Senator.

"Well, we're glad to have you back here in Oregon.

We've talked to your son, and it sounds like you were all very lucky to make it out of Columbia."

"I'll say."

"Senator," I said. "We know that you just got out of ICU, so we'll keep this short. We understand that you were involved in the trafficking of cocaine. Is that correct?

"I probably shouldn't say anything without my lawyer present."

"Okay," I said. "That's fine. Just so you know, however, Michael has already told us about his role with the CIA. Does that change things for you?"

The Senator glared at Eva and me. Despite the seriousness of his medical condition, it was obvious that he had his wits about him. There didn't appear to be the slightest trace of cognitive deficit.

"What are you talking about?"

"Look Senator, we know, okay?" I said. After letting my comment hang in the air for a few seconds, I continued. "Michael told us that he has been trying to protect you. So, look, we can have a chat right now, or, in a few more days, we can take you down to our station for a formal interrogation—your choice. If you're innocent, you have nothing to lose by talking with us right now. I'm being straight with you."

"Go ahead," said the Senator.

I turned to Eva and gave her a nod. We had played this gig before—pushing a suspect for information without first reciting his Miranda rights. That is, the two of us knew from experience that a nervous suspect would often clam up after hearing a recitation of his rights. Also, if a suspect had information, but was innocent of any serious crime, failing to recite his rights was harmless. So, in those situations, it was a win-win situation. The suspect never got charged, but if he possessed helpful information about a murder he'd often divulge it. The difficulty was in deciding when to apply the tactic.

It was certainly risky business for Eva and me, and we used the tactic only when we both were confident that the suspect was not the murderer. The risk, however, was if our hunch turned out to be incorrect. If that were to occur, we could end up botching an investigation and securing a murderer's acquittal—or even losing our jobs. In fact, the impatient strategy that Eva and I were now using on Senator Jacobsen had once backfired on us.

That is, shortly after Eva was assigned as my partner, we had investigated what appeared to be a botched burglary that resulted in the murder of an elderly woman. Although we knew that many killings are committed by people that the victim knows, in that particular case, the victim's husband appeared to have an air tight alibi. Moreover, the victim's house showed the classic signs of a forced entry. So, the husband was not a serious suspect.

Thus, Eva and I never read the Miranda rights to the victim's husband. However, after months of painstaking investigative work, we had not solved the murder. Consequently, we turned our attention back to the victim's husband. Once we placed him under surveillance it didn't take long for us to discover that he was spending nearly every night with a much younger single woman who lived down the street from his home—the scene of the murder. It turned out that the young woman had previously worked with the victim's husband.

With nothing more than that to go on, Eva and I began doggedly pursuing the guy. Once he got wind that he was under surveillance, however, he hired one of the best criminal defense lawyers in town. Within a few weeks, Eva and I secured a search warrant to search the young woman's house and property. Using metal detectors, we uncovered a .38-caliber revolver that was buried in her backyard. The ballistics from the revolver matched the impressions on the three slugs removed from the murder victim's head. Although a grand jury indicted the victim's husband for murder, the prosecution's case was later dismissed.

That is, the defense lawyer successfully argued that Eva and I had discovered the existence of the young woman by information gathered illegally—by virtue of failing to recite the Miranda rights to his client. So, according to the skillful defense lawyer, under the "fruit of the poisonous tree" legal doctrine, all subsequent evidence—including the murder weapon—had been gathered illegally. The judge agreed.

The aftermath of that bungled investigation was not pretty. I felt like some sort of a fallen hero. Even Gunny was disappointed in my recklessness. It was the lowest point in my career. Of course the Statesman Journal had a field day with the damn thing, which partly explains my longstanding dislike for the press.

Eva took my cue and started in, "Hi Senator, I'm Detective Tolento. This is the straight scoop—as we understand it. Feel free to correct any inaccuracies. We believe that you've been trafficking cocaine for approximately 10 years. We also believe that your son, Michael, cut a deal with the CIA to infiltrate the Los Hermanos Drug Cartel in order to obtain amnesty for your criminal activities."

"No comment."

"Okay," said Eva. "But, I note that you don't exactly seem surprised by what I just told you."

The Senator didn't take the bait.

Undeterred, Eva stepped a little closer to the Senator's bedside and unhesitatingly continued, "Senator, did you have anything to do with the murder of Melissa Walker?"

"Hell no! Just like you, however, I'd sure like to know who in Christ's name killed her. She was the best damn intern that I ever had. She was ambitious, bright, loyal, and attractive. Everything that she touched seemed to turn to gold. She had a bright future. It's a damn shame that her life ended prematurely."

"Senator," said Eva. "Were you in the Capitol building the morning that she was murdered?"

"No."

"What about the day before—Sunday, October 8th?" asked Eva.

"Yes, I was in my office that evening. I had a lot of work to do. The fall elections were approaching, as well as the Legislative Session. But, I left around nine or nine-thirty."

"Okay," said Eva. "Where'd you go afterwards?"

"To Magoo's for a nightcap—then home."

"So, I suppose lots of people saw you in the bar around 9:30 or 10:00?" offered Eva.

"Yeah, they did. In fact, there were a couple of other legislators over there. Steve Donald and Claudia Jolenski, as a matter of fact."

Eva continued, "Anyone at your home when you arrived there?"

"Yes, my wife."

"And that's where you were between 2:00 and 3:00 a.m. on Monday, October 9th—at home?"

"Yes."

"All right, just a couple more questions Senator," said Eva. "Was Melissa Walker in your office on Sunday evening?"

"No. I never ask my assistants to work on the weekends."

"Okay," said Eva. "Did you see her at any time over the weekend?"

"No."

Eva glanced over at me. Neither of us needed to say a thing. We both were thinking along the same lines. I cleared my throat and then addressed the Senator, "We appreciate your cooperation, senator. I have just a couple of questions. What happened down in Bogotá that caused your family to escape?

"Well, we got wind that the Cartel was growing suspicious of Michael—that perhaps they had discovered his status as a CIA agent. Our housekeeper was very loyal to us, and one day she overheard some Cartel members talking about us. Then, two Cartel goons began regularly appearing outside of our home and warned us not to leave Bogota."

"All right, one last question," I said. "Were you, or have you ever been, romantically involved with Melissa Walker?"

"No."

"Okay," I said. "That's all I have. Thanks, senator."

On the way out of town, Eva and I headed over to Jake's Steak House for lunch. We were at a low point in our investigation. We had three central suspects—Joe Martin, Michael Jacobsen, and the Senator. Yet, all three suspects had credibly denied any involvement in Melissa Walker's murder. Moreover, Senator Jacobsen appeared to have an alibi—although it could only be corroborated by his wife.

In my nearly 20 years with Salem PD, I had been at

this sort of juncture before. I always feared that I might not crack the case. Nonetheless, I had learned to just plow ahead. Experience had taught me that most of the time a criminal makes a mistake or two. A murder investigation is like a chess match—not necessarily with the killer, but with the unfolding evidence. There is often no right or wrong way to proceed. At those junctures, an investigation often seems to take on a life of its own—almost as if the inanimate evidence comes alive. Deciding how to proceed, who to question, and where to look, almost becomes more art than science. In fact, the dynamic is not unlike the discovery in quantum physics that the observer of an experiment actually becomes a participant in its outcome.

While driving back to Salem, my cell phone rang. It was Cap. He had just spoken with the FBI. The Bureau had picked up several recent cell phone transmissions from the Portland-Salem area to Bogotá. In each instance, it was the same caller. Whoever it was, they were using a "go phone" with an international calling card—like anyone can purchase at a Wal-Mart store. The FBI had tracked the location of the cell phone and its usage. It had caught the Bureau's attention due to the recent death of Felipe Guerez, the hit man from Columbia who had been on Interpol's most wanted list. The FBI had learned that the cell phone had been purchased at a convenience store in the Clackamas Town Center the day following the shootout at Flightcraft. The store's surveillance tape had been reviewed by the FBI, and it displayed a blonde-haired woman purchasing a cellular go-phone. She was wearing sunglasses and was dressed in an overcoat. The store clerk vaguely recalled selling her the phone, but, otherwise, offered no helpful information.

The cell phone had been used once that day to make

a 10 minute call from Clackamas to Bogotá. There were no further calls until yesterday, when a call was picked up from Salem to Medellin, another Columbian city that is situated to the northwest of Bogotá. Then, there was a third call that had been made today from Salem. The caller had again telephoned Bogotá.

Presently, two FBI officers were in Salem, armed with state-of-the-art electronic surveillance equipment. Their assignment was to pinpoint the location of the individual making the phone calls to Columbia.

As Eva and I turned off the Interstate and headed west on Mission Street., we decided to pay a visit to Michael Jacobsen. He lived in a new development just off of Crestview, which overlooked Minto Brown Island Park. We knocked on his door, but there wasn't any answer. Standing on the front porch of Michael's house, I turned to Eva and said, "Come on—I have a hunch where he might be."

We then drove down to Salem's Municipal Airport. Once there, Eva and I walked into the FBO, but no one was at the front desk. Consequently, we headed outside to the fuel pumps. There was an attendant there who was fueling a Grumman Tiger. I asked him if he knew where Michael Jacobsen hangared his jet.

"Yeah, I was just down there topping off his Citation," said the attendant. He then pointed to the south hangars and added, "He's right over there—about three rows down. The hangar door's probably still open."

"Was he preflighting?"

"Yep," said the attendant.

I then began running towards the south hangars. As I ran along the grassy edge of the taxiway, I listened for the sound of turbine engines. I couldn't hear any. That was a relief, because I sure didn't know what I could do to stop Michael if he was already taxiing.

I was almost there when I heard it—the unmistakable sound of accelerating turbine engines. "Shit!" I yelled out. I was breathing hard now. As I rounded the corner I could see the reflection of the Citation's flashing position lights. It was one of those typical fall afternoons in the Pacific Northwest—already overcast, drizzly, and gray by 4:00 p.m.

With my right hand I pulled out my Smith & Wesson revolver from my shoulder harness. The Citation had already started its taxi towards the active runway. Now standing directly in front of the Citation, I aimed my revolver directly at the approaching aircraft. I could see Michael in the cockpit.

The Citation was closing fast—way too fast, and the noise from the twin turbine engines was now deafening. In a last ditch effort to avoid disaster, I waved my arms back and forth in an attempt to get Michael to stop. The Citation just kept barreling forward, however. The visibility had now dropped even further, as a dark layer of cumulous clouds had moved in from the west. I had a split second decision to make—shoot at the moving jet's tires and hope that a ricocheting bullet didn't send it and its pilot up in flames, or jump the hell out of the way. I decided against firing my weapon and dove to the side.

The Citation continued to gather speed as it taxied towards Runway 31. It was probably moving at about 15 knots, and I had no chance of catching up to it.

While I was standing there out of breath and slightly bent over with my hands on my knees, Eva came running up to me. "Jack! Are you okay?" she said.

"Yeah," I said. "I tried to stop him. It was Michael. I

had a clear shot, but I wasn't sure that he was trying to escape. I didn't want to risk killing him in a ball of flames. That'd be a nice one to try and explain on top of everything else—wouldn't it?"

"Let's head back," said Eva.

Still out of breath, I nodded and managed to say, "Let's go talk to the controllers in the tower. They'll know where he's headed."

As Eva and I began walking back to the FBO, we watched Michael takeoff on Runway 31. After he lifted off and reached about a thousand feet, he put the Citation into a gradual climbing right turn to the east. Less than 30 seconds later, the Citation disappeared into the gray soup that had moved in over Salem.

After talking to the air traffic controllers, Eva and I learned that Michael had filed an IFR flight plan to Boise, Idaho. As a result, we contacted the Boise Police Department and alerted them that a murder suspect was headed their way and was possibly trying to escape prosecution.

By the time that Eva and I returned to our desks at Salem PD, it was after 5 p.m. I didn't stay long. I didn't feel like hanging around the police station. Earlier in the day I'd made plans to meet Sophie after work at Da Vinci's. That's where I was headed now. When I arrived the lounge was already packed. It was wine tasting night, which was always good business for the restaurant. Despite the crowd, I managed to find a place at the bar near the doorway. Cops always like that—an easy exit. I ordered a draft beer and began mulling things over.

As I sipped my beer, I thought about what had just happened down at the airport. I didn't really know what to make of Michael's seemingly hasty departure from the

Salem Airport. But, I figured that at 350 knots, he'd be arriving in Boise in about an hour.

While still seated at the bar, the only person that I cared to see was Sophie—not coworkers, barflies, or reporters. Unfortunately, I felt a hand on my right shoulder and somehow I knew that it wasn't Sophie's.

"Hi Jack," said Bradley G.

I unenthusiastically, said, "Hi Bradley G." Privately, I was thinking, "Just my luck. I wonder how long it's going to take the idiot to get lost?"

"Hey, tough luck with the Walker investigation, huh?" prompted Bradley G.

Playing along for now, I said, "Why would you say that?"

"Oh, c'mon, Jack," said Bradley G. "The press has been eating you alive and you have no serious suspects."

Resisting the visceral urge to punch out the little gnome, I dryly said, "Have a seat Bradley G. I'm glad you found me here. Say, why don't we roll up our sleeves and get some real work done? You know, sort of caucus right here at the bar and crime solve."

"Right, Jack," said Bradley G.

"Oh, damn. You mean that you're no longer the dedicated public servant that you used to be, Bradley G? What happened?"

"I think I'll catch you later," said Bradley G.

Lifting my head for the first time, I looked right at Bradley G. and dismissively said, "Good idea, chump. Scurry off now before I mop the floor with your face."

With that Bradley G. skulked off to the other side of lounge where he was hanging out with two other suit-and-tie bureaucrats. As he did so, I overheard him say, "What a loser." While the rap against me was that I shot off my mouth too often, it sure felt good to do so sometimes. I never lost any sleep over being direct with sycophants like Bradley G.

By now I had drained my beer and I was thinking about departing. There were plenty of places in town to enjoy the buzz of alcohol without the annoyance of pricks like Bradley G. In fact, the idea of simply going home and soaking in my hot tub was beginning to sound pretty good. I glanced at my watch—it read 5:43 p.m. I set a five dollar bill down on the counter and stood up to leave. As I did so, Sophie stepped through the doorway.

Before I knew it, she was standing next to me with her hand around my arm.

"Hi, sweet guy!" she said. "Sorry I'm late. I would have called, but I couldn't find your cell number."

"That's okay. Good to see you. Actually, the company around here's not so great. I was just headed out the door."

"Oh," she said, as she glanced around the lounge. "Well, you wanna go somewhere else?"

"Why don't we go ahead and have a drink here and then we can decide where we want to eat."

"Okay," said Sophie. "So, what's new—how was your day?"

I had to admit it. I liked Sophie—a lot. She was intelligent, successful, upbeat, and one absolutely beautiful woman. She was all legs, thin, and curvy in all the right places. She had blonde hair, blue eyes, and a button nose. It worked for me. As far as I was concerned, Sophie was Faith Hill's better looking younger sister. The way I saw it, the only problem was that I was a dyed-in-the-wool cop, who'd already seen his best days. I'd seen too much of the ugly side of humanity and I'd suffered my own share of personal losses. As a result, I was jaded and drank too much. I also wasn't exactly used to being emotionally available. That part of me had ended with the loss of Vicki.

I answered, "Not a whole lot—just an ordinary cop's life."

"Hmmm. Sounds like you're a bit down right now. Is it the investigation?"

"Yeah, I guess," I said. "It almost always happens. You know, two steps forward and one step backwards."

"So you don't have any hot new leads, huh?"

Smiling a little, I looked up from my freshly mixed gin and tonic and said, "Well, according to your newspaper, if I did, I should be running them by your editorial staff members who all seem to know how to conduct a murder investigation better than I do."

"Ouch! Feeling kind of hostile, eh? You gotta remember that I'm one of your fans, Jack Davis—and I kinda just plain like ya too."

"Feeling's mutual, Lawrence," I said.

"Well, now that we're settled on that, why don't we gulp down our drinks, have a romantic dinner, and then have earth shattering sex in front of my fireplace?"

I paused and looked at Sophie. I liked her style and I privately had been thinking along the same lines. I winked at her and said, "Now there's an invitation that I can't refuse. Let's get outta here."

I walked Sophie to her car, which was parked right in front of Da Vinci's. After exploring her inviting mouth with a lengthy French kiss, I turned up the collar on my overcoat and headed towards my car. We had agreed to meet for dinner at the Old Europe Inn.

The truth was, I hadn't felt any similar romantic

stirrings since falling in love with Vicki over 15 years ago. We had met in a coffee shop. She was only 26 back then, while I was a 31 year old rookie homicide detective. Although I had never believed in "love at first site," my view changed after I met Vicki. Something happened inside of me on that long ago day.

Vicki and I ended up buying a house and living together in Sublimity. When she was 36, however, she scheduled a "wellness" examination with her physician. Other than feeling fatigued, her clinical examination was unremarkable. But, she'd never had a mammogram. So her doctor referred her to Salem Radiology for a routine chest x-ray. The film was devastating—it revealed several lumps. Further studies established that the lumps were cancerous and that the cancer had spread to her lymph nodes.

Although Vicki fought the disease with the standard treatment regime, her cancer worsened and she eventually developed an inoperable brain tumor. Following her wishes, I had her body cremated. Both of our families and a few of our closest friends gathered together on a clear and beautiful morning out at the Oregon Coast. It was there that we "celebrated" Vicki's life. In doing so, we spread her ashes offshore near Cannon Beach.

Afterwards, I came close to taking my own life. More than once, I sat in my empty house with a loaded gun pointed at my head. Continuing to live, or to do anything, for that matter, just seemed unimportant. Eventually, however, I managed to wade my way through the grieving process and I returned to the land of the living and to my career as a homicide cop. Arresting murderers and putting them behind bars became my new passion.

While en route to the Old Europe Inn, my cell phone

rang. I'd been expecting a call from Boise PD.

"Davis, Homicide," I answered.

It was Eva. "God, you actually have your cell phone turned on Jack—and you even answered it! I'm beginning to like the effect that this Sophie Lawrence woman is having on you. Welcome to the 21st Century, buddy."

"Right, Eva. What's up?"

"It's about Michael. He landed in Boise, as scheduled. Boise PD hauled him downtown. They have him in a holding cell. He's not very happy. Claims that he was just doing what he loves—flying. Here's the phone number."

"All right. Thanks, Eva." I then hit the disconnect button and punched in the number for Boise PD. After a few rings, the call went through.

"Boise Police Department, may I help you?" answered a rapid speaking dispatch operator.

"Yes, I'm Detective Davis with Salem PD in Oregon. I understand that you're holding Michael Jacobsen. He's a suspect in a murder investigation that I'm conducting. I'd like to talk to him."

"Hold on," said the operator.

After I had nearly reached the Old Europe Inn, Michael was finally patched through. "Detective Davis?"

"Yeah, it's me," I answered.

"What the fuck is going on?"

"Well, let's see, Mike," I shot back. "For starters, how about telling me why you nearly ran me over earlier this afternoon?"

"What? What are you talking about?"

"Don't bull shit me," I said. "I was standing directly in front of you as you began taxiing away from the south hangars at Salem. I tried to wave you off, to get you to stop."

"No way! Are you serious?"

"Very," I answered. "The fuel attendant told me that he had just topped off your tanks. So, I ran over to your hangar just in time to see you taxing towards Three One. I was directly in front of you with my weapon drawn. I waved for you to stop, but you just continued on."

"I don't believe it," said Michael. "Really, I never saw you. Look, I needed to get out of 'Dodge City' and away from all the speculation. I'm a fighter jock. I hadn't flown in several days. I just needed to get in the air. So I filed an IFR flight plan to Boise—just to rock-and-roll in some IMC."

I sighed and said,"Look, I'm parked here at a restaurant ready to join someone for dinner. Get your ass back to Salem, and be at your house in the morning. I'll talk to you then. Clear?"

Michael shot back, "Clear? Are you shittin' me, Detective? Chew on this while your havin' dinner. I've cooperated with you because I'm innocent. I could have just wrapped myself in the protective shield of the CIA. If I had, you city chumps would be clueless."

Unimpressed, I volleyed back, "Talk to you tomorrow, Ace."

I had now gotten out of my car. It was raining. Water was pouring off of the Old Europe Inn's awning. While heading into the restaurant, I spotted Sophie driving up. I waited and then opened her car door. She smiled and the two of us then walked inside together with our arms around one another. We were seated at a small corner table. The table was covered with a white linen cloth and was illuminated by a small candle.

"Well, that went well," I said.

"What's that, Jack?"

"Oh, I just got off the phone with Senator Jacobsen's kid," I said. "Actually, he's not a kid—he's in his mid-thirties. It seems that he and I had a possible misunderstanding down at the airport this afternoon. I seem to be finding my share of trouble lately."

"Probably comes with the work."

"Apparently," I said.

"So what went on with you and Michael?"

Not aware that I'd mentioned Michael by name, I asked, "You know him?"

"Oh, casually," said Sophie. "You can't live in this town without hearing about the Jacobsens. I've met Michael and his father at a social function or two."

"Yeah?"

After finishing dinner I drove over to Sophie's house. She left her car at the restaurant and rode with me. Once inside it took us less than a minute to strip off all of our clothes, while we mauled each other in the hallway entry. Before we consummated our passion, Sophie said, "C'mon, sweetie."

She then led me up the staircase to her bedroom. Once there, we made love—hard against the wall, long and sweaty in the bed, and passionately on the floor. Afterwards, neither one of us ever slept more soundly in our entire lives.

In the morning, Sophie brought two steaming cups of black coffee upstairs. She then snuggled up next to me in an oversized nightshirt. It was still only six-thirty. After finishing our coffee, we made love again—like two long lost lovers. Being in an unfamiliar house, I felt a little out-of-sorts getting dressed for work. I wasn't used to showering in someone else's bathroom, which lacked my customary men's toiletries.

I arrived at work with the invigorating "chemical rush" of new love, but also looking a little rough around the edges. Not having a razor at Sophie's house, my face was unshaven and my day old clothes were a bit wrinkled.

"Hey, champ," offered Eva. "Late night?"

"Might say that."

Not knowing when to quit—a trait that I possessed too—Eva continued, "Been a while, huh?"

I can tolerate good natured ribbing as much as the next guy. But, my private life was just that—private. While I considered Eva my friend, she was also a co-worker. And the police station was one huge gossip mill. So, feeling a little irritated, I pointedly said, "What?"

"Uh, we love ya around here, Jack," said Eva. "Go slow, okay?"

Looking directly at Eva, I frowned and said, "Thanks, 'Oprah.' I'll keep that in mind."

After I had sat down at my desk, Eva informed me that Deford had interviewed some of the Senator's neighbors on Fairmont Hill. One of the neighbors was a business executive, who lived directly across the street from the Senator's house. He recalled seeing the Senator walk his dog at about 2:15 a.m. on Sunday, October 9th. Eva then added, "If that's true, Jack, then it was virtually impossible for Senator Jacobsen to have killed Melissa Walker."

"Yep. Although, I suppose he could have killed her and then hurriedly driven home with the plan to create an alibi. But, that's a stretch. It sure wouldn't have left him with much time to have made it home before 2:15 a.m."

I then walked into the break room and poured myself a cup of coffee—quite a step down from the rich cup of fresh ground coffee that Sophie had served up this morning. But, it still achieved its purpose of offering a brief distraction. After returning to my desk, I was just about to reach into my lower desk drawer to pour a shot of Jack Daniels into my coffee mug, when my desk phone rang.

It was not yet 8 a.m., so I knew that it was someone calling me on the Department's back line.

"Davis, Homicide," I answered.

"Hi Detective, it's Michael Jacobsen."

"Hi, Michael," I said, still perturbed with the hot-shot fighter jock after last evening's telephone conversation. "I assume that you're here back in Salem?"

"Yeah."

"All right," I said. "So, your story is that yesterday afternoon you didn't see me trying to stop you, is that right?"

"Yes. And it's not a story—it's the truth. I was probably copying down my clearance."

Trying to give Michael the benefit of the doubt, I said, "Okay, we'll leave that one for another day. Listen, there was a foreign male and female up at Flightcraft when you arrived. You already know that the male was shot dead. But, the female evaded capture. We have reason to believe that she is presently in the Salem area. You need to lay low. She may be here for the sole purpose of trying to kill you. Is there a patrol car parked outside your house?"

"Uh, just a minute. . . . Yeah."

"Okay, stay low," I said.

"Wilco."

I grabbed the file on Joe Martin. All detectives quickly learn that homicides are usually solved by dogged police work. It's not glamorous, it's not Sherlock Holmes-like sleuthing, and it's not lady luck. This morning, Eva and I could be found blurry eyed sitting at our desks poring over paperwork and making several telephone calls.

As I was going over Joe Martin's file, I was aware that the murderer could well be one of the people that Eva and I had already interviewed. It was one of 10 Commandments of homicide work—if no new suspects are found within a reasonable time, you've probably already come into contact with the murderer.

After coming up with nothing, Eva and I telephoned Tim Lawton, the head of security over at the Capitol. He agreed to meet us for lunch in the Capitol basement. Once there, we wasted no time in asking him about Joe Martin. Lawton indicated that he had never had any problems with Martin, and that he had no reason to suspect that he had killed Melissa Walker.

I thought that Lawton's exoneration of Martin was a little odd. After all, Martin was in the building at the time Walker was murdered, he had a motive, and he had the ability to open the rotunda glass doorway. But, I just assumed that Lawton wasn't aware of Martin's run in with Senator Jacobsen. Also, for some reason, the forensic experts were unable to definitively say whether the fiber samples collected from underneath Walker's fingernails matched those from Martin's coveralls. So, we were still waiting on that crucial piece of evidence, and hoping that something less equivocal would be established.

Eva and I asked Lawton about the Capitol Building's security cameras. We were interested in whether they would reveal Martin's location at the approximate time of the murder. Lawton said that he hadn't really examined the tapes for that purpose, because he hadn't suspected Martin. I jotted down a note to review the surveillance tapes during the 2:00 to 3:00 a.m. time period on the morning of the murder. There were eight sets of tapes that each displayed four different cameras on a split television screen. I figured that I'd start with the views of the East Wing of the 3rd floor—the location that Martin had claimed that he was cleaning during the time of the murder.

Eva then asked Lawton if he had ever seen any unusual activity by Senator Jacobsen. He hadn't. We then thanked Lawton for his time and asked him to give us a call if he thought of anything that might help our investigation.

Just as Eva and I were ready to plow through some more paperwork, dispatch alerted us about a possible homicide in a southeast Salem trailer park. We immediately took the elevator down to the parking garage, obtained an unmarked car, and headed east on Mission Street.

The trailer park was located on the Westside of I-5. It was the usual trailer park scene—run down mobile homes, worn out cars parked next to them, and several unemployed occupants. Three patrol cars had already arrived and the area was roped off with yellow crime scene tape. Two Salem PD officers were interviewing people. One of the individuals that they were talking to was the park manager, and another two were neighbors.

Eva and I said hello to the officers and carefully walked into the mobile home. The body of a young to middle-aged male was lying belly up on the sofa. The victim had brown hair and had an obvious bullet wound to his head—as the light brown floral colored sofa was saturated with blood.

A Marion County Deputy Sheriff was already inside the mobile home along with a couple of forensic investigators. I asked the deputy, "Whadaya got?"

He said, "Victim's name is Steve Hornbecker. He was shot once in the head." Motioning to the hole in the window above the couch, the deputy continued, "The bullet entered here, from the outside. That's about all we know at this point. We've uploaded his name into all of the usual databases, we've talked to the manager, and we've interviewed the nearby neighbors. He was living here with his girlfriend and her two kids. The girlfriend's been notified and is on her way. The victim was apparently unemployed. He has two priors—sale and possession, and burglary. A few years back, he served about a year in the County jail."

"Okay. Thanks, deputy," I said. "Nice work."

The forensic investigators were painstakingly searching for evidence, but it didn't look like there was much to find. It looked as though someone had simply shot Hornbecker through the rectanglur shaped window above the sofa. Doc Evans hadn't yet arrived, but he'd been notified. Eva and I both knew that we'd have to wait for the forensic analysis of the bullet slug and the autopsy report. However, we did want to question the victim's girlfriend, who was just now arriving. She skidded to a stop directly in front of the mobile home in an early-80's looking Honda sedan, with a broken headlight and an off color fender. As she did so, she hit the dilapidated picnic table located less than 10 feet from the mobile home's front door. Once inside, she screamed, "Oh my God! Oh my God!"

I had seen this kind of thing many times—and my heart ached. It always reminded me that life wasn't fair. Bad things sometimes happen to good people and, unfortunately, as a homicide cop, I have to wade into life's bad things.

As the woman's face began to turn pale, I held her arm and escorted her away from the gruesome scene and outside. She looked like she was ready to faint.

"Ma'am, I know that this is an extremely difficult time

for you. We're truly only interested in your welfare at the moment. I'm Detective Davis and this is Detective Tolento. We're with the Salem Police Department." Guiding the distraught woman over to the picnic table, I said, "Here sit down. Just take a few minutes. Take some deep breaths. It's okay to let it out—don't try to keep it in."

I then pulled out my wallet and retrieved a card for Sue Williamson, a Marion County Mental Health Therapist. Sue specialized in assisting family members with a sudden loss due to a homicide. I trusted her and had seen her effectively rebuild many peoples' lives over the last 19 years.

"Here ma'am," I said, as I handed her Sue's business card. "This person can help you deal with your loss. She's a top notch psychologist, who specializes in these types of situations. You tuck the card away and then give her a call in a day or two. I'll tell her to expect a call from you, all right?"

The woman was a mess. Eva sat down next to her and put her arm around her. After a few minutes, she walked her over to the laundry room. It was warmer in there and was removed from the busy crime scene. There were a couple of chairs in the room and Eva sat down with the grieving woman.

Meanwhile, I stayed at the crime scene for about a half hour. I knew that Eva could more easily console the poor woman, and she was doing just that. She held the grieving woman for a long time, as she heaved and uncontrollably sobbed. These kind of encounters with grieving family members were always painful—even to veteran homicide detectives. The only solace for Eva and me is that we truly feel like our jobs allow us to make the City a safer place. We track down and arrest cold blooded killers, and then place our faith in the justice system to convict and incarcerate them.

When the grieving woman finally stopped wailing and had seemed to be gaining some composure, Eva gingerly started to question her.

"Ma'am, I'm Detective Tolento. I think that you already know that I'm with the Salem Police Department. I'm very sorry about your loss and I know that it's very upsetting." About that time, I quietly slipped in the door. Eva silently gave me a nod of her head, letting me know that it was okay for me to be present. "Detective Davis has just stepped in."

The woman didn't even look up, but just kept sniffling.

Eva continued, "We won't bother you for long here, but do you think that you could answer a few questions?"

The woman didn't say anything. Her bleached hair was hanging down in front of her face. After more than a minute, she finally nodded her head up-and-down between her sniffles.

"Okay," said Eva. "We appreciate your cooperation. You're Ester Norris, correct?"

The woman again nodded her head up-and-down.

Eva, gently proceeded, "Okay, and Steve was your boyfriend?"

For the first time, Norris spoke. "Yes. He was a very kind man—very good with my children."

"That's nice. We won't take much more of your time. Were you at work this morning?"

"Yes," said Norris. "I work in Keizer at the Motel 6, in housekeeping."

"All right. What time did you arrive there this morning?"

"I work the 6 a.m. to 3 p.m. shift," said Norris. "So, I clocked in just before six this morning."

"Do your kids live here with you?"

"Yes," she said. "Steve fixes them breakfast and then they catch the bus to school. He always walks them down to the bus stop."

"Mrs. Norris, are you aware of any trouble that Steve was in, or anything else that might help us find his killer?" asked Eva.

Openly sobbing again, Norris couldn't answer immediately. After a minute or so, she finally said, "No. He was really trying to turn his life around. He had made some mistakes in his past. But, he spent almost all of his time with us. He was depressed about not being able to find any work. He had looked and looked, but could not find anything. His criminal history scared off most employers."

Eva and I then said goodbye to Norris and left her alone to grieve over the loss of her boyfriend. We entered the mobile home again to see if anything new had been found. The Forensics Unit didn't have any additional information.

Eva and I drove off in silence. We headed straight back to downtown Salem. There was nothing easy about what we had just witnessed. At the moment, neither of us felt like putting on our "cop" faces and heading directly back to the Department. So, we decided to have lunch at one of my favorite Salem hangouts.

We headed over to the Oyster Bar Restaurant on State Street. I liked the clam chowder at the Oyster Bar, as well as the privacy of its secluded seating. We ate in silence for a while, still feeling the effects of the gruesome scene and emotional pain of what we had just witnessed. Gradually, however, the two of us began talking. We agreed that it was too early to rule out anything. While there appeared to be no connection between the killing of Scott Hornbecker and Melissa Walker, we knew that it was unusual to have two homicides in the same week here in Salem. After our shop talk, Eva changed the subject and asked, "So how much longer you gonna do this, Jack?"

"You mean homicide—before I retire?"

"Yeah," said Eva. "Are you gonna put in 30 years?"

"If I could retire now, I'd do it in a heartbeat. And maybe I should. I've seen too many cops hang on too long and end up even more burned out than I am."

Eva looked at me with a slight grin and said, "Now that's hard to believe."

Nodding my head a bit and chuckling, I continued, "The truth is, I like what I do. You know that. Sure I'm tired, but I'm a cop and it's hard to imagine doing anything else. So, it's just a matter of, you know, when do I have enough money to stop. Once I do, I'll never look back. That'll be it—I'll flip a switch. I'm not one of those types who will hang on here in town and shift into PI work. I'd rather move to Costa Rica, and live out the rest of my life fishing and drinking cervezas."

Smiling and shaking her head, Eva said, "You never cease to amaze me, Jack. Not that any of that is a real surprise—except maybe for the Costa Rica part."

"Well, that might never happen. I'm not exactly eager to sell my house. I could see just wintering somewhere south of the border."

Before Eva could respond, my cell phone rang. I answered, "Hello."

"Hi, Jack, it's James Heathrow. Guess you've got another murder to investigate."

"Looks that way," I said. "It was a single gunshot wound to the head. The victim was hit inside his mobile home. The bullet was fired from outside through a window."

"Could it have been accidental?"

"Doubtful," I said. "Doc will have to verify, but it looks as though the bullet was fired from close range. Someone was standing at the window, observed the victim, and shot him."

"Do you see any connection to the Walker murders?"

I paused for a few seconds, then said, "We'll have to wait for the ballistics report. But, it doesn't seem so. Wouldn't be surprised if it's drug related, though. The victim has priors including sale and possession."

"Okay. Well, hey, the reason I called was to let you know that you don't have to worry about IA—not that Johnson and Cutright didn't push for me to place you on administrative leave."

"I wasn't worried," I said.

"Yeah, I know. But, I've been doin' this even longer than you Jack, and I still can't figure out IA. About all you can count on from those assholes is a lot of harassment."

Chuckling, I said, "Yeah, I know. Gunny always said that they all had failed to separate from their mother."

"He was right. Okay, keep pluggin', detective."

"Will do, Cap," I said.

After finishing lunch, Eva and I headed back to the Department. We pored over files, worked the phones, and reviewed the data that we had gathered. I was looking at Michael Jacobsen's financial records. It appeared that Michael had done very well for himself after leaving the Navy. In the last two years he had reported an annual income around of $250,000.

As I delved further into Michael's assets and liabilities,

I could see that he had an extensive array of investments through the Jacobsen family empire. Moreover, much of it was difficult to assess because it was hidden by a complex array of trusts, foreign business ventures, and executorships. What was apparent, however, was that about two years ago Michael began making large monthly deposits into numerous offshore accounts. The amounts varied, but seemed to range between $75,000 and $150,000 a month. It wasn't rocket science to see that those levels of monthly deposits would add up to a lot more than Michael's reported annual income.

However, Eva and I figured that Michael was merely collecting the profits of transporting cocaine into the United States. Since he was working under cover with the CIA, we had no reason to conclude that he'd done anything wrong. For all we knew, Michael's deal with CIA allowed him to dodge taxes and profit from his high risk infiltration of the Los Hermanos Drug Cartel.

I next went over Melissa Walker's autopsy report for the hundredth time. I was interested in the skin, hair, and fiber samples that had been collected. I picked up the telephone and dialed Doc's number.

"State Medical Examiner's Office," answered the receptionist.

"Hi, this is Detective Davis with the Salem PD. I'd like to speak to Doctor Evans please."

"One moment," said the receptionist.

After about a minute, Doc answered. "Hi, Jack. What can I do for ya?"

"Afternoon, Doc. I'm calling about the Walker girl's autopsy report."

With a sigh, Doc said, "Another error?" What is it this time?"

"No, Doc. I'm just callin' to confirm a thing or two."

"Shoot," said Doc.

"Okay, I can see where you gathered some samples under the Walker girl's fingernails. The report says skin and hair samples and clothing fragments."

"Yes, that's right," said Doc. Because of my snafu with the cocaine, I know that report inside and out."

"All right. I have written down here that the fiber samples collected from the janitor's coveralls may or may not match the samples collected from the victim. I think that you said that the comparative analysis was equivocal and that further study was needed. So, I'm wondering, has anything more conclusive been determined?"

"Not yet, and I apologize for the delay. I'm coordinating things with forensics. The samples collected from Walker's fingernails are cotton based and consistent with a dark color, definitely something like black or navy blue. The fabric samples from Martin's coveralls are not inconsistent with that, but they do appear to have more polyester in them than do the samples from Walker. So, we just want to make sure before we rule out a match. As soon as we can make a definitive conclusion, I'll let you know."

"Is there anything else Doc, that you might have found that didn't make it into the four corners of your report?"

"Nope," said Doc. "I mean, hell, there's a ton of esoteric biological findings that are not the least bit relevant to your murder investigation or a State compelled autopsy. But, as far as relevant findings, it's all in there. If anything, I err on the side of including information, rather than excluding it. But, I think that you already know that about me. So, trust me, I've been doing this for over 35 years, and I know what might help you and what won't."

"Right, right, of course, Doc."

"Well," said Doc. "My ass is hangin' out on this one, Jack, and I won't forget that you kept things to yourself."

"Come on, Doc. You're the best in the business and you know it. Have a good evening."

"You too," said Doc.

As I hung up the phone, Phyllis buzzed me. She had an FBI agent waiting to talk with me on line four.

"Davis, Homicide," I answered.

"Detective Davis, this is Special Agent Barnes with the FBI. I believe that your police chief has informed you that we've been tracking the wireless messages of an unknown individual in Salem. The unknown individual has used a cell phone to communicate with a branch of the Los Hermanos Drug Cartel, located in Bogota, Columbia."

"Yes."

"Well, just 20 minutes ago, we intercepted a wireless e-mail transmission from a Salem hotel—the Mill Creek Best Western. It was sent to Bogotá. We presently have the place surrounded and are talking with the hotel manager."

"I'll be there in five minutes," I said.

Motioning to Eva, I grabbed my navy blue sports coat and walked hurriedly out the door with her. It took us less than 10 minutes to head out Mission Street and to arrive at the Hotel. There were no less than 15 patrol cars already there with City, County, and State Police markings. Eva spotted two men in FBI jackets. We approached them, and I asked, "One of you Agent Barnes?"

The more muscular one of the two said, "I'm Agent Barnes."

Extending my right hand, I said, "Detective Davis, and this is my partner, Detective Tolento."

"Right," said Barnes. He then handed me a hardcopy of the e-mail that the FBI had intercepted. Only glancing at the document, I promptly folded it up like a business letter and slid it into my inside coat pocket. Barnes then continued, "This is what we have. The internet transmission that we intercepted came from Room 324. There's a woman registered there under the name of Rhonda Johnson. The hotel manager recalls checking her in late yesterday afternoon. He described her as an attractive brunette, about 5'-6" tall, slim build. The woman paid in cash, and didn't register a vehicle. Your SWAT team is in place."

"Okay. I'll want to talk with you more when this is over."

"I'll be here," said Barnes.

With that, I walked over to the SWAT force leader, Lieutenant Mitch Jolinsky. I liked Jolinsky. He was a "no nonsense" military type who had enough upstairs to always initially try and diffuse a situation, rather than to march in with guns blazing.

Before I could say anything, Jolinsky asked, "You have anything to give me, Jack."

"Yeah, if it's who I think it is, I nearly tagged her up at PDX. We think that she's a professional assassin with a Columbian drug cartel. So, expect her to be armed and dangerous."

"All right," said Jolinsky. "Stick around." He then began telephoning Room 324. He let the phone ring 30 times or so, but no one answered. After waiting for five minutes, he tried again without success.

Meanwhile, all remaining hotel patrons were evacuated. Jolinsky then tried the loudspeaker, stating: "Rhonda Johnson, occupant of Room 324, this is the police. We have the hotel surrounded. Immediately exit your room and give yourself up."

Jolinsky then turned to his SWAT team and said, "Okay, Lucas, Zelks—can you detect anything in there?" The two SWAT team members each aimed hi-tech rifles towards the exterior window of Room 324. The rifles were something that I'd heard about, but had never seen used before in the field. They detected heat and displayed the form of any living target. After scanning Room 324 for about three minutes, the two officers shook their heads and indicated that no one was in the room.

With that, Jolinsky gave the order for the SWAT team to storm Room 324. Two team members then shot gas canisters through the room's window. Two more members wearing gas masks then entered the room's front door. The room was empty.

The news media then began arriving. I spotted Sophie approaching with her briefcase in hand. In less than two minutes, Jolinsky was being peppered with questions from the pack of television and newspaper reporters. Meanwhile, Eva and I began combing the immediate area along with several police officers.

"Damn it!" I muttered. "How does this broad do it? Every car in the parking lot needs to be checked. If nothing turns up, we're going to have to contact the taxi companies. She had to get here somehow. It'll be just our luck if she hitchhiked. Let's go talk to the hotel manager and see if we can't get a decent description. Maybe we can flood the local TV stations with a composite sketch of our Jane Doe."

"Jack, what if she's still in the building?"

"Yeah, she could be. Maybe we're making this too difficult? She might be up there right now busting a gut, while watching us run around down here like chickens with our heads cut off."

Jolinsky was already on top of it, however. He had sent 10 patrol officers inside the hotel to conduct a door-to-door search. In addition, he'd sealed off the whole area. It was now getting dark outside and the temperature was dropping by the minute. Two large floodlights had been trucked in and were now aimed up at the hotel's two wings.

Turning up the collar on my P-coat, I began looking for Sophie. I wanted to say "hi" to her before I headed into the hotel to interview the manager. But, I couldn't find her. I figured that she was probably mixed in with the pack of news reporters. Before I could navigate my way through the throng of reporters, however, one of them recognized me. Within seconds, I was surrounded.

"Bad idea," I said to the pack of reports, as I strained to catch a glimpse of Sophie. I still didn't see her. Consequently, I turned away and gave the reporters a dismissive wave of my hand.

By eight-thirty the search effort was halted. The police had found no sign of the suspect, no suspicious vehicle, and no tangible evidence. The Forensics Unit had scoured Room 324, however, and had collected several samples. But, it all looked routine.

After dropping Eva off at the Department's parking garage, I telephoned Sophie. It was now just past nine. She didn't answer. So, I left the following voice message: "Hi Sophie. It's Jack. Sorry I missed you out there at the hotel. Nothin' turned up. Well, I'm headed home. Hey, give me a call."

I then drove out of the garage onto Liberty Street to head down to Bentley's. Once there, I entered the lounge and found a seat near the far end of the bar. I slipped on my reading glasses and ordered a draft beer.

After a couple of minutes, I reached into the inside pocket of my sports coat and unfolded hardcopy of the e-mail that the FBI had intercepted. It read as follows:

Janet Taylor

From:	*<jataylor@dtp.com>*
To:	*<raulespinoza@bog.com>*
Sent:	*Wednesday, October 18th 2:12 PM*
Subject:	*Re: Cactus Still Wet*

Raul,

Both cactuses are still wet, as I've been unable to reach either of them. Also, the temperature is way too hot here and may not cool down in time for the next package. See you soon.

Janet

I found the e-mail a bit amusing. The cloak-and-dagger aspects aside, it seemed to corroborate what Eva and I already knew—that the Los Hermanos Drug Cartel was a common denominator in the mix of recent murders, attempted assassinations, and espionage. While staring at the e-mail, I was interrupted by the bartender.

"Another drink, Jack?" he asked.

"Yeah, a gin and tonic."

"House or something else?" he asked.

"House is fine."

"Comin' up," said the bartender.

I folded up the piece of paper and stuffed it back into my coat pocket. I took the last swallow of my beer and began to mull things over. "She's on the run," I thought. "But, she'll have to spend the night somewhere. It's October, and it's cold. She'll probably avoid hotels and will end up breaking into someone's home."

While the bartender placed my gin and tonic in front

of me with a new coaster, I pulled out my cell phone. I then punched in the number for Chuck Gonard—Salem PD's finest sketch artist. Gonard had a knack for accurately sketching a suspect's portrait. Basically, he had the ability to "picture" a suspect in his head from an eye witness description, or even from mere characteristics of the suspect's behavior. I knew that it was imperative to begin displaying a sketch of the unknown woman to the public.

While still at Bentley's, I stared down at my drink. I thought about my life, about driving home in the rain to my empty house, and about Melissa Walker. I felt for her—for her soul. She hadn't been given a fair shake in life. But, I intended to do what I could to bring her killer to justice.

In truth, I often reflected on death and dying—especially after a drink or two. I'd always figured that my philosophical leanings were the result of my upbringing, as well as my line of work. I mean, it wasn't every working stiff who dealt with death twenty-four seven.

I had been raised as a good Free Methodist kid. Free Methodists were an offshoot of mainstream Methodists. They started their own church back in the mid-1800's. Back then, the Methodist Church charged a "pew rental" fee and supported slavery. So the wealthy parishioners with enough money to pay the rental fee, sat in the choice front row pews. But, the less wealthy parishioners, many of whom were Black slaves, were relegated to the back row pews. As a result, a growing number of congregants became dissatisfied with the Methodist Church, and eventually formed their own church—calling themselves *Free* Methodists.

Still seated at the bar, my thoughts turned to my own

life—a divorced 48 year old who was a veteran homicide detective and far from "lily white." However, I did know right from wrong and I could be counted on to take on the Establishment. Unfortunately, my maverick tendencies didn't always help my career or go over so well with most of the Department managers.

14

A Meth Lab

THE NEXT MORNING, I received a call from Doc.

"Good morning, Jack. I'm callin' about the Walker investigation."

"Sure," I said. Whadaya got?"

"The skin fragments under the victim's nails do not match the janitor's skin. The victim had skin under her nails from two individuals. One of the individuals is Michael Jacobsen. His sample matches. So, she has skin fragments from another unidentified individual. Also, the clothing fibers did not come from Martin's coveralls—they do not match."

"Okay," I said. "Does the semen match the sample that we collected from Walker's bedroom?" I asked.

"Yes it does—it matches Michael's DNA."

"All right," I said. "So, what you're telling me is that Michael Jacobsen's skin and semen were on Melisa Walker's body, but there's no forensic evidence linking Joe Martin."

"That's right. Based on the autopsy findings and the forensic evidence, the janitor is not implicated."

"Okay, thanks, Doc," I said.

"You bet. Goodbye."

I hung up the phone and let out an audible sigh. Eva noticed my reaction and said, "That bad?"

"Oh, not really," I said. "That was, Doc. He said that Joe Martin's clothing fibers do not match those that he extracted from Melissa Walker. But, Michael Jacobsen's DNA matches the skin and semen samples taken from her body and at her apartment. No surprise there I guess—since Michael admitted to getting into a brawl with Walker out on the observation deck. The twist is that there's another skin sample that was collected from Walker that came from another individual."

"So, what are we gonna do with Martin?"

"Nothing for the time being," I said. "We're gonna have to focus on other possible suspects. Time will tell about Martin."

"C'mon, Jack! What about Michael? I mean, here's a guy in bed with the victim a few hours before her death. He was also with her at the time of her death and the forensic evidence proves that. Plus, according to Palmer, he was dating the victim. Didn't he say that they'd both gotten stoned? Maybe he got pissed off and threw her through the open window? You could even argue that he did so with the belief that he was immune from prosecution!"

"I hear your pain, Eva," I said. "But, there's apparently another individual that had physical contact with the victim shortly before she died. I'm also not seeing that Michael had a motive to murder Melissa Walker—at least, not yet. Personally, I don't trust Michael and I believe that the whole Federal espionage scenario is dubious. But, who is the other individual that we haven't identified?"

Eva and I spent the rest of the morning going over the Hornbecker murder investigation. It seemed totally unrelated to the Walker investigation. While tracking down all of Hornbecker's friends, acquaintances, and enemies, I came across the name of Ron Tichner. Tichner was familiar with law enforcement—from the wrong end. He was a 33-year-old thug, who was presently an unemployed former car wash attendant. As a teenager, Tichner had experienced several run-ins with Salem PD. Back then, he was a member of the 17th Street Gang. While still a minor, he was convicted for the sale and possession of methamphetamines, assault, and car theft. Then, as an adult, things only got worse for him. He'd already served six years in the Oregon State Penitentiary for attempted murder, after nearly beating to death another local methamphetamine seller.

After a call to Tichner's parole officer, I learned that he resided on Cordon Road in southeast Salem—about two miles from the location of the trailer park where Hornbecker had been killed. Thus, Eva and I decided to pay Tichner an unexpected visit.

Heading east on State Street, Eva and I kept unusually quiet. We were both feeling frustrated and glum about the rash of recent murders and our apparent lack of progress towards solving any of them. I came to the T-intersection at State Street and Cordon Road. I turned right. After proceeding about a quarter of a mile, I came across a dilapidated old house on the left side of the street. There was smoke coming out of the chimney and an old beat up Ford pickup truck parked in front of the separate one-car garage. I pulled into the driveway—directly behind the pickup.

Cautiously, I approached the front door to the house while Eva provided cover. I knocked on the door, but no one answered. After waiting half a minute I more forcefully knocked on the door five times. Again, however, there was no response. I then motioned to Eva to go around to the back of house and cover the back door. I then pounded on the door a few more times to no avail.

"Shit!" I muttered, as I was pretty certain that Tichner was in the house, but I didn't have a search warrant.

Out of options, and unable to enter the house, I carefully returned to my car never turning my back towards the house. I then grabbed my cell phone and telephoned Phyllis. I needed a search warrant—and in a hurry. So, I dictated the essentials of a probable cause affidavit to Phyllis and told her to type it up and take it to Cap.

Unfortunately, Cap wasn't in. So, Phyllis dutifully modified the affidavit and printed out a boilerplate search warrant and took the documents to Deford, who immediately signed the affidavit. Deford then hopped in a patrol car and drove the short distance down to the Marion County Courthouse. Meanwhile, Phyllis had telephoned Judge Aldus Lever's assistant and explained the situation to her.

Judge Aldus Lever was a well-respected trial judge. He was also near retirement, having served on the bench for more than 30 years. While highly intelligent, he was also one of the most unpretentious individuals that I had ever met. In fact, I'd enjoyed a few Cuban cigars with him over the years while playing a round or two of poker. Any lawyer in town felt like they'd received a "good draw" when Judge Lever was assigned to their case.

As it turned out, Deford managed to catch Judge Lever just before he left the courthouse for lunch. Judge Lever took a couple minutes to look over the affidavit and then looked up at Deford and said, "Don't bullshit me Curt. Is this solid?" Deford then nodded his head and Judge Lever signed the warrant.

Deford then raced the warrant out to Tichner's house. When he finally arrived, I was hunkered down behind my patrol car and Eva was still covering the backside of Tichner's house.

Handing me the warrant, Deford said, "Here it is. You owe Judge Lever and me, Davis."

"I know. Look, I think the scum bag is inside. Tolento's got the back door covered. I'm goin' in. Can you cover me?"

Deford didn't even have to answer, he just gave me one of those "of course" looks on his face.

By then, I had put a bullet proof vest on. I again cautiously approached Tichner's house. I walked up onto the front porch and stood with my back against the house's siding, between the front window and door. With the search warrant in hand, I was done playing games with Tichner. I drew my Smith and Wesson, turned towards the house and planted my right foot as hard as I could into the front door. It took two kicks and then the rusted out door hinges splintered away from the frame, with the door falling inwards. I raised my Smith & Wesson revolver directly in front of me—holding it with both of my hands and my arms outstretched. Within seconds I heard footsteps running towards the back of the house followed by Eva yelling, "Freeze—police!"

I then bolted back outside the house, hopped over the porch rail, and ran around to the back of the house. As I turned the corner to my right, I found Eva standing over Tichner, who was lying face down on the ground. Eva was already handcuffing him.

After Deford departed with Tichner in the backseat, Eva and I searched the house. What we found was a methamphetamine storehouse. In addition to all the drugs, we found a payload of weapons—automatic rifles, sawed off shot guns, pistols, revolvers, and hunting knives. The lab was down in the basement and was strewn with beer cans, Playboy magazines, and dirty clothes. There were also three laptop computers up and running in one corner of the basement, which were situated on a 3 x 8 foot piece of plywood supported by two small file cabinets on each end. Fluorescent lights hung from the ceiling. The flat screen computer monitors emitted an eerie blue glow. The neatly arranged computer equipment seemed out of place in the otherwise garbage strewn basement.

Eva sat down in front of one of the computers and began perusing the various document files. She discovered a list of names in two documents titled "CIO" and "DCIO." In the document titled "DCIO," Steve Hornbecker's name appeared with the number "6" next to it. None of the names on the "CIO" list were followed by numbers. But, all of the names on the "DCIO" list had numbers next to them. Most of the numbers had a "1" or a "2" after them. Hornbecker's name was only one of three names with a "6" next to it. We theorized that the names were Tichner's drug "customers" and that the numbers next to some of the names concerned "delinquent" payments.

Eva and I spent the rest of the day tracking down known Meth-heads in Salem. Afterwards, we felt like we'd developed a pretty clear picture. Hornbecker had started "using" again. Like every Meth-head, he'd eventually gotten into trouble. Despite his desire to turn his life around, he couldn't kick the habit. As a result, he'd used what little money he had to keep his habit alive. After exhausting his own money, he turned to borrowing and eventually to stealing. A number of people that Eva and I spoke to had indicated that Hornbecker owed large sums of money to drug sellers—like Tichner.

With the new information that we'd uncovered, Eva and I drove out to the trailer park to talk with Norris. Yellow crime scene tape was wadded up and lying on the ground by the picnic table. I knocked on the door. Norris appeared along with one of her children—a little girl about two years old, who had tangled hair and food stains all over her face and shirt. I had to fight the urge to scoop the kid up, take her home, and return her all cleaned up in new pajamas and with a teddy bear in her arms. But, I wasn't a social worker—I was a homicide cop.

"Hi, Mrs. Norris," I said. "Sorry to bother you at the dinner hour. Could we come in? We just have a few questions for you."

"Yeah, come on in. I'm sorry about the mess. Good Lord! I wanna keep it together, but, how am I gonna make it without Steve?"

"We're very sorry, Mrs. Norris," said Eva. "We know that this is a very difficult time for you. If there's anything we can do either personally or professionally just let us know. I mean that."

"Call me, Ester. And thanks. I appreciate that."

I nodded at Eva to continue her questioning. Norris was grief stricken, but was also eager to talk. There's nothing harder in life than dealing with the loss of a loved one—as I knew. "Okay, Ester," said Eva. "This might be a little rough, but I need to ask you a few questions. Was Steve using drugs again?"

"I think so. He'd begun disappearing for long periods of time and his behavior was becoming erratic. I've been around users before—I've even done drugs myself. So I know the signs. But, I think that I was in denial with

Steve. How could I have been so stupid?"

"It's all right, Ester," said Eva. "You're not the first person to love someone and to wear rose colored glasses. Okay, uh, I know that Steve was unemployed. Was he hitting you up for money?"

"Yes, yes . . . and worse. At first he began asking me for a five or a ten on the pretense of needing to buy some milk or bread. But, he never came back with any groceries. In the last few months, he'd begun stealing my money. I confronted him and he . . . he got angry. So, I stopped carrying much cash in my purse. I just used my ATM card."

Eva continued, "Okay, Ester. You've been very helpful. That's all I wanted to know. We're going to leave now. Hey, is there anything that Detective Davis and I can do for you and your kids right now? Really, I mean it. You name it . . . food, clothes, or whatever."

"No. We'll be fine. I just got paid and I've got food in the house. We'll get through this."

Putting her arm around Norris and hugging her, Eva said, "All right, take care."

It was past 6 p.m. now, but instead of heading back to the Department, Eva and I drove over to the Marion County Jail. We needed to interrogate Tichner. After gaining entrance to the facility, we entered the interrogation room. Tichner had already been pulled out of his cell and was waiting for us. He looked agitated.

The truth was, Tichner was a lost cause—a career criminal. In his case, "rehabilitation" was a euphemism. He'd been physically abused as a kid, he'd gotten into drugs at an early age, and he'd failed to finish high school. His mindset was far removed from that of most ordinary citizens.

I began the interrogation by saying, "Looks like you landed yourself in a bit of trouble, Ron." But Tichner didn't respond. He just sat there behind the rectangular shaped table and stared straight ahead. I then said, "Well, you can do this the stupid way or the smart way. You're in a shit load of trouble. If you want to piss us off, the prosecutor will have no interest in a plea. But, if you're smart, Ron, you'll cooperate. And by doing so, you might just keep your ass out of prison for the rest of your life."

Tichner, looked like a time bomb that was ready to explode. He wasn't the sharpest tool in the shed and he was clearly angry—real angry. He lived by the creed of physical intimidation, a skill that he had perfected during his many years in prison. He was an imposing figure, at 6'-2" and 220 pounds. He had the whole tattoo thing goin' on too—down both of his arms and on each set of his knuckles.

"Why don't you and your prissy little fuck here get lost." said Tichner. "Or, why don't you just leave us alone, Davis, and I'll have my way with her." Turning his taunting gaze towards Eva, Tichner continued, "I'll bet you taste real good baby."

I knew what was about to happen. The Tichners of the world were a dime a dozen—sociopathic and stupid. Unbeknownst to Tichner, however, Eva was much more than a pretty face. She was also very smart and a second degree black belt in Tae Kwon Do. To that end, she had always done very well in Salem PD's biennial self-defense classes.

But, first and foremost, Eva was a cop. She didn't take kindly to intimidation. She walked straight towards Tichner, who readily accepted the challenge and stood up with his fists clinched. In the bat of an eye, Eva planted her right knee hard into Tichner's groin. Before Tichner could even hunch over, however, Eva followed up with an elbow strike to his throat. In a matter of seconds, Tichner was free falling to the concrete floor with his arms barely deflecting the severe blow to his face. The impact knocked the wind out of him and he reflexively curled up into the fetal position.

I looked at Eva with raised eyebrows. While privately applauding what she'd done, I didn't want to see my partner slapped with a charge of police brutality. Eva just looked at me, however, shook her head, and made an "X" motion with her hands—meaning to stay out of it.

She had backed off now, and we were both content to let Tichner recover without any assistance. Eva had hurt Tichner enough to bruise his trachea, but she'd also refrained from inflicting any more damage. As far as I was concerned, she'd acted in self-defense.

After a minute or so had elapsed, Tichner finally let out a gasp and began coughing and gagging. He then writhed on the floor for several seconds and began to get up. As he was doing so, he said, "Shit, you Goddamn bitch!"

I just shook my head. Eva again walked directly towards Tichner. Apparently too stupid to have learned his lesson, Tichner let out a guttural sound and lunged at Eva. However, Eva spun around and planted a hard foot strike into Tichner's upper chest area. Once again, Tichner fell hard to the floor—this time hitting the back of his head. Standing directly over him, Eva looked down and said, "You moron. You make one more derogatory remark and I'll kill you. Do you understand? Or, are you too stupid to understand that Detective Davis and I are your only hope to avoid spending the rest of your life in prison?"

Tichner slowly sat halfway up and crawled backwards towards the corner. Eva and I waited. After nearly a half hour, he finally started talking and asked, "What do you wanna know?"

Given the dynamics of what had happened, I looked at Eva and gave her the nod to interrogate Tichner. It was a simple measure of my respect for her. She'd been the object of the dirt bag's intimidation, but she'd met the challenge. She now had psychological control over him.

"Did you kill Steve Hornbecker?" asked Eva.

Still sitting on the floor with his knees drawn and his head down, Tichner said, "If I admit to the crime, what's in it for me?"

"Probably your life, instead of the gas chamber or maybe a shot at parole," said Eva.

Hesitatingly, Tichner said, "Yes."

"All right, do you mean that you murdered Steve Hornbecker?" asked Eva.

"Yes. I killed him," said Tichner.

"Okay, Ron. Okay," said Eva. "That's probably the smartest thing that you've done in your entire life . . . to admit the truth. Now, we've read you your rights and you've declined to have an attorney present. Are you still waiving your right to counsel?"

"Yes," said Tichner.

Continuing with her questioning, Eva asked, "And even understanding those rights, you've confessed to murdering Steve Hornbecker, correct?"

"Yes, that's right," said Tichner. "I killed Hornbecker. He owed me a lot of money. He'd been warned. He was in for over $50,000 and my reputation was on the line. People were already talking and were suggesting that I'd gone soft. I couldn't let that happen."

"Okay, Ron," said Eva. "A businessman lives by his reputation."

"Damn right!" agreed Tichner.

"I have a written confession for you to sign. While I can't make any promises about what you'll be charged with or what sentence you'll receive, I can promise you that I'll tell the D.A. that you ultimately cooperated with us."

"Yeah," said Tichner.

"And it might go even better for you, Ron, if you tell us the name of your accomplices. You know . . . the distributors above you and the sellers below you?"

"Holy shit, in prison a snitch is considered about as low as a child molester. I'm not going to rat out anyone unless the D.A. will promise me in writing that he'll accept a plea of something less than murder one."

"Okay, Ron," said Eva. "Detective Davis and I will be talking with the D.A. As I said, we'll tell him that you eventually cooperated with our interrogation. Here's the confession. Read it over. You don't have to sign it without the presence of a lawyer. In fact, I'd recommend that you do not sign it without a lawyer—do you understand?"

"Yes, and I'll sign it."

After Tichner scribbled his signature on the typewritten confession, Eva and I walked out of the interrogation room.

I drove Eva back to the Salem PD parking garage. Before leaving, I watched her safely get into her car and depart. I then headed south, turning left onto Commercial Street. I drove out past Kuebler Boulevard to the Stonefront Tavern. The Stonefront was an anomaly. No windows— just a stone building right off of the main south arterial heading in and out of Salem. But, the place had ice cold beer and great food. I seated myself in a booth and began to mull over the Melissa Walker investigation. Here I was, a supposedly first class sleuth, and, yet, I had virtually no clue about who had murdered Melissa Walker. Virtually, every initial suspect seemed to have an alibi.

15

Sophie—A Black Widow?

THE NEXT MORNING it was raining. I drove out my driveway with my windshield wipers swishing back-and-forth. It was not yet daylight. I was headed out early, before 6 a.m., to meet Sophie over in Bend—a resort town in Central Oregon. Sophie was attending a conference and was staying at a condominium located on a bluff overlooking the Deschutes River. I liked Bend. Although I had not been there for a couple of years, it was one of Vicki's favorite places. As I headed out Highway 22 towards Santiam Pass, I turned up the volume on my CD player. The trip went fast, as the highway was still bare and dry.

After arriving in Bend, I drove straight to the Westgate Café. I had agreed to meet Sophie there at nine. When she arrived, I knew that I was hooked. I had been thinking about her. But, it was difficult for me to acknowledge my feelings.

I hadn't always been that way, but Vicki's death had changed me. When she died, something inside of me died along with her. I was certain that I'd never love again—

at least not in the same way. I also knew that by staying emotionally closed, I could avoid the pain of losing anyone again.

After Sophie arrived, we ate breakfast and then spent the day together in Bend. The downtown streets were already covered with snow. We spent most of the morning laughing and strolling down the sidewalks hand-in-hand while visiting the various stores. After returning to Sophie's condominium, we opened a bottle of champagne and made love in the living room. We then fell asleep together underneath a down comforter and next to the flickering gas fireplace—our arms and legs all entangled and stuck together.

On my way back to Salem, I picked up a phone call from Eva. She said that Joe Martin had passed a polygraph test. While such evidence had limited probative value in court, I knew that it corroborated what we already believed—that Martin was not the killer. The truth was, from a personal standpoint, I was happy that Martin was no longer a suspect. I liked the guy. From my standpoint, he and his family had been shafted by the INS.

After arriving back in Salem, I spent the rest of the day at my desk. So did Eva. We were both poring over information and telephoning individuals who might have witnessed anything unusual on the morning that Melissa Walker was killed. At the end of the day, however, we hadn't uncovered anything new. It had now become dark outside and the office was quiet. Eva and I were both frustrated with the lack of progress in our investigation.

Eva looked up, yawned, and said, "Okay, my eyes are shot. Another action-packed day for Gotham City's super heroes."

"Yeah, riveting," I chimed in. "You wanna head up to

the Roadhouse for a drink?"

"Wish I could," said Eva. "That actually sounds pretty good, but I agreed to meet a realtor after work. I'm thinking about moving—you know, finding something a little nicer."

"Oh," I said. "Well, good luck. I'll see you tomorrow."

"Hey, that reminds me. I keep forgetting to ask you this: Did Sophie ever work as a realtor?"

"Don't think so," I said. "Why?"

"Well, I came across a document last week concerning Senator Jacobsen's purchase of his house. It was back in the early 90's I think. Anyway, it listed a 'Sophie Lawrence' as the realtor."

"Huh," I said. "Probably the same name, but a different person."

"Yeah, that's what I thought too. Okay, detective, I'm outta here."

"I'll be right behind ya," I said. "Goodnight, Eva."

"Goodnight."

As Eva walked out the door, I slipped on my P-coat—the same one that I'd worn the day before in Bend, while holding Sophie's hand and strolling along the downtown sidewalks. After fastening the buttons to my coat, I opened my desk drawer and pulled out the phone book. I flipped through the pages to the name, "Lawrence." There was Sophie's name and home number, along with her business number over at the Statesman. In addition, there was a listing for a "Sophia" Lawrence, as well as two other listings for an "S" Lawrence. I ran the three listings through Salem PD's computer identification system. The two "S" names were for "Sharon" and "Shelly."

I then walked over to the four-drawer file cabinet that contained the files on Senator Jacobsen. I sat back down, loosened the top buttons on my P-coat and began going through the files. In about 10 minutes, I uncovered a document entitled House Sale Contract. On page 4 of the document I saw the name "Sophie Lawrence," listing her as the agent. The document indicated that the agent worked for Century 21 Realty Company, and that the house had been purchased by Senator Jacobsen for $491,000 in April, 1991. The agent's signature looked like Sophie's.

Without hesitation, I picked up the phone and dialed Sophie's home number. No answer. I then tried her work number and got through to her.

"Hi, Jack!" said Sophie.

"Hi, gorgeous . . . whadaya wearin'?"

"Wouldn't you like to know," shot back Sophie. "Not much really."

"I'm already panting."

"Hmmm," said Sophie. "Don't tempt me, sweetie. I've got to head over to the Capitol to interview a legislator for tomorrow's edition. But, I'd love to see you afterwards. My place okay?"

"Why don't you call me when you're done."

"Okay," she said. "Talk to you then."

"Uh, Sophie, one more thing."

"Uh-huh," said Sophie.

"Did you work as a realtor back in the early 1990's?"

"Yeah. Why, sweetie?" she said.

"Well, did you happen to help Senator Jacobsen buy his home up on Fairmont Hill back in 1991?"

"Uh, I don't think so," said Sophie. The lightness in both of our voices had now disappeared. Sophie continued, "I did sell a couple of houses up there back then, but I don't recall meeting the Senator. Well, I guess he wasn't a senator back then. But, why are you asking me all of this,

Jack?"

Evading her question, I recited the address of the Senator's home on Lincoln Street and asked, "Ring a bell?"

"Actually, it does," said Sophie. "There's a large house up there on Lincoln Street that I listed. The owners were moving. I think the husband was a professor at Willamette's Business School, and he had accepted a teaching job back East."

"Okay, well, Sophie, the buyer of that house was Senator Jacobsen."

Sounding truly astonished, Sophie said, "Wow, I sure didn't know. But, I was new to Salem back then and the 'Jacobsen' family name wouldn't have meant anything to me back then."

"Okay, Sophie. It was just something routine that came up in our investigation. Give me a call when you finish over at the Capitol."

"Jack," said Sophie. "I think that I need some clarity. Listen, you're not thinking that I'm in any way involved in the death of Melissa Walker are you?"

"It's just something that my partner discovered and innocently brought to my attention. That's all."

"Uh, okay," said Sophie. "I trust you, Jack. I'm looking forward to seeing you tonight."

I turned off my desk light and headed down to the parking garage. It was still raining—a pretty customary sight here in the fall. In fact, nearly every year around Thanksgiving the two-lane road near my house becomes flooded. I really don't care for the Pacific Northwest's constant gray drizzle. I like to see that yellow radiant ball up in the blue sky. By February, I'm usually "done" with overcast skies and begin to fantasize about retiring early and moving to somewhere like Costa Rica or Cozumel.

Driving home, I instinctively headed towards Gunny's house. Before I got there, however, I pulled out a piece of scrap paper that I'd used to write down the address of Senator's Jacobsen's house. After looking at it, I turned the corner. There it was—a near mansion with a long brick walkway and a white pillared porch. It was a stone's throw from both Gunny's house, as well as the Governor's mansion.

I pulled my car over to the curb and sat there for a bit with the quiet hum of the Talon's idling engine and the steady pelt of raindrops. My mind flashed to the nice time that I'd just had earlier in the day with Sophie. I could close my eyes and see her beautiful face and skin, and hear her easy laughter. But, I now felt a growing uneasiness, which was barely perceptible. Slowly, I pulled out from the curb and drove around the block to Gunny's house. He answered the door.

"Hi, Jack. Hey, I was just thinking' about ya. Come in. Hell, this rain is such a drag. June's been telling' me that I've been a royal pain in the ass—and she's probably right."

Laughing, I figured that Gunny was suffering from "cabin fever" and had probably gotten sideways with June. In my opinion, June was a gem. I knew firsthand that not many women put up with a career homicide cop. But, June had managed to do so. Even at 64 years old she was still gorgeous, kind, and smart. In fact, Gunny always professed that she outranked him.

"Hi, Gunny," I said. "Sorry to bother you. Got a minute?"

"Of course—care for a drink?"

"A gin and tonic would be great," I said.

"Sure," said Gunny as he reached into his liquor cabinet to grab a bottle of Beefeater. "So, are you keepin' your head afloat in the Walker investigation?"

"Not sure," I said.

Plunking some ice into a glass, Gunny continued, "The newspaper said that you'd solved the Hornbecker murder—is that right?"

"Yeah, well . . . with Eva's help. As far as homicide investigations go, it's actually pretty airtight. The victim was a meth user. He was trying to clean up his act. He'd met someone nice, but fell into old habits. He got behind in his drug payments, borrowed some money that he couldn't pay off, and pissed off too many of the wrong kind of people. So, a middle distributer shot him."

"That's what I read," said Gunny. "But, that's not why you're here—is it son? What's on your mind?"

Gunny's affectionate reference caught me a little off guard. He used to call me "son" when I first began interning for Salem PD. But, that was a long time ago. As I gained experience with Salem PD, Gunny used the affectionate term less-and-less. But, he never completely dropped it. And that was okay, because he'd earned the right to use it. He also seemed to use the term only at times when he knew that something was bothering me.

"I don't know. The investigation is still in its early stages. You know that. We had some early suspects, which fooled Eva and me into thinking that we were going to quickly find the killer. That hasn't turned out to be the case, however. And the Statesman didn't exactly help with its slanted reporting and editorializing."

"The Statesman's never been much a friend to the Department," agreed Gunny.

"Yeah."

I then looked directly at Gunny before proceeding—and he looked right back me. As our silence grew, both of us knew that there was something more. Not the usual type of thing either, but, something much more. The type of thing that can unravel lifelong friendships.

I finally broke the ice and asked, "Gunny. When did you buy this house?"

Gunny cocked his head and gave me one of those "Say what?" glances. He then said, "Uh, well, it was back in the early 90's. Why?"

"Was a realtor involved with the transaction?" I asked.

"Uh, let me think about that one. We bought the house from a couple that was going through a divorce. Yes, I believe that they did have it listed with an agent."

"Was it Century 21, by any chance?" I asked.

"Yeah . . . I think it was, as a matter of fact. What's up, Jack?"

"Bare with me," I said. "Do you recall anything about the realtor?"

"Yes. It was a woman and she was very attractive—slender, pretty, dark hair."

"Are you sure about the hair?" I asked.

"Are you kiddin'? I'm a cop, Jack. Plus, you don't forget a looker like that."

"Do you happen to have a copy of the sales contract that I could look at—to check the realtor's name?"

"Yeah, sure," said Gunny. "It's in my file cabinet. But . . . tell me what's goin' on?"

"It's probably nothing," Gunny. "I'm dating Sophie Lawrence. Was she the realtor that sold you this house?"

"What? How could that be?" asked Gunny. "The realtor had dark hair and didn't appear to look Scandanavian."

"Well, Sophie's already acknowledged that she used to work in real estate for Century 21 back in the early 90's, and that she sold more than one home up here on Fairmont Hill."

"Really?" asked Gunny.

"Did you know the Senator before you bought this house, Gunny?"

"Yes, in fact, he's the one that told me about it," said Gunny. "He and Susan had just purchased their home down around the corner. I think that he knew that June and I were looking to purchase a new home too. Is that the other house up here that you're talking about—the Senator's place?"

"Yes it is."

Motioning for me to follow him into his study, Gunny said, "C'mon." He then sat down in his leather chair and pulled open a file drawer. He thumbed through it, closed it, and opened another drawer. He thumbed through that one too and then pulled out a file. He opened it, flipped through some documents, and then said, "Here it is." He then flipped to the back page of the stapled documents, while I walked around his desk and looked over his shoulder.

There it was, at the bottom of page 2: the name, "Sophie Lawrence," with "Century 21 Realty" listed underneath her name.

"Wow, you're right, Jack," said Gunny.

I put on my reading glasses and looked at the signature. I then unfolded the copy of the sales document on Senator Jacobsen's house, which I'd retrieved from Salem PD's file. The two signatures looked identical.

"Whadaya got, son?"

"Don't know," I said. "It's probably nothing. Sophie

apparently sold both your house and Senator Jacobsen's house.

"Like I said, the realtor who sold us this house had dark hair. But, her face and build were similar to Lawrence's. God, I never connected the two."

"Okay, Gunny. It's probably just one of those coincidences in life that has no significance."

Obviously not as convinced of the "coincidence" angle that I was desperately promoting, Gunny said, "Right, right—that's true."

"All right, Gunny, you have a good evening. Talk to you later."

"You too, Jack," said Gunny. "Hey, son, just remember to follow your instincts."

"Yeah, thanks Gunny. Sorry to come up here and talk shop. You know that you're more than some retired cop to me, right? You know that, don't you?"

"Yeah, I do. Feeling's mutual, Jack."

"Okay. I just need you to look me in eye Gunny, and tell me that you're clean on this. That this coincidence isn't going to unravel into some sordid tale involving you, the Senator, and Sophie."

"Jack, I'm clean," said Gunny. "All of this is news to me. But, if I was in your shoes, I'd be asking the same thing."

"Okay, that's all I needed to hear."

"Jack," said Gunny. "Ask yourself how you first came into contact with Lawrence. You know, was it something that she could have orchestrated, or did you initiate the contact?"

"Thanks, Gunny. And hey, take it easy on June. They don't come any smarter or prettier. Maybe the two of you should become snowbirds and head somewhere tropical?"

"I hear ya," said Gunny. "Watch your backside now."

I headed back towards home. It was miserable outside and I didn't feel much better on the inside. My heart told me that all I'd uncovered was a "coincidence"—that Sophie had merely sold a house to both the Senator and Gunny. I trusted Gunny and I wanted to trust Sophie too, but I knew better.

While driving home, my cell phone rang. I picked it up and looked at the screen to check the caller ID—it was Sophie. I set the phone down in the passenger's seat and let it continue to ring. After a half a minute or so, the phone let out a chirp—indicating that Sophie had left a voice message. I picked up the phone, scrolled through the prompts, and retrieved the following message from Sophie, "Hi, Jack! And where might you be? I've got homemade lasagna in the oven and a bottle of Merlot next to me. But, I'd rather have you next to me. Give me a call."

Something wasn't right. I didn't know if it was just me—with all of my emotional baggage, or if it was something more. I loved Sophie, or at least I had allowed myself to start going down that road. But, I also didn't know much about her. Good homicide cops had a sixth sense, or a streak of paranoia—depending on how you looked at it. My problem at the moment was that I wasn't sure which characteristic was rearing its head.

On impulse, I hit the brake pedal and made a U-turn on Skyline Drive. I decided to head back to the office. Gunny's question kept running through my head, "How did you first come into contact with Lawrence."

I vaguely recalled meeting Sophie several years ago at a couple of social functions. But, those introductions were brief and unremarkable. We had never had a conversation until <u>she</u> telephoned me immediately following the press conference that Cap had arranged. And what did the press conference concern—her newspaper's reporting of the Walker murder investigation. "What was it that Sophie had said?" I asked myself. Something was there and I knew it, but I couldn't figure it out. It then dawned on me. I remembered her saying something about being on a vacation in the Caribbean when the slanted editorial was published."

Engrossed in my thought processes, I was startled to find myself already pulling into the Department's underground parking garage. Accident reconstruction experts call it "highway hypnosis." My car's headlights panned the concrete retaining wall as I headed down the driveway and into the garage. I took the stairway instead of the elevator, needing all the fresh air that I could get. I headed straight to my desk and flipped on the computer. I then spent the next several hours searching every data base available for anything that I could find on Sophie.

The Statesman Journal's website had a fairly good biographical description of Sophie, along with a portrait like picture of her. Although I knew some of the details already, the bio revealed that Sophie was born in Sweden, that she was fluent in Danish, Spanish, and English, that she obtained a baccalaureate degree in Journalism from Stanford, and an MBA degree from Willamette's Atkinson School of Business. The bio further confirmed that she had worked as a realtor between 1990 and 1993, while she was going to Business School and working as a reporter for the Statesman Journal. It listed her current age as 39, and also revealed that she was single and the mother of one child—a daughter named Sandra.

I had never heard Sophie mention anything about a daughter. That was news to me. I leaned back in my chair. It was late now, after 11 p.m. I had been at my desk for several hours. I pulled out my flask of Jack Daniels and took two large swallows. Sophie was pervading my thoughts. I was desperately clinging to the idea that all of this stuff about her sale of a house to Senator Jacobsen was innocent. After all, nothing that I'd uncovered really gave me any reason to distrust her. It wasn't clear that she'd lied to me. So, almost as if I was on automatic pilot, I picked up the telephone and dialed her home number.

With a somewhat weary sounding voice, Sophie answered, "Hello."

"Hi, Sophie. It's me. Sorry about our evening. I ran into a snag and I had to return to work."

"Oh. Well, I was wondering what had happened," said Sophie. "You missed a really nice dinner. So did I actually . . . I never ate any of it. I kept waiting for you, Jack, figuring that you'd show up. I finally fell asleep here on the sofa."

Sheepishly, I asked, "Too late for me to come over?"

"I guess not. I mean, only if you're still up for it, though," she said.

"I'll be there in 15 minutes."

"All right," she said. "See ya then."

I was torn—on the one hand I was leery of Sophie, and on the other hand I was falling in love with her. In the end, however, I knew that the disquieting feeling that I was having was telling me something. So, I resolved to talk to Sophie—and to listen. After all, why hadn't she told me about her past work as a realtor, about her old acquaintanceship with Senator Jacobsen, and about her daughter?

But, then, I took a hard look at my own life. The truth was, I was often chided by others for being reclusive-like and overly private. More than once, someone had discovered something about my past and had expressed surprise. So, after all, who was I to think that Sophie had done anything other than what I'd always done—which was to keep my own counsel?

When I arrived, Sophie met me at the front door. She was wearing a loosely tied silky black robe. "Hi, sweetie," she said.

"Hi, baby. God, you're a sight for sore eyes." I then kissed her on the lips, loitering with my tongue for a few seconds before withdrawing.

"Take your coat?" she asked in a sleepy voice.

"Sure."

"So," said Sophie. "You had to head back into work, eh?"

"Yeah, it's one of the curses of detective work—you're never free unless you vacation somewhere that is too remote for pagers and cell phones."

"Well, Detective Davis," said Sophie with a mischievous smile on her face. "Maybe we'll just have to arrange for a romantic tropical vacation—just the two of us.

"When do we leave?"

Never to be outdone and not entirely joking, Sophie said, "Tomorrow too soon?"

"Well, that might be pushing it."

"Oh, you <u>really</u> need to get a life, detective," said Sophie. "How about if we settle for a night of tropical savagery then—right here?"

Tilting my head back and draining the last drop of wine in my glass, I smiled and said, "You've got my undivided attention."

Within seconds, Sophie and I were making love. It didn't stop anytime soon either. We were up throughout the night enjoying each other's bodies. I knew that I was falling down the slippery slope of infatuation, and Sophie seemed to be doing the same thing. Usually, the two of us would wake up in the morning, make love, and then talk for a half hour or so while sipping fresh brewed coffee. This time, however, I awoke just after 5:30 a.m. and slipped on my clothes. Somehow, I managed to do so without waking Sophie. Before leaving, however, I took out my ballpoint pen and began scribbling a note to Sophie on a paper towel. I wrote:

"Sophie,
I find myself falling head over heels for you. Thanks for a great night. Sorry, I missed your lasagna. I'll make it for you next time.
Can't wait to see you again. Have a great day.
Love, Jack"

16

The Senator

It was still dark outside. The morning commuters were still tucked away in their beds. Consequently, I was able to cruise along toward downtown with hardly any stops. White's Restaurant was my destination. On my way in the door, I picked up the morning's newspaper. It felt good to clear my thoughts and sip some fresh black coffee. After polishing off my eggs and bacon breakfast I drove on up the street to the Department.

When I got there, I noticed a phone message on my desk. It said to call Tim Lawton over at the Capitol. I also noticed that there was an e-mail in my GroupWise "in box" that had been transmitted overnight. It looked like it concerned some information that I had requested concerning Sophie's daughter, Sandra. There was a part of me that felt disloyal for snooping into Sophie's personal life, especially after the wonderful night that we had just spent together. But, her name had officially surfaced in the Walker murder investigation and I didn't have much choice in the matter. Convenient or not, Sophie had some dubious connections to at least one of the initial murder suspects.

Reluctantly, I sat down at my desk and opened up the e-mail concerning Sophie's daughter. Four possible matches for the name "Sandra Lawrence" had been uploaded. I scanned all of them. Only one fit. It appeared that Sophie's daughter was currently living in Cancun, Mexico. As soon as I read that, I recalled that Sophie had told me that she was vacationing in Cancun when the Statesman Journal's story was published about the Walker girl's murder.

Again, I internally wrestled with the information. "After all, what did it prove?" I unconvincingly told myself. Everything in me wanted to pick up the telephone and talk to Sophie. But, I didn't. Instead, I diverted my attention and returned Lawton's call.

"Chief of Security, Tim Lawton," he answered.

"Hi, Tim. It's Jack Davis with Salem PD returning your call."

"Yes, thanks," said Lawton. "You may have already discovered this, but I wanted to pass it along just in case. I've just reviewed the surveillance tapes. Specifically, tape numbers 4 and 11. They show that on the morning of Melissa Walker's murder, Michael Jacobsen did not enter the 4th floor restroom—the one nearest the observation deck. He did enter his father's office, however. He was in there for about 10 minutes."

"Does Senator Jacobsen's office have a private restroom?" I asked.

"Yes," said Lawton. "It's one of the few that do."

"All right, thanks Tim," I said. "I appreciate the information."

"Sure," said Lawton. "Glad to help."

Eva then walked into the office with a cup of coffee.

I informed her about my conversation with Lawton. Changing subjects, I then asked her, "Tell me straight out Eva—no bull shit. Do you think that I've been played by Sophie?"

Wincing a little and showing some discomfort, Eva said, "God, I don't know, Jack!" She then continued, "I mean, big deal, she worked in real estate when she was younger. She hasn't exactly denied that, right? So, it's not like you caught her lying or anything. But, for her to have a connection to Senator Jacobsen, and to fall into your life just when you start to investigate him for murder . . . I think that raises a suspicion."

"I thought you'd see it that way. I do too."

Trying to soften the impact for me a little, Eva added, "It still could be coincidental, Jack."

"Yes it could, but I think we'd better pay Senator Jacobsen a visit."

"Damn right," said Eva.

"Uh, Eva, there's another thing. Sophie also sold Gunny his house."

Eva looked at me with one of those, "You've got to be kidding looks," and simply said, "No way."

"It's true," I sheepishly said. "I've spoken with him. He's not involved, however. I trust him."

Eva didn't say anything. I'd seen her in dozens of difficult physical and emotional situations and had never seen her cry. But, her eyes were now moistening up—as she had always looked up to Gunny and carried a soft spot for him.

Senator Jacobsen had just been released from the hospital. He was now resting at home and was doing as well as could be expected. After all, he was in his mid-sixties and he'd suffered both a gunshot wound to his chest and a brain concussion. He was lucky that he hadn't died out on the tarmac at PDX.

I rang the doorbell to the Jacobsen home. Mrs. Jacobsen answered.

"Good morning, Mrs. Jacobsen. I'm Detective Davis and this is Detective Tolento. We're with the Salem Police Department. We'd like to ask the Senator a few questions. Would that be possible?"

"Yes. Come on in. Just a minute, let me tell Allen that you're here."

After a few minutes, Mrs. Jacobsen returned and escorted us down a short hallway and into the Senator's study. It was very elegant with cherry bookshelves, a wet bar, and an executive-style desk. The Senator was lying on the sofa covered with a blanket up to his chest. He was propped up slightly at one end, with a couple of pillows underneath his head. He had his reading glasses on and was reading the newspaper.

As Mrs. Jacobsen led Eva and me into the study, she politely announced, "Allen, the two detectives are here."

The Senator promptly folded his newspaper across his chest and said, "Right. Detective Davis, Detective Tolento, it's nice to finally meet both of you. And thanks, by the way, for saving my life up there at the airport. Truly, I appreciate what you both did there, which was nothing short of heroism."

While shaking his hand, I said, "Good morning senator." Eva then extended her hand, smiled, and said, "Hi, senator. We're glad that you're recovering. How are you feeling?"

"I'm doing better, thanks. I apologize for appearing like this. I'm just glad to be out of the damn hospital and back home. So, what can I do for you two hardworking public servants at this early hour?"

Eva took over the questioning. It was something that she and I had discussed in the car on the way over to the Senator's house. Diplomacy wasn't always my strong suit.

"Senator . . . . ."

"Call me Allen," interrupted, the Senator. "Here in my home, and away from the Capitol, my first name works fine."

"Okay, Allen. I'm placing this recorder here. Do you voluntarily agree to give your recorded statement absent legal counsel?"

"Certainly," answered the Senator.

"Okay, well, let me get right to the heart of things. Were you ever romantically involved with Melissa Walker?"

With all of the slickness of a career politician, the Senator calmly answered, "How do you define 'romantically involved'? Sure, I liked the kid. But, I kept it professional and never crossed the line."

"Would you like to explain these then?" asked Eva, as she handed the Senator a large manila envelope containing several compromising pictures of him and Melissa Walker. As the Senator looked over the pictures, she asked, "Now that I've shown you some pictures of you and Melissa Walker embracing and kissing, would you like to change your statement?"

Obviously, we had caught the Senator off guard. We had earlier obtained a search warrant to inspect his home. While he knew that we had searched his home, he clearly didn't know that we had seized any compromising items. But, we had. We retrieved the photographs up in the attic above the master bedroom's walk-in closet.

Looking downcast, the Senator finally answered, "Look, I wanted to keep this private. It is true that I had a brief affair with Melissa. She was a beautiful woman. She cut it off. It only lasted a few months. I have no idea who took these photos. I've never seen them before. Where did you find them?"

"Well, we can't divulge that information. But, let me get this straight, senator. Are you denying that you were being blackmailed?"

"Yes," said the Senator. "I've never seen these photographs until right now."

"Senator, did you murder Melissa Walker or did you conspire to have her killed?"

"Absolutely not!" said the Senator. I was as shocked to find out about her death as you were."

"And when was that?"

"After we arrived in Bogota," said the Senator. "The State Police contacted me and informed me that Melissa was dead and had likely committed suicide or suffered an accidental death."

"So, your story is that you had nothing whatsoever to do with Melissa Walker's murder, is that right?"

"It's not a story," shot back the Senator. "It's the truth. All you'll accomplish by publicizing my indiscretion with Melissa is a lot of unnecessary pain."

"All right, senator. Let's move on. Are you acquainted with Sophie Lawrence?"

"Of course!" answered the Senator. "What kind of inane question is that? What half-wit in this town wouldn't know who Sophie Lawrence is?"

"Yeah, but do you know Ms. Lawrence personally— beyond just knowing her professionally?"

"God! You cops—always beatin' around the bush. Maybe I should have my lawyer present after all? Yes, I know Sophie, and she knows me. We've met dozens of times over the years at various social functions. She's also interviewed me several times. I first came across her over at the Business School years and years ago. Back then, she was a real estate agent and she sold me this house."

The Senator had become agitated—just as we had anticipated. Undaunted, Eva kept up the full-court press, "Yeah, we discovered that, Allen. Ms. Lawrence worked for Century Twenty One and she had the listing for this house, which you purchased back in the early 1990's?"

"And your point is, detective?" shot back the Senator.

"And you initially met her at the business school over here at Willamette?"

"Yes, I just said that!" said the Senator.

"Could you tell us about that?"

Defiantly, the Senator answered, "What's there to tell? I was a frequent guest lecturer at the Atkinson School of Business. I have an MBA and a law degree. I own my own law practice. I periodically lecture there. I met Sophie there in the early '90s. She was bright and damn attractive."

"Okay. How was it that she ended up selling you this house?"

Shaking his head, the Senator said, "Look, I came across this house. My wife and I wanted to move up here—to Fairmont Hill. I don't recall if I had already met Sophie and she told me about the house, or if I just coincidentally found it."

I could see that Eva was now the one who was becoming agitated. The Senator was smoothly placing a spin on everything, but was clearly being evasive about his relationship with Sophie.

Eva continued, "All right, Allen. May I be direct with you?"

"Please do."

"Good, then you can cut the crap, buddy," sharply said Eva. "Perhaps we should invite your wife in here—would you like that? Or, should we just haul your miserable ass downtown right now so that you can more formally explain your relationship with Ms. Lawrence?"

The Senator was accustomed to privilege and respect. What he wasn't used to, was what was happening right now—a dressing down from a cop who he undoubtedly felt had half the brains that he possessed. The Jacobsen family, extending back several generations, had helped build Salem into the City that it is today. Moreover, the family was still prominent and influential. The three Jacobsen brothers tirelessly and generously contributed their time and money to the community. Between the three of them, they served on many important and notable commissions, boards, and philanthropic organizations that existed in the Salem area.

Nonetheless, Eva was undeterred. She and I could both tell that the Senator was stonewalling—always a favorite tactic of any seasoned politician. The only problem was that the Senator was too proud to capitulate. Instead, he angrily responded, "You're a fool, detective. I could have you and your better known accomplice here immediately thrown out of my house by merely making a phone call to the Governor. More importantly, I could also see to it that both of your careers are ruined! So . . ."

I'd had enough. I couldn't continue to stay silent while this slick politician without a moral compass insulted and threatened both me and my partner.

"Listen, jerk off," I said. "I think we both know that you already tried that underhanded tactic with the Statesman Journal, and it backfired. So, this is the deal, big shot. I couldn't care less about your reputation. You have exactly five seconds to start talkin' before I arrest you for Conspiracy to Commit Murder and haul you outta here in handcuffs. Got it? The clock's tickin', my friend!"

Eva looked over at me. My interjection was not scripted, but it plainly had succeeded in keeping the heat on the Senator, who was by now fuming.

"Look, Allen," said Eva. "He's right. Cooperate right now—or we'll have to take you downtown in your pajamas and handcuffs. If that happens, I guess your wife can just find out the hard way about you and your indiscretions."

There was a point in every interrogation when a subject blinked—and the Senator had just blinked. Although we didn't have anything more than some weak circumstantial evidence on him, we were at least as good at bluffing as he was.

Trying to save face, the Senator finally answered, "The two of you are real prizes. You know that? Like Batman and Robin. What a joke! Look, I've known Sophie for a longtime. I actually met her down in Palo Alto, while she was attending Stanford. We became friends. I sort of became her mentor. I encouraged her to follow her dreams of higher education and a career in journalism. That's partly why she moved up here to Salem. I had connections with the Statesman Journal and I helped her get a job there. She also was accepted into the Business School here at Willamette. And, yes, she sold me this house. Eventually, we got involved—had an affair."

Eva realized the impact of the Senator's words—and not just as they related to the Walker murder investigation. That is, she knew what effect the Senator's admission would have on me—a man who had recently fallen in love with Sophie. For my part, I didn't flinch. A part of me had seen it coming, although I had privately hoped that my suspicions about Sophie would be disproved. That didn't turn out to be the case, however.

"Are the two of you still involved?" asked Eva.

"Beats the hell out of me, you'll have to ask her that one."

Unimpressed with the Senator's vagueness, Eva said, "Let me rephrase that. Have you recently slept with Ms. Lawrence?"

I felt my guts squirm. Here I was investigating a murder and I was sleeping with a woman who was intimately connected to a key murder suspect. At the moment, everything inside of me wanted to leave the Senator's house and find a quiet place to drink a couple shots of whiskey.

Gunny had always warned me about the dangers of getting romantically involved with anyone even remotely connected to a murder investigation. I never pursued the matter with him, but I'd always felt that his sage advice flowed from the wisdom of some personal experience.

"No," answered the Senator.

"Okay. Just a few more questions," said Eva. "We know about your cocaine activities and your ties with the Los Hermanos Drug Cartel in Bogotá. Does Ms. Lawrence have any involvement with that?"

"Not that I'm aware."

Looking right at the Senator, Eva asked, "Did you murder Melissa Walker?"

"I already told you that I did not."

Eva and I decided not to ask the Senator any more questions. Not only was the evidence against him sketchy, but there was also the fact that he had federal immunity for his drug trafficking. And the truth was, we weren't sure how broad it was. The last thing that we wanted to do was to haul the State's beloved longtime senator down to the courthouse jail in his pajamas, only to end up releasing him the next day without charging him with a crime.

We departed the Senator's house in silence. Despite his denial, Eva and I knew that the revealing photographs raised the specter of a blackmail attempt that had resulted in the Senator conspiring to commit murder. And his initial evasive statements about the extent and nature of his relationship with Sophie didn't bolster our view of his credibility. But, we also knew that I was standing on the edge of an emotional cliff—one that I'd nearly thrown myself off of a few years ago after Vicki had died. Privately, I was wondering if it had been a mistake to not take myself off of the Walker murder investigation.

That is, with all of the richness of a Shakespearian play, Sophie had beaten me at my own game—and had very likely played me for a fool. I had finally come across an individual who led a more private life than me and the twist was that I also happened to be very much in love with her. Yet, despite her involvement with one of the key suspects in the Walker murder investigation, I still unshakably trusted her.

Eva finally broke the ice and asked, "Whadaya say we head down to Minto Brown and take a walk? It's a warm sunny day out—it'd be nice down there."

I ran my hand over my jaw and simply said, "Why not?"

Salem is an anomaly—it is the only sizable city in Oregon that has both lots of prisons and lots of protected wilderness areas. The prisons were long ago forced on the City by the State Legislature. So there wasn't much that the City Planners could do about that. But, they did have the ability to protect the City's green belt—and they certainly had done that. There are many beautiful parks in Salem, such as Bush Park and Wallace Marine Park. But, the crown jewel is Minto Brown Island's Wildlife Refuge. The park at Minto Brown seems endless with its vast array of trails, woods, and fields. On any given day it's not unusual to see deer, rabbits, and a variety of birds.

I drove my Talon into the front parking lot and Eva and I got out and began walking. Eva was trying to help—I could see that. She was one of the few people in my life that could do that without rankling me. After crossing over the wooden foot bridge, she said, "Jack, I don't want to intrude. Okay? I'm just here for you. Lord knows that you've been there for me. God only knows how many times I've wanted to quit police work and find some normal job. The only reason that I didn't is because I drew on your strength. You always believed in me—even when no one else did."

"Eva, I did what any partner would have done. We all go through that stuff. I certainly did. Gunny was always there for me. So, you should probably thank him more than you should thank me. Besides, by any measure, you're one hell of a detective."

"Thanks," said Eva. "Look, maybe you should just talk to Sophie. You know—lay it on the line. I don't mean to pry, but the way I see it we've truthfully uncovered nothing other than that she once worked as a realtor and was manipulated by a powerful older man. Unfortunately, that's not a particularly unusual dynamic."

"I know. I hear what you're saying. But, we both know why we are having this conversation." I then stopped, faced Eva and with outstretched arms placed my hands on her shoulders. "It's because we both suspect that there's more. It's the 'more' that we are worried about. Here's your homicide partner involved with a woman that you realize is going to have to be formally interrogated in one of our murder investigations."

"Okay. Jack—listen to me! Believe it or not, I'm suggesting that you give Sophie the benefit of the doubt, okay? But, no matter what, I'm here for you. I also trust your judgment. That's the bottom line."

Still looking directly at Eva, I said, "When Cap asked me several years ago whether I'd be willing to take you on as a partner, I didn't hesitate. I've never regretted that decision."

Eva and I drove back to the Department. We hadn't been there very long before Cap called us both into his office.

"Jack, Eva—sit down," he said. "You need to be in the loop on this. It concerns Michael Jacobsen. We have a Departmental Policy that requires me to inform the AG's office about certain situations. One such situation is a suspect's immunity from prosecution. So, shortly after the CIA arrived here a few days ago and flashed the immunity documents for Michael, I immediately contacted the AG's office. Were either of you aware of the Policy?"

Eva and I looked at each other and both shook our heads.

"Well, Gunny, helped draft the policy back in the mid-1970's. It came about as a result of one of his murder investigations. Some Army veteran who had Special Ops training went nuts up in the Cascades and murdered a couple of hikers. Gunny collared the dude and began questioning him. Before he was done, some military officials showed up with immunity papers—similar to the ones the CIA just used on behalf of Michael."

I interrupted, "What was the outcome, Cap?"

"Gunny released the guy. But, after the fact, the AG's office said that the immunity was bogus—that it wasn't a true Executive Order from the President."

"So what happened with the vet?" I asked.

"We never saw the guy again. He virtually disappeared. We also never identified the two apparent agents that escorted him away—and not for any lack of effort. The AG's Office even helped out, but, even our combined efforts couldn't get to the bottom of it. The Army just stonewalled our requests for information. Whatever military missions the guy had performed they were apparently so clandestine that the Army brass could not acknowledge them. Further, I subsequently learned that the vet was either killed or locked away for life by the Army."

"Makes ya feel all warm and fuzzy inside about ol' Uncle Sam, doesn't it?"

"No shit," said Cap. "So, this time around there was no way in hell that I was going to let those CIA goons just waltz outta here. I demanded to see their identification. Their names were Mitchell and Stoddard, and their IDs looked legitimate. I even telephoned the CIA. My usual contact wasn't in, so I spoke to an Agent Donald. He vouched for the two guys. But, here's the kicker—since then, I've been unable to verify that the two guys were actually CIA agents. The CIA will neither confirm nor deny anything, and I've even been unable to re-contact Agent Donald—if there was an actual agent by that name."

Shaking my head, I said, "I guess we've been around long enough to know that this kind of stuff really happens, Cap. But, even so, to have it happen right here in the halls of our own department? I sure missed it."

"Well," said Cap. "I'm the one that's responsible for

everything that happens around here—not you. But, we do have something. I learned a lesson from that incident with the Army veteran. So I photocopied the immunity documents that the two apparent CIA goons trotted out. I then passed them on to the AG. The AG then contacted President Bush's Chief Legal Counsel who confirmed that the President did not sign any such document for a Michael Jacobsen."

As I listened to Cap, I found myself internally wrestling with the shifting sands of the investigation. I felt that it was premature to say anything about Sophie. Similarly, regarding Michael, there was still a paucity of evidence incriminating him with murder. The fact that he was Melissa Walker's boyfriend cut both ways: it linked him to her, but it also gave him a defense against the forensic evidence. That is, he merely had to claim that he had engaged in consensual sex with Walker shortly before her death—knowing that the sex video would confirm his story.

"Cap," I said. "You realize that we don't have much on Michael?"

"Yes, I know. But, you now have some information that you didn't have five minutes ago."

"Sure," I said. "Looks like Eva and I better pay him a visit."

"You're playin' catch up, Jack—just like I've been doing. Less than 20 minutes ago, I dispatched two Units over to Michael's house, and another over to the airport. He's gone. He's not at his house and his jet is not hangared down at the airfield."

"Shit!" I said.

"You're tellin' me. I've put out an APB on him. But, no one that we've talked to has seen him in the last 24 hours."

17

Sophie's Story

AFTER LEAVING CAP'S office, Eva and I didn't linger around
the Department. It had been a long day and neither of
us had stopped to take a lunch break. Eva headed home,
while I drove down to Da Vinci's Restaurant. Once there,
I took a seat at the bar and ordered a gin and tonic along
with a Caesar salad. While sitting there, I flipped open my
cell phone and called Sophie. She agreed to meet me at Da
Vinci's. She arrived about a half hour later.

After some small talk, I figured that I had nothing to
lose by asking Sophie some difficult questions.

"Baby, I need to ask you some things—personally and
professionally."

Hesitantly, Sophie, said, "Okay."

"The investigation into Melissa Walker's murder has
necessarily caused me to also investigate the Jacobsen
family. In doing so, I've come across your name . . . ."

"And?" Sophie sharply interjected.

"Well, Senator Jacobsen has confirmed that you sold
him his house back in the early 1990's."

"Okay, we talked about that, Jack," said Sophie. "I just
couldn't recall whether I'd sold a house to him. I guess

you're telling me that I did?"

"Look, Sophie, the Senator admitted that the two of you had a longstanding affair and he implied that it was still going on."

Sophie froze. Her cheeks immediately flushed and she averted my eyes by looking downward. The two of us, very much in love with each other, then sat there in awkward silence for several minutes.

"I'm leaving," said Sophie.

Feeling like a heel, I said, "Hey, baby, talk to me. Look, I didn't invite this—it just fell in my lap. I'm a homicide detective. I'm investigating a murder and Senator Jacobsen is under a microscope. Your name surfaced. I'm just doing my job."

"Is fucking me just doing your job too, detective?"

I was the one looking down now. After a few seconds, I said, "You know it's not like that, Sophie."

"No . . . No I don't!"

"Look, can you just explain it all to me so that I'm not left in the dark making false assumptions? I certainly don't want you unnecessarily dragged into a murder investigation."

"Your sympathy is overwhelming, detective. Gee, I wouldn't want to inconvenience you or to jeopardize your smoothly run murder investigation."

"Sophie . . . .," I said, while shaking my head. Another period of silence then followed, before I continued, "Why don't we move back there? The sofa's open. It's more private."

Sophie nodded her head without speaking, and I picked up her glass of Pinot Gris and walked behind her the few steps into a more private overflow room. For the next several minutes, we just sat next to each other sipping our drinks in silence. The gulf between us was almost palpable. We were both hurting. After a while, I nodded to the bartender to bring us another round of drinks.

"I feel pretty let down by you, Jack," she said. "I've done nothing wrong, and I don't owe you or anyone else an explanation. I've made some mistakes in my life. What you're unwittingly doing is treading into an area that I've tried very hard to live down for the last 20 years. But, it has nothing to do with the murder of Melissa Walker."

"I'm sorry about this. I really am. When your name surfaced, I tried to ignore it, but other details began to crop up."

"Such as?"

"Such as the fact that you have a teenage daughter," I said.

Again, Sophie looked like she had been kicked in the stomach. Her face had nothing additional to show, however, as tears were already running down her cheeks. She then said, "Jack, I'm beginning to feel sick. I trusted you. I've come too far in life to be put in this position."

I looked into Sophie's eyes, held her hand, and said, "Okay, should we go?"

Ignoring my question, Sophie continued, "I was 20. I met Allen in a florist shop down in Palo Alto. I was completing my Journalism degree. I lacked confidence and I was way too trusting. Allen was charming, persistent, and flattering. He started regularly coming into the shop to buy flowers. Soon, he started flirting with me and made me feel attractive and desirable. Believe it or not, he was a pretty handsome guy back then. He eventually began taking me out to lunch. However, not a lot happened down in Palo Alto. After he moved up here to Salem, he stayed in touch with me. He'd visit me now and then."

"Uh-huh," I said.

"I moved up here, in truth, to be near him. I had a serious crush on him—and I'm sure that he knew it. He was very smooth, very convincing, and seemed very genuine. He landed me an entry level reporter's job with the Statesman and he also paved the way for my acceptance into Willamette's MBA program." While letting out a sigh, Sophie then said with a slight shrug of her shoulders, "We got involved. He encouraged me to get my realtor's license, which I did. I was actually very good at selling houses and I made a lot of money."

I swallowed the last bit of my gin and tonic and then said, "Look, Sophie, don't be overly hard on yourself. You're not the first attractive young woman to be manipulated by an older influential man."

"You don't know the half of it, Jack."

"I'm sure I don't," I said. "But, I'm generally a pretty good listener." I then placed my hand on the back of Sophie's neck and gave her a gentle squeeze.

Sophie continued, "Jack, I've been honest with you. I haven't been playing games. I don't do that—and I'm certainly not involved in any criminal activity. There are things about my life that are personal—very personal. I'm sure that you can relate to that?"

"I can."

"Yes, I have a teenage daughter," said Sophie. "She's my whole life. Allen Jacobsen is her father."

I tried not to flinch. It was pretty obvious that this lovely woman had carried a painful secret for most of her adult life.

"Does she know?" I asked.

"Yes. I really wrestled with that one. You know, whether to tell her or not. But, in the end, I felt that it wasn't my right to play God. I felt that my daughter would benefit from knowing who her father was, and to make her own choices as to what to do with that information."

"Does the Senator know?" I asked.

"Yes—he sends support payments every month."

"Okay, Sophie," I said. "I think I've put you through enough. I'd love to hold you the rest of the night. But, if you'd like to be alone, I'd understand."

"No, that'd actually be nice."

Putting my arm around her and giving her a gentle squeeze, I said, "Why don't you leave your car here? Let's head over to my place. I'll bring you into work bright and early tomorrow morning."

"Sounds like a plan."

After arriving home, I walked Sophie up the circular stairs to my bedroom. Once there, we embraced and quickly began stripping off each other's clothes while stumbling towards my bed. After making love, we collapsed together with our bodies pressed together and our limbs intertwined. We then fell asleep that way—neither one of us waking up for several hours.

The next morning, I drove Sophie downtown to retrieve her car. After I pulled into the empty parking space next to her car, we kissed each other in the way that only true lovers do—deeply and passionately. We both knew that we had just weathered an emotional tsunami and had become stronger as a result. All we really wanted at the moment was to be together. But, our daily routines beckoned and required our individual attention.

On my way back to the Department, I stopped by the Liberty Mall Starbuck's to get a cup of coffee. When I arrived at work, Eva was already there. I could tell that she'd been there a while too—as her desk was covered with paper, files, and phone messages.

"Morning, Jack," said Eva. Before I could return her greeting, however, I felt her gaze pierce right through me. She then tilted her head back slightly, rolled her eyes, and exaggeratedly let her head drop back down. "Jack, what are you doin'? Have you completely lost your grip?"

Obviously, Eva had taken one look at me and had figured out that I'd spent the night with Sophie. I chalked it up to a "woman's intuition." I really didn't care, however, what Eva or anyone else thought about my relationship with Sophie. My professional life was one thing, but my personal life was another. I generally tried not to mix the two. So I blew off her comment and began looking over my phone messages.

Unfortunately, some people just don't know when to quit. After sitting quietly for a minute or two, Eva approached me and whispered into my ear, "Look, handsome. Your personal life is your business. But, your involvement with Sophie might be clouding your judgment. I've been doing some diggin' here. Did you know that Sophie was in the Capitol Building on the morning of Walker's murder?"

On the outside, I remained poker faced. But, on the inside my heart sank. I had just made love to Sophie. More importantly, I had just convinced myself that she was not a murder suspect. But, here again, I was faced with additional information about her that implicated her.

"What are you talking about?" I asked.

"I've been reviewing the list of persons that were in the Capitol Building at the time it closed on Sunday evening, October 8th. One of the persons is unidentified, but is generically listed as 'SJ-1.' I just got off the phone with Lawton. He said that certain members of the news media are given temporary access cards to enter the Capitol Building. When I asked him about the person listed as 'SJ-1,' he said that it was Sophie Lawrence."

"Does Lawton know when Sophie left the Building?" I asked.

"Yes—want to venture a guess, playboy?"

"Uh, between three and four?" I reluctantly asked.

"Three seventeen to be exact." With that, Eva stood up, grabbed her overcoat, and said, "C'mon, we need to talk."

We headed up Commercial Street to White's Restaurant. Once there, we both ordered coffee and toast. For the moment, I was willing to take a backseat and to hear whatever it was that Eva wanted to tell me. With both of her hands wrapped around her steaming cup of coffee, she said, "Jack, this is what I see. You tell me where I might be off track. Sophie Lawrence was in the Capitol Building when Melissa Walker was murdered. She left shortly thereafter. She was Senator Jacobsen's mistress—and may still be. Heck, I don't know. Maybe you do, sexy guy? Then, there's the Senator's longstanding involvement in cocaine trafficking. Also, he's been sending a large monthly sum of money to Sweden every month. Maybe it's blackmail money—who knows? If that's not enough, Jack, consider this—I just discovered that Sophie met with the Senator *the day after Walker's death.*"

"What?"

"Yeah, that's right! Sophie flew the coup to Cancun— the same day that the Senator flew down to Bogotá. Then, the next day, on October 10th, she rendezvoused with him in Belize."

"Are you solid on that?"

Eva reached into her side coat pocket and pulled out

two pieces of paper. She then said, "Here," and handed the papers to me. They were photocopies of credit card receipts from a resort and a few restaurants in Belize City. There were five transactions. Three of them were signed by the Senator and two of them by Sophie. The evidence proved that both Sophie and the Senator had, in fact, rendezvoused in Belize City on October 10th.

"All right, I'm going to take myself off of the case," I said. "You need to bring in both Sophie and Senator Jacobsen for questioning. But, let me call Sophie and ask her to come over here on her own quietly, so that the media doesn't have an orgy. I'll tell her that she has 30 minutes to do so. As far as the Senator, I don't feel quite as charitable towards him. Let's just send a patrol car up to his house and haul his ass down here."

"I'm fine with all of that, Jack—except for the part about you taking yourself off of the case. You can't do that. Whether you're compromised or not, we both know that you're the best homicide detective we've got and you're also familiar with the case. No one in the Department knows about your relationship with Sophie. Just reassure me that you won't divulge anything confidential to her."

"That's my business, Eva."

"Have it your way."

After returning to the Department, I picked up the phone and dialed Sophie's number. She answered after the first ring.

"Hi sweet guy! Lookin' to have a romantic lunch?"

I swallowed hard. I could feel a lump in my throat. It was one thing to be mister tough guy and collar a dirt bag. It was another thing, however, to tell the woman that you loved that she was about to be arrested for suspicion of murder.

"Sophie," . . . Unable to say anything more, I cupped the telephone receiver with my right hand and turned my head away in anguish.

Hesitantly, Sophie asked, "What is it, Jack?"

"You need to come down to the Department right away—within 30 minutes. We have to question you. I didn't want an officer to show up and escort you out of your office in handcuffs."

"You're not joking are you, Jack?" she asked.

"No, I'm afraid I'm not. You need to trust me. You need to come over here to the Department. If you have nothing to hide, everything will turn out okay."

"Should I call my lawyer?" she asked.

"Definitely."

"So," she said. "You're telling me that I need to drop whatever I'm doing and turn myself in—or I'll be arrested."

"I'm afraid so."

"Okay," gravely said Sophie. "I trust you, Jack."

Sophie arrived within 15 minutes—just as she said she would. I met her at the reception area and walked her back to my desk. I then introduced her to Eva. After a few moments of resigned silence, I escorted Sophie into one of the interrogation rooms. As I exited the room, I turned back to her. We locked eyes. Everything in me wanted to hold her in my arms and get her out of the Department. But, events had now moved beyond my ability to control.

Meanwhile Senator Jacobsen had also been brought in and was waiting in one of the other interrogation rooms.

I had already spoken with Cap about my involvement with Sophie. Despite our longstanding friendship that spanned nearly 20 years, he removed me from the Walker investigation. In doing so, however, he said that if

Sophie's interrogation did not implicate her, he'd consider reinstating me.

Eva was assigned to question Sophie. After questioning her for nearly an hour, she hadn't learned much. Sophie appeared credible, as well as smart and articulate. Those same attributes enabled her to easily earn her MBA and to quickly rise through the journalism ranks to obtain her current post as the President of the Statesman Journal.

"Okay, Ms. Lawrence," said Eva. You see the predicament we're in here, right?"

"Not really."

Undeterred, Eva asked, "All right, tell me where you were on the night of Sunday, October 8th—the night that Melissa Walker was murdered?"

"I was in the Capitol Building."

"And what were you doing there," asked Eva.

"Two things—I had a scheduled interview with the Speaker of the House—Jeff Newton. That took place at 8 p.m. in his office. Check with him. I then met Allen in the VIP lounge. I don't know why he wanted to meet there instead of in his office. I just figured it was because the lounge had a great liquor cabinet—all at the Taxpayer's expense. Anyway, Allen and I needed to discuss some . . . some personal things concerning our daughter. We met around 9 p.m."

Caught off guard, Eva said, "Your daughter?"

"Allen is the father of my teenage daughter."

"Okay," said Eva. "When did you and the Senator finish talking?"

"We didn't talk very long—maybe 15 minutes or so."

"So when did you leave the building?" asked Eva.

"Very late—into the morning. I believe it was around three or so."

Hoping to trap Sophie in a lie, Eva asked, "Why'd the two of you stay there so late?"

"Allen and I got into an argument. We don't particularly care for one another. We had an affair when I was 20 years old. He was already married. The really awful part about it was that when he found out that I was pregnant he turned his back on me. He wanted me to have an abortion. I refused, however, and he balked at paying me any child support."

Eva couldn't get a handle on Sophie. She didn't know whether to feel sorry for her or to loath her. Hiding her internal dilemma, she continued, "So, on the evening of October 8th, the two of you got into an argument, but remained together in the VIP until three or so—is that what you're telling me, Ms. Lawrence?"

"No. You've got it wrong. Allen left after we argued. Probably 9:20, maybe 9:30. We may not care much for each other, but we do have a certain amount of respect for one another. He saw that I was very upset and he suggested that I stay in the lounge, enjoy a cocktail or two, and then leave when I felt like it. And that's what I'd planned to do—but, I fell asleep on the sofa after my second glass of wine."

More than a little frustrated by now, Eva asked, "So, what you're telling me is that you innocently went to the Capitol Building on the night of October 8th. You interviewed the Speaker of the House around eight or eight-thirty, and you then met Senator Jacobsen in the VIP lounge around nine. The two of you discussed your daughter and got into an argument. He left after 15 minutes or so, but you fell asleep and stayed there until about three the next morning?"

"Yes," said Sophie.

At that point, Eva stepped out of the interrogation room. Deford had already finished his interrogation of the Senator. Eva and Deford then compared notes on their interrogations and quickly deduced that both suspects had independently corroborated each other. In addition, they had failed to implicate themselves in the murder of Melissa Walker. Although Sophie had been inside the Capitol Building when Melissa Walker was murdered, it now seemed plausible that her presence there might truly have been a "coincidence."

There was also the problem of motive. Eva had failed to uncover any reason why Sophie would have wanted to murder Melissa Walker. The "jealous lover" angle just wasn't there. Sophie seemed to genuinely loath the Senator and was certainly no longer carrying a torch for him.

The facts surrounding the Senator, however, were more troubling. For many years he had profited from the sale and distribution of cocaine. He also seemed to have a penchant for attractive young women—like Melissa Walker. Then there was the ambiguous activity of his son, who was apparently spying on the Los Hermanos Drug Cartel on behalf of the United States Government— although a long shadow of doubt had been cast on that story.

In addition, there was the bizarre fact that Walker had apparently ended her affair with the Senator only to fall in love with his son. It didn't take a rocket scientist to consider that the Senator might have been overcome with obsession and jealousy that led him to kill Melissa Walker.

Armed with the statements of Allen Jacobsen, Eva returned to the interrogation room. She had been questioning Sophie for over two hours. After sitting down, she said, "Just a few more questions, Ms. Lawrence. Your recent Cancun trip—what caused you to head down there?"

"Same reason as most people, I guess—to take some vacation time and relax on the beach."

Eva continued, "Did you meet anyone down there?"

"Well, I always meet some new faces down there. But, if you're asking me if I traveled down there with anybody, No I didn't."

Eva had to hand it to Sophie. The woman was cagey and difficult to pin down. Undaunted, however, Eva said, "Look, we know that you sandwiched in a trip to Belize, while you were down there."

Sophie didn't say anything and, for the first time, Eva felt like she had Sophie on the defensive. "Would you like to explain why you met the Senator down there the day after Melissa Walker was murdered?"

"I'd like to have my lawyer present before I answer any more questions."

"All right," said Eva. "But, this is the way I see it. I think that you've had an ongoing partnership with Senator Jacobsen, who we know has been a key player in the distribution of cocaine here on the West Coast. For some reason you saw Melissa Walker and her parents as a threat. So, you killed them—all three of them."

"Really? That's very interesting, detective. You've just about got it all wrapped up don't you? Except, 'oh shit,' there's something called 'evidence,' which you seem to be a bit short on. And the reason that you are, is very simple—I <u>didn't</u> kill anybody!"

"We have proximity, motive, and no alibi," said Eva. "For Jack's sake, I hope that you're telling the truth, Sophie."

18

Zuni

I was already headed home and was driving past the Wild Pear Restaurant. I'd had it with police work. I didn't even want to know the outcome of Sophie's interrogation— the whole thing just hurt too damn much. After turning up Orville Road, my cell phone rang.

"Davis, Homicide," I answered.

"Hi Jack. It's Jim Heathrow."

"Hi Cap," I said.

"Jack, Tolento has completed her interrogation of Sophie Lawrence. She's not sure what to make of it. She said that Lawrence handled herself very well and steadfastly maintained her innocence. Her story basically checks out, although Eva said that Lawrence refused to explain why she met Senator Jacobsen in Belize, the day after Walker's murder. The bottom line is that we don't have anything on her, save for some weak circumstantial evidence. She's obviously high profile and I don't think she'll skip town."

I felt my stomach muscles tighten as I crested the hill near River Springs Road. I'd been a homicide detective for a long time. But, I'd never previously fallen in love with a murder suspect.

"All right, thanks, Cap," I said.

"Jack, that's not the main reason that I called."

It had been one of those days—the kind you'd just as soon forget. I was looking forward to a gin and tonic or two, or even three, and some much needed solitude.

Cap continued, "I primarily called to tell you that we've located Michael Jacobsen. He's apparently in New Mexico, in a small town not far from Gallup."

"New Mexico?" I repeated.

"Yeah, we have a credit card transaction from there that went through yesterday. He's apparently in Zuni, a small town on an Indian reservation. He used his credit card in a tavern down there called the Crow's Nest."

"Are you sending Eva down there?" I asked.

"Yeah, I am, as well as a certain homicide detective named Terrence Davis."

"Cap, I know what you're tryin' to do," I said. "You've saved my butt more than once in this investigation, but I should stay off the case."

"Lawrence isn't out of the woods yet, Jack. But, it is beginning to look like she wasn't involved in the murder of Melissa Walker. Either way, what's important is that you didn't do anything wrong. You informed me of your conflict shortly after you became aware that there might be one. Moreover, you're the best homicide detective that I've got. And right now I need two of my best ones to travel to New Mexico to collar a murder suspect. Are you on board?"

"Yes," I said.

"Good. I was hopin' you'd see it that way. Listen, I've contacted Zuni PD and the New Mexico State Police. They're on the lookout."

"All right, Cap," I said. "I'll try to catch a flight outta here first thing in the morning. Are you sure that you can spare Eva goin' down there too? I mean, I'd love to have her come along, but there's a lot of stuff goin' on here."

"No, that's why you have a partner. You don't know what you might get into down there. You both need to go. We can handle things here."

"Okay, goodnight Cap," I said.

I headed straight for the kitchen liquor cabinet. After mixing a "double" gin and tonic, I slid off my shoulder harness. Out of habit, I checked the chamber in my Smith & Wesson to make sure that it was fully loaded.

There'd been only one occasion out here at my country house when I had fired my revolver. A few years back, a chocolate colored pit bull wondered down my driveway and decided to take on my Siberian Husky named Elko. Huskies resemble wolves in appearance, but they are typically non-aggressive and friendly. They are also very rugged, however, and if forced to fight they can usually hold their own against almost any dog.

On that particular morning, I heard the dog fight erupt as I was getting dressed. I looked out my bedroom window and could see that the pit bull was getting the upper hand with Elko. Once a pit bull wraps its powerful jaws around anything—it's all over. Consequently, I grabbed my revolver, ran downstairs, and sprinted the 30 meters to the location of the canine brawl. Hoping to avoid firing my gun, I picked up a shovel and took a couple of good whacks at the pit bull's head, but the powerfully muscled critter wouldn't back down. As the pit bull finally began to turn Elko over onto his back and was tightening his jaws around his neck, I took aim at point blank range and fired. The pit bull was instantly killed and slumped to the ground. Elko then immediately righted himself and proceeded to inspect every inch of the motionless dog. After he was satisfied that the intruder was no longer a threat, he trotted over to me and nudged his wet nose against my hand—as if nothing had ever happened.

As I slid the bottle of gin back into the liquor cabinet, my telephone rang. "Hello," I answered.

"Jack?"

Recognizing Sophie's voice, I said, "Yeah, it's me baby. I . . . I really . . . ."

"I know. I didn't do it, Jack. I didn't kill anyone. I've done nothing wrong. Yes, I've made mistakes in my life—a very big one nearly 20 years ago. But, I've tried to live that one down, and thought that I had. I forgave myself a long time ago."

"Sophie," I said. "We can't talk until this is all over."

"I know. I love you . . . and you love me too, don't you?"

"Yes, I do," I said.

The next morning, I headed down to the Salem Airport. It was early, just after six. The FBO operator always saw to it that a fresh pot of Boyd's Coffee was available, and I helped myself to a cup. I had spent a fair amount of time down at the airport back in the days when I was working as a part-time flight instructor. I had even tried to change careers and was ready to start flying cargo at night. But, in the end, I was too far along in life and too experienced at detective work to really justify doing anything else.

With a cup of coffee in my hand, I walked out to the fuel pumps. I saw my old acquaintance, Kevin Hilbrandt, a fuel attendant who had topped off my Cessna 172 on many occasions.

"Morning," I said.

Hilbrandt looked up, took in my shadowy frame and finally recognized me. He then said, "Hi, Jack. What brings your ghost out here at this hour?"

"Hi Kevin," I said. "Long time."

"You're tellin' me," said Hilbrandt.

"Hey, I'm tryin' to locate Michael Jacobsen. I'm guessin' that you've fueled up his Citation several times."

"Sure—lots of times," said Hilbrandt.

"Do you know if he ever made runs down to New Mexico?"

In a matter of fact tone, Hilbrandt said, "Yeah, frequently."

"How do ya know?"

Looking kind of sheepish, Hilbrandt explained, "Well, when I place the fuel receipt in the pilot's seat, I often sneak a peek at the yoke clip to see what approaches he's been flyin'. You know . . . part of my pilot education. Anyway, I've frequently seen the approach plate for Albuquerque, while fuelin' up Michael's Citation."

"Okay. Thanks, Kevin. Oh, and don't worry—your secret's safe with me."

With an embarrassed smile on his face, Hilbrandt replied, "Hey, you should take a few lessons and start flyin' again."

"Yeah, I think about it once in a while—especially on sunny days when I see you and the other folks around here liftin' off the runway. But, it's a pretty expensive hobby."

Hilbrandt nodded his head in agreement, as I turned and walked back to my car.

Shortly thereafter, Eva and I headed up to PDX. Continental Airlines had an early morning flight direct to Albuquerque International. But, with all of the added airport security measures, we barely made our flight. After arriving in Albuquerque, we rented a Toyota Camry and headed west on Interstate 40 towards Zuni. The trip took a little over two hours.

Zuni is a town of 12,000 inhabitants on the Zuni Indian Reservation, which is located in northwestern New Mexico. Most of the residents are Native Americans. The Zuni are thought to be descendants of the Pueblo tribes that roamed the Southwest more than a 1,000 years before the Europeans arrived. The Zuni maintain a high level of autonomy. Their language is unique and does not resemble that of other Native American tribes. They also view women as the life of the tribe and expect them to take care of all trading, financial matters, and disputes. Whatever possessions the men build, gather, or collect— they are considered as belonging to the women. The Zuni are also mystical and look to their shamans for wisdom and medicine.

After arriving in Zuni, Eva and I were headed down Highway 61. We were looking for the Crow's Nest tavern, which we found without difficulty. The tavern was centrally located near the only intersection with a traffic light. Several dusty pickup trucks and cars were parked out front.

As Eva and I walked towards the tavern, I noticed an older looking motorcycle parked near the front door. I stopped and looked at it—spokes, drive chain, and a round headlight. I flashed back to a time nearly thirty years ago when in my early twenties I had driven a Honda CB550-4 motorcycle from Bellevue, Washington, to El Paso, Texas. I recalled driving through the expansive Navajo Indian Reservation just to the north of Zuni.

Interrupting my reverie, Eva, said, "What is it, Jack?"

"Oh, nothing," I said.

When Eva and I walked into the tavern, it was like one of those old network television commercials with the line, "When E.F. Hutton talks, people listen." That is, everyone in the smoke filled place suddenly stopped whatever they were doing and silently looked directly at Eva and me—a couple of pale faced strangers. After hesitating for a few seconds, I grabbed Eva by the arm and escorted her up to the bar. I looked at the bartender and said, "Hi, how 'bout a draft beer and a Chardonnay for the lady?"

He responded, "Sure, Coors, Bud, IPA?"

"A Bud's fine," I said.

The bartender poured a cold Budweiser and uncorked a new bottle of chardonnay. He then asked us if we wanted to order lunch. He recommended the special of the day—a meatloaf sandwich.

Most of the tavern patrons had resumed their activities and were no longer staring at us. The bartender, a burly sort with a crew cut and tattoos covering nearly every inch of his tree-trunk sized forearms, then asked, "Where you folks from?"

"Salem, Oregon," I answered.

"Hell, I have a nephew who lives in Rhododendron, at the base of Mount Hood. What brings the two of you all the way down here?"

I considered saying something vague like, 'Just passin' through,' but acting on instinct I said, "We're homicide cops. We're investigating a recent murder that took place in Oregon."

For the second time in fifteen minutes everyone in the Crow's Nest Tavern stopped talking and stared at Eva and me. I took out my badge and displayed it to the bartender. "Name's Terrence Davis," I said. "This is my partner, Detective Tolento." I then extended my right hand and firmly shook the bartender's beefy hand, as did Eva. Next, I asked, "We're looking for a white man, about 5'-10", short cropped dark hair, in his mid-thirties. Ring a bell?"

"Don't know," said the bartender. "I'm not here all the time."

I reached into my shirt pocket and pulled out a 2 x 3 picture of Michael. "Here's his picture," I said. His name's Michael Jacobsen. Have you seen him?"

The bartender looked at the picture for a few seconds and said, "Yeah, I have seen this guy. He keeps to himself. He shows up every couple of months and stays for maybe two or three days."

"When did you last see him?"

"Oh, it's been a while," said the bartender. "Last July or something like that."

I kept pressing, "You haven't seen him this week?"

"No," said the bartender. "But that doesn't mean he hasn't been here. Hey, hold on—just a minute."

The bartender then went down to the end of the bar. He showed the picture to someone sitting near the end— towards the door. I leaned back and craned my head behind the guy seated next to me. I couldn't see very well who the bartender was talking to, or even whether it was a man or a woman. But, it looked like he was talking to an individual with a long gray braided ponytail.

After a minute or so, the bartender walked back towards me. He then said, "Yeah, he's been in here. He was here a few days ago."

"Anyone know where he is, or where he's stayin'?"

"I doubt it," said the bartender. "Like I said, he keeps to himself."

"Okay, thanks."

The bartender then said, "Everyone around here calls

me 'blow.' When I was a kid, I'd always take off runnin' while saying 'hair running blow.'"

"Okay, Blow," I said. "We appreciate your help. We'll probably be here for a day or two. Is there a hotel in town?"

"Nope, just a campsite," said the bartender. "You'd have to head up to Gallup for a hotel. It's about a half hour's drive up six-o-two."

"All right, thanks. Say, can you tell me how to get to the local airport?"

"Yeah," said the bartender. "Turn right on the main drag out here. Go to the next stop sign. Turn right and keep goin' about two miles. Can't miss it."

"Thanks, Blow."

As Eva and I were headed out the door, someone said, "Victoria says to follow the crow."

I froze. I then looked at Eva for a split second, while placing my right hand around the handle of my Smith & Wesson. I slowly turned around to see who had spoken. Again, everyone in the tavern suddenly stopped talking and stared at us. Everyone except one individual, that is. The individual with the long gray ponytail was still comfortably seated at the bar with his back turned to us. I still couldn't tell if it was a man or a woman. The individual was wearing a tan coat, jeans, and cowboy boots. While standing just a few feet away from the stranger, I said, "What did you say?"

The individual finally turned around to face me—it was an older, stately looking Native American male. I guessed that he was in his early 70's. However, his face was not weathered or lined, like commonly seen in many indigenous older people from the Southwest. Instead it was smooth and had an olive colored glow. He also had brown eyes that sparkled and seemed almost translucent. While seeming to look right through me, the old man repeated, "Victoria says to follow the crow."

As the words flowed out of the stranger's mouth and into my brain, I slowly slid my right hand off of my revolver and walked up closer to him. I said, "Tell me more."

The stranger responded, "You are not schooled in the Shamanic way. Your mind will not accept what I am about to tell you. You must try to listen from your spirit."

I stood there in silence, not sure what to make of the mysterious stranger. How the hell did he know anything about me? Particularly, that I had once loved a woman named Victoria? My mind began to explore the possibility that the stranger was a member of the Los Hermanos Cartel, or perhaps the CIA. But, something inside of me knew that he was not an adversary.

The stranger continued, "You once lived in this place that we now call Zuni. So did Victoria. She has come to me in spirit. She is worried about you and she has pierced the veil to tell you to follow the crow."

I could feel a lump in my throat. The patrons in the tavern had once again slowly resumed their activities. They could see that there was no threat of violence. But, what the stranger had said was nothing short of incredible.

"Who is Victoria?" I asked.

The stranger answered, "Do not pretend to be a fool or to think that I am one. You know the entity as Vicki. In this life, you met each other in a coffee shop. She has communicated through me and has said what she felt was necessary."

"Who are you?"

"I am Red Moon," said the stranger. "I've lived here all of my life. I'm a Zuni shaman. Do not be distrustful."

"Is this a joke?"

"Far from it," said Red Moon. "Why would I joke with you about such a thing? I'm 104 years old. I have experienced many realms, and I know that we ultimately shed our physical body in the same way that a butterfly sheds its cocoon. The entity lives—and she chose me as a vessel. Do not discount her admonition."

I was thinking, "What the hell?" I felt uneasy—not the type of emotion that a homicide detective particularly enjoys. Usually it means that bad things are about to happen.

As I turned to leave, Red Moon placed his hand on my arm and said, "Do as the entity has instructed."

19

The Crow

NONE OF WHAT had just happened fit within my construct of the world. Some things have to be shoved to the back of your mind, however. At the moment, Eva and I needed to focus on our mission—arresting Michael Jacobsen. We drove the rental car down the road towards the Zuni Pueblo airport. The airport was deserted. There were three small general aviation airplanes tied down next to the 4,800 foot long asphalt runway. The airstrip sat on a mesa at 7,300 feet above sea level. There was no control tower. There were two hangars down at the west end of the runway—near runway 7.

"Jack, I don't like this," said Eva. "It's eerie. It doesn't feel right. That stuff in the tavern with the old medicine man . . . and now this deserted airstrip. I dunno."

"Well, we're here, right? We've traveled a long ways. Let's at least check out the airfield. We should probably start with the hangars. If we find Michael's jet, maybe we'll be able to snare him."

I stopped the car about 50 yards away from the nearest hangar and parked it next to some brush. We checked our weapons, exited the car, and guardedly walked over to the hangar. I tried to open the side door, but it was locked. I wasn't about to let a locked door stop us, however, so I kicked it in. Search warrant or no search warrant, I figured that I could at least argue that we were in hot pursuit of a murder suspect. Eva and I then entered the hangar, but it was empty.

Consequently, we headed over to the next hangar. This one was larger and newer. Like the other one, it was all locked up. But, the side door was solid—I didn't even try to kick it in. Although we couldn't see any nearby cars, we detected fresh tire tracks. While Eva kept an eye out, I began trying to pick the lock. After about three minutes, I succeeded.

It was pitch black inside, as the hangar did not have any exterior windows. We stood motionless for several seconds trying to give our eyes an opportunity to adapt. Everything seemed okay, so I began fumbling for the light switch. I finally found it and several overhead florescent lights started to slowly flicker on.

Sure enough, there was Michael's Cessna Citation, N1732T. We carefully searched the hangar, but found nothing incriminating. I then went over to the Citation and opened the door to the cabin. I went inside. It was an extremely nice business jet with leather seats, a wet bar, and a built in flat screen television. I entered the cockpit. There was a flight bag sitting in the co-pilot's seat.

Inside the flight bag there were three large leather bound Jeppesen notebooks that were standard equipment for any jet pilot. The notebooks contained approach plates for instrument landings, which were used to help a pilot safely land in low visibility conditions. On the outside of the notebooks, Michael's name was embossed in gold. The other items in the flight bag consisted of standard things like a knee board, a flashlight, and some High Altitude Airway maps and VFR charts. There certainly weren't any bags of cocaine lying around.

I then crawled out of the cabin, exited the Citation and said, "Let's get outta here. Maybe we can collar Michael back in town. Otherwise, we're going to end up on a stake out here at the airport."

"I've been ready to leave since we got here."

"I hear ya," I said. "It sort of feels like we're walking into a shootout at the Okay Coral, doesn't it?"

"Yep," tersely replied Eva.

The two of us then drove back to town. We ended up stopping about two blocks west of the Crow's Nest tavern. There was a corner drug store, a gas station, and a post office there. We figured that we'd flash Michael's picture around and see if we got lucky. We both walked into the drug store. The cashier, who was also the owner, recognized Michael's face. Similar to the bartender, he said that Michael was not a regular, but that he had appeared in his store several times over the last year or so.

After leaving the drugstore, we decided to split up. Eva agreed to head over to the post office, while I went over to the gas station.

It seemed that we were slowly tightening the noose around Michael. The gas station owner also identified him. In fact, he said that Michael had stopped in just yesterday to fill up his SUV. He thought that the SUV was a Tahoe or an Expedition.

My pulse was beginning to quicken as I could sense that the chase was on. As I headed back towards the post office to meet up with Eva, I saw a crow swoop down right in front of me. I stopped dead in my tracks. Red Moon's words came back to me—"Follow the crow."

The crow hovered in front of my face for a few seconds, cocked its head to one side, and let out a kah-kah sound. But, it wasn't a threatening gesture. The crow then flew on up the road about 50 yards and began swooping directly overhead two cars that had pulled off to the side of the road. It then shot straight past me in the other direction. I spun around to watch it. Two more cars were just pulling off to the side of the road and the crow began swooping directly above them too.

I pulled out my Smith & Wesson. Two men then walked out of the post office. I wondered where Eva was. Just as I was starting to move laterally and out of the two men's line of sight, one of the men suddenly turned and fired at me. The bullet ripped through my right collar bone area. I managed to fire off two bullets at the shooter and dropped him dead. His accomplice was now raising his automatic weapon at me and I shot and killed him too.

I then dropped hard to the ground, groaned, and could feel blood oozing down my chest from my shoulder wound. I rolled amidst additional bullet fire and ended up behind the cover of a steel trash dumpster. Bullets sprayed off the dumpster. I sat up and managed to look over the top of the chest high dumpster. I aimed my gun at one of the shooters who was running towards me. I dropped him dead. I then fired off two more shots at another shooter and wounded him. I then heard the squeal of car tires.

Pressing my hand against my wound, I cautiously stood up. One of the suspicious cars was now gone and everything seemed quiet. Three of the bad hombres had been killed, one wounded, and two had sped away in their car. I ran over to the post office. Eva had Michael in handcuffs. I could now hear sirens. Two police cars had arrived. Michael appeared compliant, and Eva said that he had not resisted arrest. He was then placed in one of the patrol cars and was transported to the Zuni Police Department.

Meanwhile, I was taken to a hospital in Gallup to have my collar bone wound treated. X-rays revealed some bullet fragments. Against the surgeon's wishes, I refused to stay overnight for observation. Instead, I tossed off the ridiculous hospital gown that they had placed me in and slid back into my Wrangler jeans. It wasn't the easiest thing to do with my right arm in a sling, but I managed. On my way out the door, I caught site of the charge nurse who flashed me a disapproving look. Feeling like a grade school kid that had just been caught playing hooky, I sheepishly shrugged and mouthed the words, "Thank you."

Shortly thereafter, a New Mexico state trooper drove me back to the Zuni Police Department. Eva had been interrogating Michael for several hours. She said that he was sticking to his story that he was a CIA agent assigned to infiltrate the Los Hermanos Drug Cartel. Meanwhile, Zuni PD had verified that the four men that I'd either killed or wounded were Columbians with known ties to the Cartel. Road blocks were in effect by the State Police to try and capture the remaining two men that had escaped by vehicle.

I entered the interrogation room. "All right, Michael," I said. "You're in pretty deep here. You're CIA story seems farfetched and doesn't exactly check out—including your apparent immunity."

"And that surprises you?" he shot back. "Look, all I can say is that I'm an undercover agent for the CIA and that the operation that I'm on is off the books. Of course you're not going to find anyone there at the Company who is going to confirm my status as an operative. If you push hard enough, however, I guarantee you that the Company will contact the Governor. The Company would never allow me to stand trial. You can count on it. But, none of that really matters—because I *didn't* kill anybody!"

"Why'd you fly down here?" I asked.

"I'd rather not say."

"You can't have it both ways, Michael," I said. "Even if your CIA story is legit, you're going to have to answer some questions. I don't exactly see any agents in dark suits here at the moment to spring you."

"No? Who do you think the three men in suits were that you shot and killed?"

"Nice try, asshole," I shot back. "We've already confirmed their identities."

"Believe what you want, detective. Ignorance is bliss."

I had to hand it to Michael. He was pretty quick on his feet. The bottom line, however, was that he was in captivity and would be returning to Oregon to likely face murder charges. I was no longer buyin' his story. And Salem PD sure as hell wasn't going to release him again into the custody of a couple of goons in aviator sunglasses. If Michael truly was a spy for the United States Government, then it would take some pretty high level communication with the Oregon Executive Branch to obtain his release into federal custody.

"So, what do you know about your father's involvement with Melissa Walker?" I asked.

"Look, I know what you're drivin' at. My father has some frailties. He's caused some pain for my mother."

"Okay, Michael," I said. "I'll give you one last chance here before we arrest you for the murder of Melissa Walker and for suspicion of the murders of Albert and Gloria Walker. This is what we have: You were the victim's boyfriend and you were alone with her near the scene of the crime just minutes before her death. You admit that the two of you had been intimate both earlier in the day and immediately prior to her death. You also admit that she took cocaine and that the two of you struggled. We have solid forensic evidence that corroborates all of that. I don't think that it would be very difficult to convince a jury that your alibi is bogus, you know, the part about you supposedly trotting off to the little boy's room just before the victim is mysteriously murdered."

"I understand your predicament, detective. But, I didn't do it!"

"All right, Michael," I said. "You're under arrest in Oregon, for the murder of Melissa Walker and for suspicion of the murder of her parents."

"Understood," said Michael.

Sometimes timing is everything in an investigation. With that in mind, I asked, "Michael, did you know that Melissa was one month pregnant at the time of her death . . . with your child . . . a boy?"

Michael burrowed his eyes directly into mine and held his gaze for several seconds. It was probably the first genuine reaction that I'd gotten from him. Everything else had seemed rehearsed. He then lowered his head and mumbled, "No, I didn't."

On the commercial flight back to Salem, I walked up to Eva's seat and sat down next to her. I had a nagging feeling that I couldn't shake. Everything seemed to point to Michael as the murderer. Although he hadn't confessed, I'd seen flimsier cases of Murder One result in a conviction. Even so, something wasn't right.

"Does it seem to you that Michael has given us too much incriminating information and that he hasn't really attempted to defend himself?" I asked.

"I don't know? I mean, everything seems to point to him. We've accumulated quite a bit of forensic evidence, in addition to placing him at the crime scene. And his alibi is shit."

"Who do you suppose took those pictures of the Senator and Melissa Walker?" I asked.

"Good question. I haven't really given it much thought, but, I'd venture that it was either a crook lookin' to blackmail the Senator or a private investigator?"

"That's what I've been thinking," I said. "Given that we found them in the Jacobsen's bedroom closet it stands to reason that either the Senator or his wife put them there. You know, it's usually the cheater's spouse that hires a PI."

"So, we need to have a visit with Mrs. Jacobsen?"

"Yep," I said.

Tightening the Noose

AFTER ARRIVING IN Salem, Eva and I drove straight to Fairmont Hill and parked in the driveway of Senator Jacobsen's home. We walked up the walkway together and rang the doorbell. The Senator's wife, Susan, opened the door.

"Good afternoon, Mrs. Jacobsen," I said.

"Hello."

"Detective Tolento and I would like to talk to you," I said. "May we come in?"

As if she had not heard me correctly, Mrs. Jacobsen said, "I'm sorry, Allen is resting at the moment. Besides, I don't mean to be rude, but I doubt that he would be willing to talk to you without his lawyer present."

"Uh, we'd like to talk to *you*, Mrs. Jacobsen," I said.

"Me? Oh, well, I've already given you my statement. I really don't have anything to add. Why would you want to talk to me?"

Now seated in the living room, I said, "Mrs. Jacobsen . . . . ."

"Please call me Susan."

"All right," I said. "Susan, could you tell us where you were between midnight and 3 a.m. on Monday, October 9th?"

"Well, I've already provided that information in my previous statement. As I said, I was here sleeping with Allen."

"If I told you that a surveillance camera in the Capitol Building shows that you left the building around 3:15 a.m., what would you say?"

"I'd say that you're bluffing, detective. I was right here with my husband."

"What can you tell us about your husband's relationship with Melissa Walker?" I asked.

"Whadaya mean?"

"Susan, let's not play games. I don't wanna make this any more painful than it must already be. We know that your husband had an affair with Melissa Walker."

Mrs. Jacobsen sat poker faced and in silence.

"Look, we have the pictures of your husband and Melissa Walker," I said. "Did you hire a private investigator to check up on him?"

I waited for over two minutes, but Mrs. Jacobsen did not respond. She appeared collected and composed. In fact, I had to hand it to her—she remained in eye contact and displayed no emotion. But, I'd been down this road a few times in my lengthy career and I had little doubt that she was scared. I concluded that I'd have to break the ice.

"All right," I said. "I'm going to read you your Miranda rights and we're going to have to take you downtown for processing, Susan."

"Wait!" said Mrs. Jacobsen. "I've stood by my husband for over 40 years now. He's a good man, an honorable man, and a great man. But, he has weaknesses."

"Okay," I said.

"I didn't hire an investigator. But, I did discover the photographs and I confronted Allen about them. He told me that Melissa had hired an investigator to take some compromising photographs of the two of them. He had become obsessed with her. She was finished with their romantic relationship and had threatened Allen with public exposure if he didn't stop pursuing her. Honestly, I felt that he had taken advantage of her. But, I also could see that she had used him to advance her career. He even told me that she had warned him that if she was ever harmed, her parents would publish a set of the same photographs that they had locked away in their safe."

Eva and I sat there and just listened. Mrs. Jacobsen paused and blotted her tears with a tissue. While she took a moment to compose herself, I looked over at Eva and shook my head. This homicide investigation had already resulted in more than its share of twists and turns. And right now, I wasn't sure what to make of Mrs. Jacobsen's assertions. Truthfully, I had overlooked her as a suspect. If she had killed Melissa Walker, I was already considering that she wouldn't be the first jealous spouse to commit murder. Often, the anguished spouse even rationalizes that their murderous act is a noble effort to save their marriage. I actually felt some sympathy for Mrs. Jacobsen, given the longstanding pain that she'd obviously endured at the hands of her philandering and creepy husband.

"Susan," I said. "Did you push Melissa Walker through the glass doorway?"

Mrs. Jacobsen did not answer. No doubt, it was a painful moment for her. Mrs. Jacobsen was like a trapped lioness. If she was a murderer, I knew that she needed to be brought to justice. But, I also knew that she was not some low life—a molester or a serial killer. I had no interest in making the situation more difficult for her than it already was. If she had murdered Melissa Walker, I wasn't going to get any joy out of seeing her sent to prison for the remainder of her life. But, I could tell that she was about to crack. So, it was with some reluctance that I asked, "Susan, did you know that Melissa Walker was pregnant with your son's child at the time of her death?"

Mrs. Jacobsen began trembling and moved her right hand up to her mouth. Tears began streaming down her face. In a subdued voice, she said, "No, I didn't know that. Are you sure? You're not bluffing?"

Standing up and placing my hand on her right shoulder, I said, "Susan, I'd never bluff about something like that. The Medical Examiner confirmed the pregnancy, as well as his paternity. The embryo was only three to four weeks old – it was a baby boy."

While crying and blowing her nose with a tissue, Mrs. Jacobsen said, "You earlier asked me if I'd pushed Melissa through an open window in the Capitol Dome. I suppose that if a motivated person was in the right place at the right time, something like that might happen."

With a sense of both relief and sorrow, I asked, "How 'bout her parents, Susan? Did you have any involvement with their murder?"

"Well, I was in Bogota—so I sure didn't personally kill them. But, again, if a wife knew that a couple of other people knew something about her husband that could destroy him, his career, and her marriage, she might be prompted to hire someone to do something about it."

"I see," I said.

Before I could add that she was under arrest for the murder of Melissa Walker and for the conspiracy to murder her parents, Mrs. Jacobsen abruptly rose to her feet and said, "If you don't mind, I'd like to have my husband by my side." She then briskly walked upstairs to her bedroom. Not seeing any harm in allowing Mrs. Jacobsen the modest comfort of having the Senator next to her as she was arrested and handcuffed in her own home, I let her go.

Eva and I then sat there in the living room and waited. A fire was burning in the fireplace. A portrait painting of the Senator was prominently affixed above the fireplace mantel. On each side of the mantel were several family pictures. The pictures displayed Allen and Susan Jacobsen's wedding, their parents, and their son Michael. While waiting for Mrs. Jacobsen to return with the Senator, I inspected the pictures. Mrs. Jacobsen had been a beautiful bride and a lovely young woman in her early years. In fact, she was still a very attractive woman who had aged gracefully.

Then it happened. The sound of a gunshot rang out. I instinctively unholstered my Smith & Wesson and ran up the stairway taking two steps at a time. Eva was running with me nearly shoulder-to-shoulder. Before I reached the upstairs level, however, a second gunshot rang out. Seconds later, Eva and I entered the master bedroom and stopped in our tracks. Blood stains were all over the wall behind the bed, the headboard, and the pillows. Mrs. Jacobsen was lying motionless with her face down and her body slumped over the Senator's chest. A still smoking pistol was in her right hand. I turned her body over, but could not detect a pulse in either her or the Senator. They each had bullet wounds in their heads. It was obvious that Mrs. Jacobsen had shot her husband in the head and had then turned the gun on herself. Eva telephoned 911 and we each administered CPR. But, it was pointless. In less than five minutes, the paramedics arrived and took over. Although the hospital was just minutes away, both the Senator and Mrs. Jacobsen were pronounced DOA— dead on arrival.

After leaving the hospital, Eva and I returned to the Senator's home to inspect the crime scene. We then spent that night, the entire next day, and the next night at the Department buttoning things down with our Forensic Unit and giving our recorded statements.

It was now five-thirteen in the morning—two days after the murder-suicide of Allen and Susan Jacobsen. I hadn't stepped outside in over 36 hours. The Melissa Walker murder investigation was now closed. I walked out of the Department and headed down to Bentley's for a cup of coffee and a Bloody Mary—or two. The crisp air felt invigorating as I strolled down the Liberty Street sidewalk. Although Susan Jacobsen's suicide had prevented us from knowing everything, Eva and I had solved the puzzle of the three murders. During the last 36 hours, we had debriefed the marital counselor for Allen and Susan Jacobsen, as well as a private investigator that had been hired by Melissa Walker. We had also re-interviewed Michael Jacobsen, as well as Lynn Palmer. Finally, we had seized the Senator's office computer and had obtained a forensics analysis as to what had taken place with the computer on October 8th and 9th.

What we learned was that Susan Jacobsen had endured a painful four decade long marriage to the Senator. Although she loved him, she had suffered through his countless liaisons and affairs with other women. More recently, however, she had optimistically felt that their ongoing marital counseling had finally healed their relationship and that the Senator had been rehabilitated. Unfortunately, however, she discovered that the Senator was having yet another affair with Melissa Walker.

The pictures that had been retrieved from the Jacobsen's home had been taken by a private investigator named Peter Fontain, who was hired by Melissa Walker. She had then given a set of the photographs to the Senator, in an attempt to force him to leave her alone. Moreover, as a precaution, she had given her parents a sealed manila envelope which contained the negatives of the pictures. She then asked them to place the sealed envelope in their safe and to never view its contents unless she was harmed. Her parents complied with her request.

Melissa Walker then told the Senator that if he didn't leave her alone or if he ever tried to harm her, her parents would publish the incriminating photographs. Once Susan Jacobsen confronted the Senator with her knowledge of his affair with Melissa Walker, he admitted to the affair and explained that he was in a mess that could ruin <u>both</u> their lives.

Already feeling the loss of her husband's affection, Susan Jacobsen then learned that her son, Michael, was dating Melissa Walker. At that point something snapped inside of her and she felt compelled to protect her marriage, herself, and her son from any further pain and rejection at the hands of Melissa Walker.

On Sunday October 8th, Susan Jacobsen innocently entered the Capitol Building during public hours. She did so from the parking garage and the stairwell, which coincidentally avoided detection by the security cameras. She spent the afternoon with the Senator in his office. Although he left shortly after 9 p.m., she remained. She had been researching some things on the Internet and hadn't yet finished. So, she decided to stay a while.

She then sent an e-mail to one of her friends. While doing so, she noticed that Michael had sent an e-mail intended for the Senator. She opened it. Michael had e-mailed his father to tell him that he and Melissa were coming over to the Capitol to take in the view from the observation deck. He also stated that there was something that he and Melissa wanted to discuss with him.

In our re-interrogation of Michael, he admitted that he had subsequently discovered that his mother was in the Capitol Building on the morning of Melissa's Walker's murder. He figured out that she had probably murdered Melissa. Desiring to protect his mother, he flew to Zuni in an attempt to steer Eva and me towards him as the central suspect. He figured that he stood a good chance of beating a murder conviction since he hadn't killed Melissa, and especially given his status as a CIA operative with immunity.

So, while Mrs. Jacobsen found herself in the Capitol Building late into the night on October 8th, and realized that her son and Melissa Walker were going to arrive, she hatched a plan to commit murder. She locked the office door, turned out the lights, and stepped around the corner. When Michael and Melissa arrived they unlocked the Senator's office door, but could see that no one was present. So, they headed up to the observation deck. Susan Jacobsen then followed them. She kept her distance, but followed the pair up most of the 121 steps to the observation deck. On her way up, however, she stopped at the last landing that was directly behind the Capitol Dome's glass windows. Next, she opened the window on the side of the landing, which is the size of a small glass door. She then hid.

Michael then came down the stairs to use the restroom and walked right by her. While he was gone, Melissa Walker also decided to leave the observation deck. It is unclear why she did so.

Of course, all of that made it easy for Susan Jacobsen. In order to commit the murder without detection, she needed to separate Michael from Melissa Walker. Eva and I didn't know how she expected to accomplish that. But, we theorized that she might have planned to telephone Michael to ask him to retrieve something from the Senator's office. She could have then planned on calling out Melissa Walker's name, to lure her down the stairwell. And maybe she did just that—we'll never know. Or, perhaps Melissa Walker departed the observation deck on her own initiative simply because she too needed to use the restroom?

In the end, it all conveniently worked for Susan Jacobsen. As Melissa Walker reached the landing, Mrs. Jacobsen rose up and shoved her through the open glass window, which is when Melissa Walker let out her blood curdling scream—as she fell 100 feet to her death.

The final sad saga is that Susan Jacobsen hired a professional assassin to murder Melissa Walkers' parents. On her way home from the Capitol, she had made a phone call from a pay phone at a nearby gas station. Eva and I had already traced the number and had connected it to an individual named Richard Santee, who was a known assassin for hire with a military background and a criminal history. He had now been captured, however, and transported back to the State of Washington. He had already spilled his guts in an effort to plea bargain.

After finishing my second Bloody Mary at Bentley's, I drove straight to Sophie's house. It was now just after 6 a.m. I rang her doorbell and stood there. My hands were shoved deep into the pockets of my P-coat and my collar was turned up. It was nearly freezing outside. I looked rumpled with an unshaven face and dark circles under my eyes. I needed to sleep.

I rang the doorbell a second time. The sun was just beginning to appear over the horizon and everything was covered with frost. I felt like I was returning home from a war—one without a clear winner. Sure I had solved the murder of Melissa Walker, but at what cost? It was one thing to solve a murder and to then have the killer convicted and incarcerated. It was entirely another thing to solve a murder and to then have the killer commit a murder-suicide.

"Jack!" exclaimed Sophie. "What are you doing here? Hey, are you all right? Come on in."

THE END